CRAZY FOX REMEMBERS

Don and Sue Preston

PRENTICE-HALL, Inc., Englewood Cliffs, New Jersey

Book Designer: Donna Kurdock
Art Director: Hal Siegel

Printed in the United States of America

Prentice-Hall International, Inc., London
Prentice-Hall of Australia, Pty. Ltd., Sydney
Prentice-Hall of Canada, Ltd., Toronto
Prentice-Hall of India Private Ltd., New Delhi
Prentice-Hall of Japan, Inc., Tokyo
Prentice-Hall of Southeast Asia Pte. Ltd., Singapore
Whitehall Books Limited, Wellington, New Zealand

10   9   8   7   6   5   4   3   2   1

Library of Congress Cataloging in Publication Data

Preston, Don, date
    Crazy fox remembers.

    I.   Preston, Sue, date   II.   Title.
PS3566.R398C7   813'.54   81-1590
ISBN 0-13-188896-X   AACR2

To Rachel, Laura, Amy and all
those who led the fight for law and order
in the early days of the West

Contents

Introduction

In at least one sense, the genesis of the present volume was a late-night educational television program to which we had been invited to discuss our special field: the social mores of the Indian Nations between 1850 and 1900. In answer to a question, I stated that we did indeed sometimes encounter, in our research, material of a more than scholarly interest. In illustration I mentioned a remarkable document that had only recently come into our hands, a nonprofessional writing putatively recounting the adventures of various Western characters, some of whom had previously been thought fictional. The host of the show (and subsequent mail) expressed incredulity and pressed us to go into greater detail on our next appearance. Although we promised to do so, after some discussion with a literary agent, we have decided first to make this remarkable work available to the lay reader as a public service.

 A few words of explanation may be in order. In 1979, prior to the publication of our widely discussed paper, "Eating Ceremonies of the Blackfeet Indians" (Preston and Preston, 1980), we had spent many tedious but rewarding months perusing both printed and handwritten documents in the Indian Archives in Flagstaff, Arizona. One day, after a newspaper account of our activities had appeared, a package was mailed to me at the museum. The accompanying note, signed by a woman, explained that the journal contained therein had been written by an old man of her family some years before and had been left amongst his meager belongings at his death in the 1930s. She thought the document might have historical value, but at the same time she was fearful that it might be attacked as fraudulent or made the subject of ridicule. Since clearly this good woman was not seeking pecuniary reward and merely wished an expert's opinion as to the manuscript's authenticity, we decided to read it.

It was often difficult to decipher, for it was handwritten on lined paper that was already beginning to yellow, as cheap paper will; but we nevertheless persisted. Initially we were irritated both by the writer's tendency to skip about in time, telling whole episodes out of sequence, and by his apparently arbitrary shifts in the use of grammar and syntax. Sometimes his writing would appear to be the work of an educated Caucasian, sometimes almost a translation of formal Indian speech, and sometimes a solecistic scumble of pidgin English. However, within a short time we were engrossed in the old man's spikey scrawl. After a second reading we were dumbfounded. After discussing what we had read, we were forced to the conclusion that this diary, if indeed authentic, appeared to establish the actual existence of one of America's best-known fictional heroes! True, the person described in these writings did not possess the qualities or character depicted in the later popular entertainments, but nevertheless the similarities seemed greater than could be accounted for by mere coincidence.

Clearly this was a matter of sufficient importance to warrant delaying our departure, even at the risk of missing a most remunerative lecture engagement scheduled for the following day. We drove immediately to the address given by the woman who had sent the parcel, but when we arrived at the place (a roominghouse) no one there knew her present whereabouts. Apparently she had moved, leaving no forwarding address. Dismayed, we were compelled to face the fact that additional corroboration would be unlikely. Nevertheless, even though we have been advised by legal counsel to change some of the names used in the manuscript, we yet hold forth hope that the publication of these diaries may encourage the lady to come forward and join us in the inevitable discussions required by this electronic age. Of course, since such a public-spirited gesture could only enhance the commercial value of the property, we should willingly offer the lady a position in the enterprise: 2.5 percent of the net would seem reasonable.

We have often pondered, as any reader might surmise, whether the author of those well-known popular entertainments drew entirely from his own imagination, or whether, indeed, some stories of the actual man may have reached him through the familiar, if often distorting, medium of oral history. Clearly, if the adventures recounted herein are true, then there would have been ample opportunity for such word-of-mouth transmission (and transmutation) to have occurred.

And, indeed, there can be little doubt, to anyone familiar with the history of the post-Civil War West, that a great many of the events recorded by Crazy Fox *are* grounded solidly in fact. A sizable number of the people concerned are known even to the general reader, and virtually every episode involving them is a matter of established historical record. The research required to infuse such a staggering amount of authentic material into a literary hoax would clearly have been beyond the resources of this aboriginal author, despite his fragmentary formal education.

Unfortunately, both Crazy Fox and the author of those popular fictional works are now dead, so speculation as to the possible influence of the first upon the second must remain forever within the realm of conjecture. But it does seem unlikely that the popular author could have had access to these particular source materials, since the lady asserted that the papers had never been out of the family's possession.

Thus, despite persuasive internal evidence, we shall never have certain knowledge of the authenticity of these diaries. You, the reader, will have to be the final judge. Did the old man record all these events faithfully, or could the pages that follow be no more than the ramblings of an aging Indian who, for reasons we shall never know, played the red fox with us?

Don Preston
Sue Preston

By the time I was born, many of the old ways had been lost. The white man had come, first as a Spaniard and then as an Englishman or a Frenchman or a Dutchman; but whatever his language, he wanted our land, our souls or our lives, though not always in that order. In return he gave us promises, mostly broken, and the portions of land he did not yet want, to hold forever until he changed his mind.

The white man has learned much about us, because almost from the time he put us on his reservations his scholars have come in a steady stream to study our ways, to get us down on paper before we are gone from this earth entirely. So let the white man write of us; perhaps it will help to ease his conscience. But it has long seemed to me that we, too, should write of The People, so that our children may know of the old ways and their minds may bear traces of our footsteps. And this I have decided to do.

It is a story I had thought never to tell. I had thought to take it with me to the home of the Ancient Ones beyond the sky. But something has happened that has made me think of this matter again. The lady whom I call my granddaughter and with whom I live out my days, went recently to a home where they have a talking box. From the box, she supposedly heard my old friend's story. Remembering that those times had been spoken on in the family when she was a child, she came to me and recounted the things she had heard from the voices within the box.

Until that night it had never occurred to me that this sort of thing might happen. It was all so long ago, and I had thought it buried deep in the dust of all the men and horses that have passed along those trails since my friend and I first rode them together. So I too went to where people were listening to the talking box, and I too heard the voices pretending to be other people in another time. How strange and how sad to hear others trying to be like him and me. And how wrong it all was.

There is another reason why I must speak now of those times. My Children, you listened to the talking box and you cheered as those voices hunted down an Apache and took him with tied hands before the white judge. You, who have been born into a world where The People have been scattered and have become few, have forgotten that the sun of our People was once high in the sky. You have forgotten where we began on our Mother Earth, and you must be helped to remember. You must keep our prayers and our ways safe in your hearts, so that you and your children may know how to find the path of the Ancient Ones. And you must not clap your hands to talking boxes when an Indian is in trouble.

I set down these words so that you may see where I have walked, in a long life full of strange people and events. I have told some of these stories around cookfires, in the tongue of our people, but now I will put them down in the white man's language, which all now learn in school. It may be that when my granddaughter's children are old enough to read, she will show them these words. And they will truly know how it was for me, because I have tried to recall those times exactly as they happened. Perhaps when they have read of my wanderings on this earth they will come to understand that when a Potawatomi gives his word to another, he is bound by it forever.

Perhaps, too, they will see that not all white men are devils, even though the ones they have known may have seemed so. Things were different in other times, and in those days it was sometimes possible for men, no matter what color their skins, to meet as brothers. Or at least as cousins. Maybe the children will learn this from an old man's words after he is gone.

I am old now and will soon go. So now I will start to tell you how it was.

Crazy Fox
Potawatomi Reservation, 1933

Chapter

1

*In which Crazy Fox returns
to Texas, meets an old friend, and
explains how it all came to begin.*

In 1871 I was one of the men delegated by my Cherokee relatives to buy enough Texas cows to get our herd up to strength again. I was chosen because I had been to Texas and had worked Texas cattle, and also because I spoke English and Mexican and would be able to arrange a deal that wouldn't leave us too short on money or cows. White men were sometimes known to take advantage of Indians in trading, especially when the Indians were far from home and the tribe. But even at home in the Nations, the white law could be sometimes sympathetic and at other times indifferent to wrongs done to an Indian—not that it mattered very much, since whichever way it leaned on any particular occasion, it seldom did anything. In fact, we were going on this trip to Texas because our herd had been rustled to the point where we could see more of our stock by riding around the country than by looking over our own fences. And even though things had changed a lot in the past few years, we rode mostly at night to avoid any white men who hadn't heard how much things had changed. Many of them were still inclined to defend themselves violently against peaceful, even unarmed, Indians.

After many nights of riding I began to recognize the countryside. We were in Texas, probably not far from the outer edges of the CK Ranch, and I suddenly began to think about the Knights, whom I hadn't seen for several years. I wondered how they were, and whether they would remember me. I had changed some and had learned many things since my time with Jack Knight and his father, but I found myself looking forward to seeing them again.

3

My friends and I had camped on high ground among some rocks. There was enough grass for the horses and a clear spring bubbling down into a little pool among the rocks. The morning felt good. As I made water in the early light, the birds were already beginning their songs. Life could almost have been what it had been before the white man came. I had no way of knowing then how completely my life would change that day.

As the horses drank from the little pool and munched clumps of grass near its edge, Two Moons and I leaned against a big rock and listened as Walker Clark told of a dream he had had. He felt that the Great Spirit was trying to tell him something in the dream, and he wanted to know what we thought it meant.

We three had been walking together through some woods, he said, when a raccoon came out into our path and began to do a strange little dance, running back and forth with jerky little steps and spinning around. The raccoon said he needed a brave man's help. Then he started to cry and rub his face against a tree. What did we think it meant?

Just as Two Moons was about to answer, we heard gunshots not far away. We scrambled up on the rocks to get a better view, and that was the first time we noticed that we had camped not more than an arrow's flight from a coach road. I saw then that we were near the same spot where I had camped eight years ago, with two other friends.

A stagecoach was stopped in the road, its horses snorting and jumping around while the driver fought to keep them from tangling the reins. A man in white was standing in front of the coach, yelling and waving his guns. The shotgun rider must have thought he meant business, because a moment later a big square box came flying off the side of the coach and hit the ground with a loud thump. Then the driver snapped his whip and the horses lunged ahead, nearly pitching the guard right off the seat. The man in white jumped out of the way but then started running after the coach, shouting and shooting off his guns. He ran for a little while and then stopped, still yelling, as the coach disappeared behind a big cloud of dust. Finally, he sat down on a rock, and I could see he was disgusted. And now I could also see that he was wearing a black mask over the top part of his face.

Even with the mask, though, I was pretty sure I recognized him. I had thought he looked familiar right off, with the white clothes and hat, but I wasn't really sure until he started shooting. Bullets had been flying all over, whining off rocks and kicking up puffs of dust right at his own feet. No one except Jack Knight would be that careless with guns. But was it possible that Jack had turned outlaw? If he had, he was going about it in a strange way, out here on foot like this.

After a bit he got up and walked back up the road toward the strongbox. He looked at it a little and then suddenly gave it a good swift kick, which set him to yelling and dancing around, taking little hopping steps and holding his boot. After he'd calmed down, he reached down and got hold of a handle on the end of the box and started dragging it off the road. But after a little of that he let go of it and slumped against a cottonwood tree, holding his masked face in his hands. Then he gave the tree a little kick.

"YiEee," said Two Moons softly. "Could that be the raccoon of your dream?"

"He wears the raccoon's little mask, and he acts as strange as the animal in my dream. It may be that the Great Spirit means us to help this man." Walker Clark paused to think about that. "Or it could be the Great Spirit means us to kill him, to end his unhappiness. What do you think, Crazy Fox?"

"I think he needs help, like the raccoon said in your dream," I answered.

"But what help, and which of us? We cannot all follow him around. He would not understand, and he might not care about dreams or even the Great Spirit." Walker Clark stopped to think again. "One of us should go with him, and watch to see what the Great Spirit will direct. I will go, since it was my dream. It may be that I am the brave man the raccoon said he needed."

"YiEee," said Two Moons. "You might follow long and far. What will your new wife think when you don't return to the wigwam?"

Walker Clark thought about that, too, and I could almost see the pictures of his young wife that ran through his head. "Tell her I will return when I can," he said. "I have no wish to go, but if the Great Spirit calls a man he cannot pretend he is deaf."

He didn't move to go, so I could see we were going to sit on that rock a long time debating the wishes of the Great Spirit. I could also see that he was headed for trouble if he decided to stay in Texas, since he had never been out of the Nations before and he spoke no language except Cherokee.

"Brothers, let us talk further of this dream," I said. "As you told it, we were all walking in that forest, and the raccoon spoke to all three of us. So we cannot know who he meant. But the Great Spirit is wise, and it seems to me that he would have wished for the man to go who could be of the greatest help. I think I may know that man down there, and I speak his tongue. I think I should go down to see if he needs help. My brothers should stay here and watch. If he does not need us, I will return. But if I go with him, then I will meet you at camp tonight. There is a big rock a half day's ride that way, near a bend in the stream. Camp there and wait for me."

Walker Clark looked like he wanted to argue, but I guess more pictures of his young wife danced before his eyes because he stayed silent. A man could not always know what a dream was telling him, and after all I *was* unmarried. The honor of helping the raccoon was to be mine.

As I rode down, Jack was sitting on the strongbox, one boot in his hand, rubbing his foot. When he heard my horse he hurriedly put his boot back on and started waving his hat at me.

"Good morning, Jack," I said as I got near. "How have you been?"

He peered at me through the mask, tilting his head back to see better through the eye slits. "Speakum English?" he said at last.

I sighed. "Me Crazy Fox. Me come back."

"Oh, Crazy Fox. I thought I knew you from somewhere." He stopped to straighten his mask. "Say, do you think we could ride double back to the house? I've lost my horse, and it's a long walk home."

He didn't seem particularly surprised to see me, or to wonder where I had been for the four years since we'd last met.

"Why you hold up stage?" I asked him.

"I wasn't trying to hold up the stupid stage," he wailed. "All I wanted was a ride into town, but that guard must have been new. He didn't recognize me."

"Why Jack wear mask?" I asked. "Man think you outlaw, think you shoot him."

"Everybody knows I'm not an outlaw," he said in disgust. "I can't think what got into that man."

I tried again. "But why Jack wear mask?"

"That's a long story. Listen, maybe we could catch Whitey before he wanders back to the ranch. He might go back to Benton's Canyon."

Benton's Canyon? Whitey? "Why horse go there?" I asked.

"Because that's where I caught him in the first place," Jack said. "He's this really big white horse, and one day . . ."

I didn't hear the rest, because I was remembering the huge silver stallion that had roamed the area around Benton's Canyon for years. He had become almost like one of the spirits of my People. He had led a wild herd larger than any known in this country before, and nearly every man I had met on this range had tried to catch him at least once. No one had ever even come close.

"You catchum white stallion in Benton's Canyon?" I asked stupidly. "How you catchum?"

"I've been telling you about that, don't you listen? Like I said, it was after the—uh—trouble up there. The folks in town had sent out extra horses to carry in the dead and wounded, but they didn't have one for me so they suggested I walk home. That night I camped near the opening to the canyon, and I waited the next day to see if they'd changed their minds and sent someone back for me. That was when I noticed this big white horse watching me from between the rocks."

He stopped, as if that was all. "Go on. How did you catch the horse?" I was getting pretty tired of repeating that question, and my grammar was slipping a little.

"Didn't have to. I just sat down and looked back at him, and after a while he came over and nuzzled me. So I climbed on and rode him home."

I stared at him as if he'd just explained how to saddle a cyclone. Could it be that Jack truly was touched by the Great Spirit? I began to wonder if Walker Clark's dream *was* meant for me.

"Well, can I ride with you or not?" he was asking impatiently. "It's not very far."

I gave him a hand up behind me, and then had my hands full with my pony, who didn't like the smell of a white man. When I got him quiet and we were heading toward the canyon, I remembered my original question and tried it again. "Why Jack wear mask?" I asked over my shoulder.

I thought for a while he wasn't going to answer, but I guess he had just been thinking of how to tell it. "You remember I mentioned the trouble at the canyon, when the people from town came out to get the dead and wounded?"

I nodded.

"Well, that was a posse, led by some men who used to be Rangers with Father's old company. Or what was left of it, anyway, after it was disbanded."

I waited.

After a bit he said, "I just didn't think folks would take on so.

I mean, it was surely a tragedy, but nobody could have thought I had anything to do with it."

"With what?" It was like pulling stickle-pig quills off a dog.

"With the massa— With what happened." He paused again. "To the posse, I mean."

I pulled another quill. "What happen posse?"

"Well, we were riding up near the canyon, following up a rumor that John Wesley Hardin and some of his friends had been seen out that way. At the time I didn't even know who Hardin was, but everyone seemed all fired up to find him. And my father kept saying I had to hold up the family name with those Rangers, just like he'd done when he was younger. So I volunteered to scout the canyon for signs of anyone camping there."

Another quill. "You findum sign?"

"Well, sort of. So I went back down to tell the leader that I thought the gang was up at the head of the canyon. He didn't ask me how I knew, so I didn't tell him about this Indian I'd met up there who'd told me where to look for the Hardin gang." He paused, thinking. "Kiowa, I think. Or maybe Apache. Something like that."

I wanted to grab a handful of quills and rip them out of him, but I waited.

"Anyhow, what happened was that we rode into the draw and all hell broke loose. Hardin must have had fifty men with him, and they were all whooping like Indians and shooting guns at us from behind every rock and tree." He shivered, and his hand clenched my shoulder. "It was like hell's supposed to be. When it was over, most of the men were either dead or close to it. Except me, of course. I'd fallen off my horse and landed behind some rocks."

Something still didn't quite make sense. "Why everybody mad?" I asked.

"Well, just before he died, the leader of the posse got all excited and he told everyone I'd led them into an ambush. But I didn't," he said plaintively. "I mean, I wasn't the leader, and all I did was pass along this information I'd been given. How could they blame me?"

How indeed?

"Why you wear mask?" I asked for about the twentieth time.

Jack's voice was solemn. "You probably won't understand this, being an Indian and all, but it's a matter of honor. Wes Hardin took away my good name, and my father's, too, in a way. So until I can catch Hardin and clear my name, I have to wear this mask."

I felt I must have missed something. "Why?" I asked.

"I'm coming to that," Jack said loftily. "You see, in the olden days when a noble knight made a vow, he'd wear an eye patch or give up hard liquor or some such until he'd finished the job. Well, I've made a vow, and my name is even Knight. You see?"

"Not quite," I said.

He sighed. "I knew you wouldn't understand. Well, the point is, the mask stays on until I've had it out with Hardin. Besides, it will make it harder for him to recognize me."

I had read some of those tales of knighthood in the Cherokee school, and at the time those vows hadn't seemed all that crazy. Men of my People often did that kind of thing, and for reasons that were probably no more sensible. I knew Jack had loved historical romances when he was a child. And being sensible was never uppermost with him.

I made one last effort. "Outlaw wear mask," I said. "People think you robber."

"That's stupid," he said. "Everyone knows I'm not a robber."

"Crazy Fox understand," I said. And the frightening thing was that I did. Jack's kind of reasoning was hard to dispute.

We decided to head up Crooked Creek, which led to Benton's Canyon, to see if the horse was visiting any of his former herd. And when we rounded a bend a few miles up the creek, there he was, all rippling muscle gleaming in the sunlight as he drank from the stream. Ah, Children, if only you had seen him. What an animal! I myself had dreamed of catching those flashing muscles that seemed to flow over the ground faster than the wind. But he was like quicksilver; elusive, always melting away from the lariat.

"Hey, Whitey!" Jack shouted as he saw the horse.

The horse looked up and snorted, then went back to drinking. I didn't blame him, considering the name Jack had given him.

Jack jumped down and gave a whistle. The horse ignored him and began munching on grass. When Jack started toward him he took a few prancing steps away and then went back to eating grass again.

"Let's just rest here a little while, Crazy Fox," Jack said. He sat on a rock with his back to the horse. I got down and squatted nearby, watching the horse who was moving imperceptibly closer as he grazed.

I asked Jack if there were cattle for sale hereabouts. I explained about our depleted herd and told him we wanted to replenish it. But in "English," of course.

"I'm sure my father will sell you what you need," he said. "But how are you going to drive them to the Nations by yourself?"

Before I could answer he put a finger to his lips. The horse was walking toward him now, lifting his forehooves high in a prancing gait and nickering softly. When he had come within a few feet Jack spun around and dived for the dangling reins. Amazingly, the horse stood quiet.

"Gotcha, you big dumb sonofabitch," Jack said happily.

We rode along together for some time, and finally we passed under a sign I remembered well: It was a big plank of wood hanging between two posts, and it had the letters "CK" burned into it. Riding down that road was a strange experience, as if I had somehow moved backward in time. And in a way I had, because I had first seen that sign eight years ago, when I was a very young boy and very far from my home. I will tell you how that came to be.

I was the first of my family to be born in the new land west of the Mississippi. True, there were other Potawatomi all around us, but it wasn't their real homeland. We had all been dumped in strange lands, and my People didn't even go together. Some went to Missouri, some to Iowa and some to the Indian Territory. Not until I was in my middle years did I see the land where The People of the Fire had once walked proudly, and it was hard to find a trace of our ancestors there in those farmlands and towns.

My mother was called Shining Moon du Sable in her girlhood in upper Illinois. (I am using the white man's names so that all will know where I mean, but in the old days these places were called by their proper names.) My father was from Indiana and at the time I'm writing about was called He Who Runs Fast. But I guess it wasn't a very good name because he failed to outrun a bear not long after our tribe was removed. My mother had no man to care for her, so she went to her sister's home in the Cherokee Nation.

My mother's sister had married a wealthy Cherokee and she welcomed her poorer sister into her big house. My early days were spent roaming over the prairie wild and free, but my mother's sister let us have no peace until I was enrolled in school. Emissaries from all the other tribes came to study the Cherokee schools and courts, and it was not hard to convince my mother that being able to attend those schools would be a real advantage for a young man from a less prosperous tribe. In the years that followed I learned to read in English and Cherokee, and I devoured their books and newspapers at a good fast pace. I learned some Spanish then, too, though most of that came later.

One of the things I learned best was to love the English language. I hope you will not blame me for this, my Children, as some others among The People have done. It was no act of betrayal. English is beautiful because it allows so many different ways of saying things. True, that may make it a language better fit for liars than for honest men, but it also makes English a very good language for poets and writers. Of course I went back among my own People whenever I wanted to hear serious thoughts expressed, because there they could be spoken in the language of wisdom. But in school I read English books of every description just for the beauty of the words, until my eyes nearly fell out of my head. I cannot think that this was wrong. I missed the days on my pony at times, but those were good years in which I learned many things.

But in 1861 all of our lives changed forever. The white man had gone to war with his brothers, and he demanded that The People choose a side. The whole Indian Territory was in ferment, some tribes going for the North and many more for the South, and my mother feared I would be caught up in the troubles. So at fifteen I went with my mother to stay with those of our People who lived the farthest from the fighting. My school days were over.

Few of the writings on the white man's war will tell you what happened when our People became involved in their fight, or how we ended up losing more than either the North or the South. But at fifteen I was unthinking and easily stirred by tales of battle, and I longed to be riding out with the Indian regiments that were forming all up and down the Territory. For over a year I heeded my mother's wishes, but eventually the news of the action going on all around us was too much for me to resist. That winter I slipped away to my Cherokee relations, and for months I rode with my uncle in his Confederate regiment. Then, in the summer of 1863, at a place history books call Honey Springs, we were defeated in the biggest battle fought in the Indian Nations during the white man's war. Those of us who survived were suddenly a People on the run. We ran southward, and some of us ran as far as Texas.

In the confusion after the battle I got separated from my uncle. But I wasn't really worried, since everyone was moving in the same direction. I rode along as part of an endless river of wagons, filled with household belongings and women and children, rushing to where no bullets were flying. I pulled my pony up alongside a Creek family and tried to console the woman, who had not seen her husband since he helped her load the wagon. She was not much larger than the two children, playing with some puppies behind the flour sacks. She tried to smile for them despite the worry lines in her face.

I reined my pony in close, so she could hear me above the noise, and told her I would ride with her and protect her until her husband caught up. She gave a fleeting smile that said I was a child to be humored. "I am called Star Shine," she said, "and I will be grateful for your protection."

I ignored that smile of a mother and said, "I am Crazy Fox and I have been with my uncle, Robert Eagle, who commanded—"

"Ah, your uncle is well-known to us. My husband, Running Deer, attended council meetings where your uncle spoke often." She stopped, as if remembering that times were much different now. Behind her the children began to cough from the dust blowing into the wagon.

"We have no water," she said, pointing past my shoulder toward some trees. "Could you see if you can find us some?"

I took the water basket from the end of the wagon and rode toward the woods. The stream was small and well back in the stand of trees, so that the noise of the human river flowing by outside was muffled. I let my pony drink while I filled Star Shine's basket, and then let him graze a while in that peaceful spot. I could catch up with the wagon easily. I even lay in the stream myself, to let some of the road dust wash away from my tired body. It was then that I heard the first of the shots.

I sat up in the stream to listen, because at first I wasn't sure it really was gunfire. All the road noises sounded so far away, so removed from those woods. Then I heard them again, a crackle of shots and distant screaming. I leaped on my pony, leaving Star Shine's basket behind on the mossy bank. As I rode dripping from the woods I knew something was truly wrong. The shots were too many and too close together for a hunting party or someone shooting at a snake.

I couldn't see too well in the roiling clouds of dust, but white faces were riding and shooting and killing along the line of wagons. I had heard about bands of white raiders in the Territories, including the army following Quantrill, which had almost wiped out a town up in Kansas earlier that year. I wondered if this could be Quantrill's Raiders so far south, but I didn't have time to wonder very long.

As I rode into the cloud, people were screaming and horses were neighing wildly. I was thinking only of that wagon full of children and puppies, and the sadly smiling woman. People were running all about, children were crying, horses were dying, and live-stock and wagons were being driven off by the raiders, who pushed the dead owners off as they fled. At last I found Star Shine's wagon. It was overturned in a gully, its wheels still spinning though the horses were gone. The top had been torn away and the contents were strewn all over the ground. And there wasn't a sound. All were dead, Children, all had been shot many times. Star Shine's arms were outstretched toward her little ones, and her eyes were wide with the horror of what she had seen in the seconds before she died. Even the puppies had been shot.

I was almost a man and I had seen many things in battle that I would long remember, but none was the equal of that look on Star Shine's dead face. I bent over her to close those horror-stricken eyes, and at that moment something hit me from behind and I went down amidst the flour sacks and the dead children and puppies, unable to fight off the blackness that came down on me.

I don't know how much later I began to see the little dancing points of light, but I remember that my head was making sounds like a running herd of buffalo. I tried to open my eyes but they would not open. I felt I was moving, riding to see my father in the land of the Great Spirit.

"He's waking up." I heard the words like a whisper across a foggy creek in the morning.

A bright light hurt my eyes. I shielded my face with my hands and looked up. I could see rolling hills and a blue sky with little bits of fluff racing beyond the trees. Was this, then, the land of our Ancestors? It looked very much like any other place. I turned my head to see more, and groaned at the pain.

When I opened my eyes again two figures were looking down at me. They were not white men, so I let my muscles relax.

"Are you all right?" the tall one asked. "We wouldn't have picked you up but we could see you were still alive and we didn't want to leave you there for the white devils to scalp."

I tried to sit up but a hammer of pain struck my head.

"I think we're all right here," the voice said. "We rode all night and no one followed us. They were too tired from killing women and children."

Suddenly I saw it, as if he had held a painting before me. Star Shine, bloody and staring, reaching out toward the jumble of children and puppies caught in one last act of play.

"Was it Quantrill?" I asked the tall man.

"I don't know. Does it matter? Our people have been dying between the white faces for a long time now, fighting their war. We are still dying." He was very tall for an Indian and his hair was like the hair of the black people I had seen around my uncle's house.

"Who are you?" I asked him.

"My name is Turning Smith and that is my cousin, Eagle Flies. We are Cherokee."

But one of your parents was not a Cherokee, I thought. No matter. At least we could understand each other.

"Where are we now?" I asked him, trying again to sit up.

"I don't know," he said. "We were trying to reach Choctaw country, but I don't know where we are after riding all night in hills I've never seen before."

We made a dry camp, building no fire lest the smoke bring the raiders to us. At nightfall, Turning Smith put me on a horse and tied my arms around its neck so I wouldn't slip off if the darkness returned. I felt weak and lightheaded as we rode through that starry night, but I stayed conscious. I thought of Star Shine, and it seemed to me that if the Great Spirit would allow such a sweet woman and her little children to be hurt so, I wasn't sure I wanted to stay on my Mother Earth.

After several days of camping in the hills, and several nights of riding, I felt stronger, strong enough to try to talk Turning Smith into heading back toward our homeland. We weren't doing anyone any good out here, and maybe we were needed at home. But he was taller than me and older, and he had a cousin along, and I saw that if there was going to be any chief amongst these three Indians it wasn't going to be me. So, not wanting to ride alone in a strange country, I stopped arguing.

One day we made camp in a natural hollow under some rocks that were tumbled around as if thrown from the Great Spirit's hand. We were shielded from the sun and the horses had been fed and watered, so I lay down to get some rest. I heard a noise far away, like an eagle making his morning dive for breakfast. I started to speak, but Turning Smith held up a hand for silence.

He slowly edged around the rocks to see what was making the noise. Eagle Flies and I followed, and we all stood looking down to where a buckboard was bumping across the prairie. The noise wasn't coming from the buckboard, though. It was coming from a rider off in the distance, galloping toward the buckboard and hallooing. The two men on the wagon seat finally heard him too (Who has the best ears, Children?) and pulled up. We all watched the rider get bigger and bigger as he rode across the valley, waving his hat and yelling.

"That's an Indian they've got tied up in that wagon," Turning Smith said softly.

"Looks like a Kiowa," said Eagle Flies.

"Maybe, but he's still an Indian," said Turning Smith. "And the white men have got him tied up like a turkey ready for the fire."

"How can you tell he's a Kiowa from here?" I asked.

"Quiet. Cousin, get the horses," he said. "We will show them how a Cherokee fights when the odds are even. And you, too, Crazy Fox."

I could see his mind was made up. These white faces were far from the burning wagons we'd left behind us, but they were going to pay for what their brothers had done.

Eagle Flies came back with the horses and we mounted silently, watching the scene below. The men in the wagon were shaking their heads and pointing the rider back the way he had come. He was waving his arms and arguing, though we couldn't hear his words. Finally the wagon started off again, the Indian rolling and bouncing in back and the rider following along behind.

"Crazy Fox will take the rider. My cousin and I will take the wagon. Three scalps will hang from our belts before this day ends." He let out a whoop that echoed off the rocks and raced off, with Eagle Flies behind him. I had not known whether I would follow or not, but suddenly Star Shine's staring eyes came into my mind. I kicked my pony and let out a whoop of my own.

They heard us coming and began whipping the wagon horses into a run. But our ponies had been moving by night, at a walk, and now they were glad for a run and flew across the prairie after the lurching wagon. The lone rider seemed confused for a minute, but then he turned his horse and started back the way he had come.

Turning Smith and Eagle Flies raced after the wagon, yelling encouragement to each other as they went. I started after the rider, glad to feel the wind stream over my body. This was better than sneaking about by night.

The rider turned in his saddle and saw I was gaining. He tried to kick more speed from his horse, but it had run far already and was in no mood to go faster. The rider turned again, and this time he turned too quickly and lost his balance. He sailed in the air, his arms flailing, and hit the ground in a heap.

I reined up and slipped from my pony. My knife was in my hand, and hate for the killers of Star Shine in my heart.

He turned to look at his doom, his eyes wide with terror.

I stopped. He was a boy. Not a child, but still younger than I was by several years. Not much older than Star Shine's son, who had played with puppies. I raised my knife and thought, Here is a boy for your boy.

"You'd better not—" His eyes were still wide, but he saw my indecision.

Show me what to do, Great Spirit! Show me the way!

The boy still stared at the knife, but I think he already knew he was not to die this day. I put the knife back in my belt.

He seemed to relax immediately, as if nothing frightening had ever happened. "Do you speak English?" he asked.

I had not spoken English for a long time, so I groped for the words the Cherokee teachers had taught. "What is our present location?" I said at last.

He looked blank. "No speakum English?" he said. "What you speakum? You Kiowa? Tonto?"

"Certainly not! I'm no Apache. I am from The People called Potawatomi."

"Not Apache." He seemed at a loss for what to do next. Then his face lit up. "Me Jack Knight," he said, pointing at his own chest. "What your *name*?" He stabbed the finger at my chest.

I began to see the problem. For this boy Indians spoke only one way, it seemed. "Me called Crazy Fox," I told him. "Me lost."

He nodded enthusiastically. "Good, good," he said. "Crazy Fox not lost. As a matter of fact, you're in Texas, almost on my father's ranch." He paused to think about that. "And I can tell you, folks are going to be plenty mad when they hear what you and your friends have done."

I remembered Turning Smith and Eagle Flies and turned to look for them, but the wagon was out of sight. I ran to my pony and raced back across the valley floor just as that boy had done minutes before. In a mile or so I saw the wagon. I slowed my pony, not wishing to approach but knowing I must. The horses were walking at a slow clop-clop, as if they had forever to reach their destination. From time to time one paused a moment to grab a clump of grass.

As I got closer I could see the two white men slumped on the wagon seat. Their shirts were stained red, but they still wore their hair. A little way off I saw the two Indian ponies grazing calmly. I tied the wagon horses to a bush and went to find my friends.

Turning Smith and Eagle Flies lay dead on the stony ground many weeks' ride from their village, staring at the last sky they would ever see. It would be a long time before their women learned of their dying and took up the keening that followed death through the door.

I stood there, seeing the whole thing as a high flying bird would see it. I was in a strange valley with four dead men, one live boy, a wagon and a team. And one trussed-up Indian. The boy was running along the trail toward the wagon, holding his side and panting. When he got there he stared with big wide eyes at the death. He poked the two white men, who didn't move, then he poked the Indian, who jumped so violently the boy almost fell over backwards.

"Hey, this one's alive," he yelled.

I went to look at the Indian. He was glaring as if angry that he had missed all the fun. I pulled my knife and leaned over him.

"You better not let him go," the boy said behind me. "My father would be real mad about that."

I cut the thongs holding the Indian's arms and legs. He jumped to the ground and danced around as if trying to get the bounces and bumps out of his joints. I held my gun ready in case we didn't understand the same language and needed a talking aid.

"Me speak white face talk," he said. "Me no do what they say. White face give horses to Bear Foot."

The boy hooted. "You bet," he said. "Happens all the time."

"You say Bear Foot tell lie?" The Kiowa looked really amazed at this.

"Lie! That's about all you people do," the boy said.

I stopped the Kiowa with a gun across his middle. "No," I said. "Boy only one know we not shoot people."

"They not care who shoot Indian."

"But boy know I not shoot white men. And he see you tied up. You kill boy, you murderer. That maybe worse than horse thief."

He gave me a hard look, but I could see he was thinking it over. "If we go back, how you make boy tell truth?" he asked.

"I spare boy's life. Why he not tell truth?"

I could see that the boy was beginning to realize what a hold he had over us. He was smiling in a way I didn't like. "Or we could kill boy and ride hard. No one left to tell then," I added.

The Kiowa considered this, too, nodding his head. The boy stopped smiling and came to my side. "My father is the biggest rancher in these parts, and if you kill me he'll have half of Texas hunting you down," he said.

"Boy right," I said to the Kiowa. I was growing tired of all this talk while my friends stared silently at the sun. "You help me, then we go talk to boy's father."

As we loaded the bodies into the wagon, I looked at Turning Smith and Eagle Flies, and I hoped they had truly thought this was a good day to die. We tied their horses behind the wagon, and I told the Kiowa to drive with the boy riding next to him. He shook his head vehemently.

"Bones hurt," he said. "No ride in wagon. Bear Foot walk."

I just wanted to get this nasty business done. "You take pony," I said. "I drive wagon."

That was how we ended up, with me driving, the boy next to me on the buckboard seat, and the Kiowa riding alongside on my horse. We rode in silence, thinking our own thoughts. I thought of my two friends, who had saved my life and then so quickly lost their own. And I wondered what was to come this day, when we delivered our freight to the Knight ranch.

I looked at the Kiowa, riding along on my horse. He was smiling, and I didn't much like that either. He saw me looking at him and said, "You not Kiowa. Where you come from?"

I told him and he thought about that for a minute. Then he said, "You not Kiowa, but Bear Foot no think you shoot Indian." He smiled again. "Sorry about horse," he said, and kicked my pony hard.

"Shoot him, shoot him!" the boy was yelling.

As he raced away I got my gun off the seat and raised it. But the Kiowa was right. If I couldn't kill the white boy for Star Shine, how could I kill an Indian for the white men? I put the gun down. Another body in the wagon wouldn't make things any better. There had been enough of dying. In a minute more the Kiowa was out of sight, and I was sure I'd never see him nor my pony again. Children, he was one lousy Kiowa.

Silence filled the valley, except for the flies buzzing around the back of the wagon. After a while the boy must have figured we were now even because he began to hum a little tune. The Kiowa was no longer there to threaten him, so he didn't need my protection. We were heading for his ranch, to tell our stories to his father, and in Texas a white man spoke first, even if he was a boy. The more I thought, the more it seemed that things were a lot more even for him than they were for me. I sat on that wagon seat, listening to the humming, with a ball of iron in my belly.

We clopped along the wagon trail for a long time, and finally we came to a sign swinging between two posts. And for the first time in my life I passed under the big letters "CK." A little farther on we saw some riders off in the distance, and the boy said, "Those are some of my father's men, and they all got guns."

The ball in my belly rolled around a little.

We began to pass some buildings set back from the wagon road among tall shade trees, and in a little while more we passed some men working on a picket fence. They put down their hammers and started walking after us. One of them saw what was in the wagon and yelled, "Hey, he's got Henry and old Gus there!"

We passed the bunkhouse, where more men were coming out to follow us, and crossed a little bridge. I could see barns and a blacksmith shed, and beyond that I could see the main house, which was large and white and had more shade trees and grass around it. The blacksmith put down his tools and came out to follow, wiping his big hands on his leather apron.

The trees gave everything a cool, peaceful look, like a park I had once seen in a white man's town. But I was out in the hot Texas sun with a whole army of Gus and Henry's friends following along behind, and that iron ball was trying to come up my throat now.

Men were coming from the corrals and barns, but I kept driving and held my eyes straight ahead to where a man was standing all alone in the middle of the house yard. He was a short man but very wide and blocky, and the wide-brimmed hat he wore made him look even heavier. As I got closer I could see he had shaggy eyebrows and a lot of laugh lines around his eyes, but he wasn't laughing now.

I reined up the horses and sat still while he walked around the wagon and looked at what lay in the bottom. The big crowd of men held back till he had finished looking, then they began to move in closer for a better look themselves. "Hell, them ain't Kiowas," I heard one of them say.

The stocky man came slowly around to the front of the wagon again and looked at me long and hard. Finally he said, "All right, I think it's about time you commenced talkin'."

The boy said, "Father, that stupid horse threw me again and—"

The man looked at him and he stopped. Then he looked at me again. "Do you speak English?" he said.

"He doesn't speak much of it," the boy said. "I know that was your special horse, but—"

The look his father gave him was nearly hard enough to punch holes in him, and this time he stayed quiet. The older man turned back to me again.

I took a deep breath and began. "My name is Crazy Fox and I come from up in the Indian Territory. I was fighting with the Confederacy, and we lost a battle up in the Cherokee country." I paused to see if the gang of men was listening or loading up their guns. They were listening. So was the old man, his cold blue eyes held on me like gunbarrels. I went on, telling of the wagon train and my rescue by Turning Smith and Eagle Flies and our travels south.

"That them back there?" Mr. Knight asked.

I nodded, and went on telling how they had ridden to free the Kiowa, and how I had spared his son's life. I watched to see if that impressed him, but he didn't seem to be filled with gratitude.

"How come you didn't shoot that horse-thievin' Kiowa?" he asked.

The men shifted about at this, and I could hear muttering. I thought hard of what to say, to make them feel I had not taken the Kiowa's side, but I could not think of anything convincing. Finally I told the simple truth.

"There had been enough killing," I said.

He looked at me for another long minute, then nodded. He walked around back and looked at the four bodies again, then said, "You men get some boxes made."

He came back to the front of the wagon and looked up at me again, sitting there on the wagon seat as rigid as a tentpole. He sighed. "Well, you might as well get down from there and tell the cook to give you somethin' to eat," he said, and motioned for his son to follow him.

As they walked away I could hear him talking to the boy. "Dammit, Jack," he said. "Ain't you never gonna learn how to set a horse?"

Since Mr. Knight was pretty much the law in that part of Texas nobody questioned his way of doing things. So the next day the two white men were buried in a dusty little graveyard outside of the town of Cottonwood with Mr. Knight saying a few words over them. I got his permission to bury Turning Smith and Eagle Flies in a little grove of trees in the valley where they had died.

I was far from my home with no friends and no place to go, so I stayed on at the Knight ranch and became a cowboy. I stayed there for four years, in fact, before I rejoined my People.

It had been many years since I'd last ridden down this road, and the grass around the big main house seemed even greener now. In some strange way, though I was far from my People, it was almost like coming home.

Chapter

2

---

*In which Crazy Fox helps
tilt a windmill, makes a curious deal, and
prepares to leave Texas behind him.*

It was just past the noon meal, and Charles Knight sat on the front porch rocking and smoking. He continued to rock and smoke while we handed the horses over to old Miguel at the barn door, but as we started toward the house he stopped rocking. And as we came closer I could see he was smiling. He got up from the rocker and stepped down from the porch to welcome me.

"I had always hoped that before either one of us got called up Yonder, you might come this way again." He gave me the hug a father might give a long-missed son.

"I too am happy to see the faces of my friends once again," I told him. "You have been in my thoughts always."

"You're lookin' no worse for wear despite all that travel." He still held his eyes on me, as if he were trying to see what kind of man I had become.

"I am well and my family is well," I said. I started to say something about him and his family, but the words stopped in my throat. Jack was standing nearby in his dusty white outfit and dirty mask-covered face, nudging a clump of grass with his boot toe. I realized he had not spoken, and that Mr. Knight had not once looked at Jack since we arrived. It seemed that things had not gone as Mr. Knight had wished during my absence.

"Let's go up there and sit down, and you can tell me what brings you back down our way." Mr. Knight climbed the steps back up to the porch, and as I followed him I realized he was reaching the late years of his life.

We took chairs and Jack, who had not been invited to join us, perched on the porch railing and began idly kicking at one of the posts.

"I have come to buy stock for my People," I told him. "Things have not always gone well for us, and in recent times we lost most of our herd. I—"

"Lost?" he said, shaking his head. "We've lost some cattle around here the same way, but our hands aren't tied like your'n. We can deal with rustlers when we can catch 'em."

I smiled, remembering that trussed-up Kiowa years ago.

"Well, how many head do you need?" he asked.

"I have only two men with me, and they are not very experienced in trail herding. I doubt if we can handle more than three hundred."

Jack began to kick harder at the post, and now he was humming a little tune.

"We can manage that," Mr. Knight said. "Where are these other two fellers?"

"My friends and I separated this morning. I will meet them tonight at that butte near the bend of the creek."

Charles Knight gave me an odd look, and for the first time he looked toward Jack. Jack stared up at the cloudless sky and hummed a little louder.

It looked like no one planned to break the silence, so I started up again. "I met Jack out on the road today, not far from the place where we had that trouble when I first came here." I was sorry I had brought that up, so I hurried on. "We decided to ride on in together so I could talk with you."

Mr. Knight didn't even look at me this time, but kept staring at Jack, who was still humming and kicking. "Did you two happen to meet up with Slim Masters on your way in?" he asked.

Jack didn't seem inclined to talk, so I said we hadn't.

"Well, he rode all the way out from town to tell us about a stage holdup out in the valley today." He glanced at me. "Probably not far from where you met Jack," he said.

"I didn't rob any stage," Jack said quickly, jumping down off the railing. "All I wanted was a ride. It isn't my fault if that driver was too stupid to listen to me, is it?"

Mr. Knight looked pained. If you are dealt a hand you have to play it, but you had to wonder if Mr. Knight wouldn't just as soon have thrown this hand in years ago.

"Jack," he said softly, "don't you understand that the only people around here who wear masks are those who mean to steal things? People don't take to play-acting unless it's on a stage in a theater."

"Father, I have explained all this to you before. You know why I must wear this mask."

"Please take the blamed thing off, Jack." It was the only time I had ever heard such a pleading tone in the old man's voice.

Jack's voice was louder this time. "You know I will take it off when I've tracked down the Hardin gang and brought them to justice."

"Hell, Hardin likely don't even ride with a gang, and he's probably long gone from Texas by now anyways."

"He does so have a gang," Jack said, nearly yelling now. "Who do you think shot . . ." He stopped himself. "Well, you know he does," he finished.

Their voices were carrying a good distance by now, and I could see figures edging up from around the outbuildings to hear better.

"I don't give a hoot in hell about Hardin, and I can't change what happened out there that day," Charles Knight said. "That's done and past. But you are ruining your life with that damn-fool mask, and mine too. So will you please take the damned thing off and—"

"No!" Jack yelled. "No I won't. When a Knight gives his word he keeps it. You may not believe me about what happened today, and maybe you don't even believe me about that other time, but you can sure believe I'll wear this mask until I've done what I have to do." He jumped down from the porch and strode off toward the barn.

Mr. Knight watched him go, then let out a big sigh and said, "Things do not always go well for me either."

I didn't know what to say so I just waited, and in a while he turned to me again. "I don't suppose you know anything about that strongbox Masters mentioned, do you?" he asked quietly.

I thought carefully and then said, "I believe it can be returned."

He nodded and turned away.

As we stood there, two puppies chased each other across the yard in a rolling tumble of growls and barks. I watched them pretend ferocious battle, then suddenly drop flat in the shade of a big oak to sleep. I thought of Star Shine's puppies and turned away quickly, trying to blot the picture from my mind.

I saw that Mr. Knight was looking at the puppies, too, with a smile that seemed to have some pain in it. He caught me watching him and shook his head. "Hell, we can't spend our days watching dogs play," he said. "Let's go look at some cows."

The afternoon passed quickly as we rode over just a small section of that sprawling ranch looking for cattle in the best shape for a trail drive. By the time the sun was over our shoulders, I had driven the start of our new herd into an old corral used mostly during spring roundups. Neither of us had said a word about Jack.

As we closed the gate on the last cow for the afternoon, I said, "I will ride out now to meet my friends by the river."

He nodded but seemed reluctant for me to go. I supposed that his days were now spent mostly over books and ledgers, and I had been a bit surprised when he had come out with me instead of sending one of the hands. He was no longer young, and the years seemed to pull at the lines of his face.

Charles Knight had come to Texas before it was Texas. He was one of those Americans who had gone into Texas when it was still Mexican territory and had somehow managed to hold onto his ranch through the Texas war for independence. He fought with Sam Houston but never had a good word to say for him, claiming the general was mostly out for Houston and it was no wonder he was run out of Tennessee. Mr. Knight had been in the Texas Rangers for a while and had served as a scout for the Confederate forces in the early days of the white man's war, until a leg wound had sent him home.

But his biggest interest from our first meeting was his son, Jack, the one who would someday inherit everything the old man had fought to build up. I was only seventeen myself then, and Jack was two or three years younger than I was. But even so, it was pretty clear over the next four years that very few men could have grown up less ready for the job. He couldn't stay on a horse, he hardly knew a cow from a buffalo, and he didn't seem to have any interest at all in how a ranch bigger than my People's whole reservation was run. He wasn't overly fond of Indians or blacks or Mexicans either, and in a country filled with Indians and blacks and Mexicans, this could sometimes cause problems. Mostly what he liked was fancy clothes and stories from books.

Jack had never been comfortable around his father. He wanted to please the old man but never seemed to know how, and every time he set out to do something he thought his father would admire he ended up riding off in the wrong direction. Like that day when I met him for the first time. His father had sent him to deliver a message to some men working on the south range, but instead of doing that he had decided to follow the wagon taking that Kiowa over to Stumpy Morgan's place for identification. Mr. Knight had told the men they were to do nothing to the Indian until Morgan had identified him positively as the one who had stolen his horses, but it seems they were muttering about a "necktie party" anyway as they left. Jack heard them, and thought that sounded a lot more interesting than riding out to a line camp. So he had saddled up his father's prize horse and followed after the wagon. The rest of that day is as I have told it, and it was only one of many such adventures Jack managed to get into over the years I worked on the CK Ranch.

His father kept trying, though. I think one of the reasons he kept me on at the ranch was that he thought I might teach Jack something. Maybe he was impressed with an Indian boy of seventeen who had been in a war, who could read and write in two languages and speak two more pretty passably. The only language Jack spoke was a kind of half-baked Eastern English acquired at school.

Jack had a lot to live up to. His father was one of the most famous cattlemen in all of Texas. He had built up the biggest ranch of its day from what had started out, in the forties, as nothing more than a couple of sod-roofed buildings, a few half-wild longhorns and two or three vaqueros. He had been successful in everything he had ever tried, except for raising the kind of son he wanted. I was sorry to see that the years of my absence had not brought them closer together, but there was nothing I could do to help him. My place was with my People who waited for the cattle I would bring them.

"I am grateful for your help," I said. "I will return tomorrow, and then you can tell me what I must pay for the cattle."

He laughed. "You never will learn how to bargain," he said.

He squared his shoulders and rode off toward the house like a man who would never give up.

Next morning before daylight I left Two Moons and Walker Clark, explaining that I had a favor to do for my white friend and that

I would return as soon as possible. They agreed to wait there for me, now that they knew we would not have to search further for the cattle.

I rode back to the CK ranch buildings and left my horse tied by the barns. I went silently into the house, which was still quiet with early morning. I went to Jack's room and touched his shoulder as he slept. He came awake with eyes wide, and instantly grabbed for his mask on the table next to the bed. Then he realized who I was and relaxed.

"We have a job to do," I said. He nodded.

We left the house without breakfast, and I waited in the yard while he brought out a buckboard and hitched two of the wagon horses to it. When we finally got the lines untangled, we drove the wagon across the little bridge and down the lane toward the prairie. The only sound was the creaking of the wheels, which startled some late-sleeping birds into their morning song. When I looked back at the silent house I saw a stocky figure standing at a window, watching us go.

The strongbox was where we had hidden it, and it didn't take long for us to get it into the wagon, even though Jack had to keep stopping to fix his mask. It was homemade out of an old hat, and it kept slipping around so that sometimes when I looked at an eyehole I saw a nose staring at me.

We drove on into Cottonwood and pulled the wagon up in front of the stagecoach office. This building hadn't been here the last time I had visited the town, but it already had the same look of neglect all the other buildings had. The hot sun and the Texas winds aged everything, buildings as well as people. A sign hung from one chain, with the other one dangling free and looking as if it had been that way for a long time. It said "We Serve All The South," and the front door stood open as if inviting the South in. The inside looked dark and cool.

The few people on the street had turned to watch us as we drove in, but nobody seemed alarmed or surprised at Jack's getup. And as we dragged the strongbox out of the wagon, no one paid much attention to that either. It looked like the word had got around about what had happened, and everyone had decided not to interfere with Knight business.

"Don't worry about all this, Crazy Fox," Jack told me. "I know Jake Hamilton, and he'll understand."

I helped him heft the box through the door and into the shadowy room. At first it was hard to make out the fat little man behind the counter. Even an Indian's eyes need a few seconds to adjust.

When they did adjust, I saw the man had been expecting us. "Howdy, Jack," he said. "Thought you might drop by." He nodded to me.

"Hello, Jake. We found this box out by the stage road this morning. Figured it must have fallen off the coach someway."

"Yep, I figgered Soapy was a mite too quick with his story about robbers. I wasn't really worried about it, but I am right glad to get it back." He thought about it a minute, as if considering relations between the Cottonwood Coach and Freight Company and the Knight Ranch. "Lord, you know I believe you may even be entitled to a reward for recovering this."

Jack held up both gloved hands in protest. "No, no, just doing my duty, Jake. I'm just glad it was us that found it and not some of the trash roaming around these days."

"Ain't that the truth." He looked at Jack for a time, then said, "You reckon your daddy will be sendin' in his supply order this week?"

"Probably," Jack said. "Why?"

"Oh, I was just thinkin' that the stage will be comin' through again on Thursday, so it might be just as well if one of the hands brought in the order." He thought about that for a minute and then added, "I mean, I know you're bound to have a lot more important stuff to attend to than jawin' with that danged fool Soapy Washington."

Jack looked puzzled for a moment, and I realized that by now he probably believed he really had found that box just like he'd said. But then it dawned on him what he and Soapy might have to jaw about, and he said, "You're right, Jake. Thursdays are very busy on the CK."

Stepping back out into that street was like poking your head into an oven, but Jack didn't seem to notice. He was obviously happy to be in Cottonwood, and not because of the dirt road and the cluster of small wooden buildings bleaching in the sun like buffalo bones. In a minute he turned to me and said, "Come on, there's somebody I want you to meet."

"Who?"

"Just the prettiest girl in Texas," he said. "Maybe in the whole world." He started toward the saloon across the street. It had not changed in four years, and I wondered if old Sam still ran it. Like most bartenders, he had never seemed to notice that I was an Indian when I put money down on his bar. I wondered if he felt the same way about Jack's mask.

Jack had walked across the street and was peeking over the swinging doors. He motioned for me to come along. I wasn't happy about entering a saloon with a masked man, but I was even less happy about standing out in that street alone. Too many Texans still used my People for target practice. I joined him at the door and we went on in and sat down.

I saw Dulsie Morgan right away, mainly because she was the only woman in the place. But she would have been pretty noticeable anyway. She was wearing more clothes than she'd had on when I'd seen her last, four years ago in Abilene, but now there was a lot more of her trying to get out of them. Her blonde hair was piled up on top of her head, and the red dress made her eyes look as green as moss. She had on little red shoes that looked like they'd dissolve in the first cow pie she stepped in. But all in all she looked like a very healthy person.

She saw Jack waving at her and started over toward us, pausing to blow in a man's ear along the way. He made a grab for the closest part of her, but she ducked out of the way and laughed.

"Jackie!" she yelled as she got near us. She grabbed him and planted a kiss on his lips that sounded like a cow walking in a mud hole. Then she stood back and looked at him. "I thought you might come into town today," she said. "I mean, I heard about some trouble out your way."

The man whose ear she'd blown in looked up from his whiskey and said, "Hey, Dulsie, ask him if he's seen ol' Wes Hardin lately."

Jack started to say something but Dulsie put a hand on his arm. She glared at the man with the ear and said, "Now you just hush up your mouth, or I ain't gonna come to your party." The man snickered and went back to his drink.

She turned back to Jack and said, "Boy, I wouldn't want to be around when Soapy comes through here again if I was you. He's one mean man, and *big*." She rolled her eyes and the bartender let out a cackle.

She noticed me then. "Say, don't I know you from some place?" she asked. "I mean, normally I don't—uh—meet too many Indians, but you look familiar."

"This is Crazy Fox," Jack said. "He used to work for us, and he's my friend even though he is an Indian."

"Yes, ma'am," I said. "I met your father on a drive to Abilene, years ago."

"Oh, Abilene." She giggled. Then she looked at Jack. "I sure would like to visit that town sometime," she said soberly.

"It's no town for a lady, Miss Dulsie," Jack said. "Stay here in Cottonwood, and let me take you for a ride on Sunday after church."

"Oh, honey, I doubt if I'll make it to church. I work late Saturday nights, you know."

"I know," he said unhappily. "These men in this place get to see more of you than I do, and it just isn't fair. Sam could hire someone else to serve drinks and clean up around here, so you'd have more time free."

Sam snickered again, but Dulsie didn't blink at the description of her duties. "Now, Jackie, you know what I told you. I like working here. I get to meet lots of nice folks. Not like if I stayed stuck out on that ol' ranch with nobody to talk to but Daddy and some ol' cows."

"Well, at least Sam could get you a nicer uniform than that to work in," he said. The man with the ear nearly choked on his whiskey.

"Don't you like it?" she asked, leaning forward so that a good part of her nearly came out of it entirely. "Most of the customers think it's real purty." She fingered the lacy edging around the top, and Jack's eyes followed her fingers.

"You know, Jackie," she said after a minute, "there is one little ol' thing I had meant to ask you about."

"What?" Jack said, still studying her fingers.

"Well, I did promise my daddy I'd talk to you about that ol' windmill your daddy put up out at Quit Well."

"Now Dulsie, you know—"

"Oh, I know, Jackie, you probably don't have time to fuss with a dumb ol' girl's problems."

"I do, I do," he said. "It's just that—"

"It's just that that ol' windmill is driving my pore daddy plumb crazy," she interrupted. "I mean, that well really was his, you know."

"My father bought it from him fair and square. In fact, your father thought he was getting the best of the bargain."

"Well how was he to know those silly ol' windmills would come along?" she said, her voice getting whiney just like her father's.

"But nobody made your father sell, Dulsie," Jack said,

his eyes back on where her fingers were playing with that lace.

Dulsie leaned across the table again. "I know, Jackie," she said, "but don't you think you could get your daddy to let my daddy use just a little bit of that water?" She was stroking his arm as she talked, and he looked like he might start purring any minute.

"Well, Dulsie, I just don't know. . . ."

"Oh, Lordy, is that a bug?" she said, her voice all high and squeaky.

"Where?" Jack asked.

"Right here," she said, leaning over and pointing. "Oh, get it, Jackie!" She took his hand and guided it to where she said the bug was, though I couldn't see anything there but a little mole.

Jack's face got as red as an afternoon sun. "I guess I could discuss it with my father," he said, looking for the bug. "I mean, it wouldn't hurt to ask him, I guess."

"Oh, Jackie, I told my daddy you'd hep us out." She fixed up the top of her dress. "I've got to get back to work now, but if you can really get your daddy to let us use a little of that water . . ." She puckered her mouth and thought about it. "Well, maybe I just *will* ride out with you next Sunday. Only, don't make it too early, honey."

Jack watched her flounce away with a look on his face like a man who has just stumbled into a gold mine. I could see the light in his eyes right through the mask.

By the time we got back to the ranch I was eager to meet Two Moons and Walker Clark and tell them about the cows. But as I helped Jack unhitch the horses, I realized he hadn't said a word since we left town. He'd just hummed quietly as we rode. I wondered if he had been rehearsing how to bring up the business of the well with his father.

He had. "Why don't you come on over to the house," he said. "I know Father will want to see you again."

"No, me go gettum cows."

"Come on, Crazy Fox. You know it's too late for that now. Come on in with me and help me talk with Father. He listens to you."

That was what I had been afraid of. It was one argument I would much rather not be part of. I knew Mr. Knight was not likely to give away water no matter how much of Dulsie fell out of her dress. But I could see Jack wasn't going to give up, so I went along with him.

Inside the house it was cool and quiet, though we could hear noises from the cookhouse out back. We went down the hallway and Jack tapped on his father's door.

"Come in." Mr. Knight was seated at a big rolltop desk, but he swiveled his chair around when we entered. "You fellers been to town?" he asked.

"Yes, Father. Crazy Fox helped me with an errand I had."

Charles Knight looked at me and nodded slightly. His eyes said thank you.

"And guess who I ran into," Jack went on. "Dulsie Morgan."

"Stumpy Morgan's little girl? I thought he'd sent her off to school somewheres."

"No, she's been home a while now. She works in town, and she's a really beau— She's a very nice person."

"Well, I sure hope she's turned out better'n her ma. Stumpy's woman ran off with some drummer back in '59. Not that I blame her much." He turned to me again. "I thought you might be gone most of the day so I had some of the boys bring in some cattle from out by Quit Well. You can look them over in the spring corral."

"It's funny you should mention Quit Well, Father," Jack broke in. "Dulsie and I were just talking about it this morning."

"Oh?" Mr. Knight had turned back to the desk and was entering figures in the ledger book again.

"Yes. Dulsie says her father has some . . . uh . . . bad feelings about that windmill you put up there." Charles Knight looked around questioningly. "Now that there's plenty of water coming from that well, Dulsie wondered if her father couldn't have a little of it." He stopped at the look on his father's face. "I mean, I'm sure Mr. Morgan would pay a reasonable rate for it," he added lamely. "And it would be the neighborly thing to do."

Mr. Knight sighed. "Neighborly? Jack, if you'd ever pay attention to anything that goes on around here you'd know that I offered to sell Morgan water at a reasonable rate, right after I had that windmill freighted in and put up there. He said he'd get by without it. Well, his idea of getting by was to try to cut the fence and slip his cattle in when nobody was looking. The boys caught him at it twice, and the second time he got some buckshot up his tail for his trouble." He shook his head. "Hell no, I don't intend to help out any man as lowdown as Stumpy Morgan. The country'd be better off without him."

"But Father, we've never had a water problem, and you don't even need Morgan's well. And how was he to know about windmills?"

"He'd know about 'em if he'd ever read anything," Mr. Knight said. "And the reason we've never had a water problem is because years ago I bought land on both sides of the crick. I knew this country would grow, and people would be after water as well as land. And Stumpy Morgan wasn't forced to sell that dry well; he was the one who came to me, tryin' to get money for what he thought was a useless piece of land. To hell with him." He turned back to his ledgers again.

"But you help out other people, returning their strays and helping them catch rustlers and—"

"Jack! The answer is no."

The room was dead silent; only a Mexican tune from out back drifted through the air.

Finally Jack sighed. "All right, Father, then will you let him have the water as a special favor to me. I won't ask anything else."

Charles Knight slammed the ledger book shut and spun his chair around. "Favor? Sure, I'll do you a favor, as soon as you do one for me. Take off that damned mask and stop making a jackass out of yourself and I'll give the well to Morgan outright."

Jack sucked in his breath. After a minute he exhaled and said softly, "Father, that's not fair."

"Fair be damned!" bellowed Charles Knight. "I want a son who'll work this ranch with me, not a clown that everybody's laughin' at across half of Texas."

"I don't care what people say," Jack said evenly. "And I'll tell you what I've said a hundred times before. I'll take this mask off when Wes Hardin's gang—"

"Crap! I just hope you never do meet up with Hardin, because he'll probably blow your head off and that damn-fool mask with it."

The room fell quiet again. The Mexican singing had stopped, and there wasn't a sound anywhere.

Finally, Jack said, "I wish you'd reconsider this business of Morgan's well, Father." I could see that his face was red and he was trying hard to keep his temper.

Charles Knight stood up and glared at his tall son, and his own face was flushed. "I will not," was all he said.

"Then I won't answer for the consequences." Jack whirled and walked out.

Charles Knight sighed. "Go with him, Crazy Fox," he said. "Try to see he doesn't make an ass of himself today. I'm still tryin' to forget yesterday."

As I went out I almost stumbled over two Mexican women dusting the hallway floor. I reached back to pull the door shut, and I couldn't help seeing Mr. Knight reaching for his whiskey bottle.

My pony was one of the best in the Nations, and if we'd been traveling many miles he might have left that big silver stallion behind. But it was only a short, fast ride to the Morgan place, and as we flew across the prairie, dodging rocks and buckthorn and mesquite thickets, the big horse pulled away from us.

I saw the windmill long before I got to it. It towered over the land, higher than the tallest trees in this part of the country. A gentle wind was pushing its fan of big wooden blades around in a slow, creaking circle. In later years these windmills would spring up all over the West, but this one was the first I had ever seen. In fact, it was the first one anyone had ever seen in that part of Texas, and it must have cost Mr. Knight a lot of money.

I crested a little rise and saw the whole windmill straight on, and beyond the big wooden tower I could see a wire fence, and beyond the fence a small board house and a few sheds. The silver horse was tied to the front porch, and I hoped he didn't get frisky. One good lunge could pull that whole house down into a pile of warped lumber.

I saw a place where the fence wires were down and rode through and into the yard. I could hear voices, and as I tied my pony, Jack and Stumpy Morgan came out onto the porch. Stumpy was waving his arm toward the windmill.

"Listen to the danged thing," he said in his whiney voice. "Hell, I not only got to look at it every gol-danged day, but I have to hear it out there a-squeakin' all the blessed night too. A-suckin' water up outta my well, and I can't have even a muddy bucket of the stuff without gettin' my butt shot off." He spat a glob of tobacco juice toward the windmill, but most of it went down his chin and onto his shirt.

"I know how you feel about it," Jack said. "And I did talk to my father, just like I promised Dulsie I would. But he says he paid you good money for the well when it was dry, and he offered to sell you water at a fair price after the tower was up. But you tried to just take it."

"Danged right!" Stumpy yelled. "And if I'm even one foot t'other side of that blamed fence they start throwin' lead at me. That ain't neighborly, Jack. And it ain't bein' neighborly to pay a man close to nothin' for his well and then not let him have any water, now is it?"

"Well, but—"

"Sure, he's the big honcho with all the money in Texas, and he can afford to dig deep and build that consarned contraption to pump up the water a poor man like me couldn't reach. But that don't make it right, Jack."

I could see that Jack was getting confused, and then he saw Dulsie in the doorway. She must have ridden right out to tell her father about Jack's promise. She was wearing a pair of her daddy's pants and a shirt that was missing most of its buttons. Jack got red in the face.

Stumpy looked at Dulsie and then at Jack, and for a minute I thought he was about to grin. But instead he fixed his face into a sad expression and sighed loudly. "But I know there ain't nothin' anyone can do," he said. "I'm just gonna have to look at that blamed thing and hear it every night for as long as I live—which won't be very long without we get some water, I guess."

"Now, Pa," Dulsie said, putting her arm around his stooped shoulders. "We probably won't die for lack of water. And Jack did try. It's not his fault if nobody can stand up to Mr. Knight."

Jack was getting even redder in the face, or what I could see of it above and below that mask. "No, by God, you won't have to look at that thing all your life," he said in a kind of wild voice. "I'll show everybody how scared I am of my father. Come on, Crazy Fox!" He ran to the white horse and jumped into the saddle, and then remembered the reins were tied to the porch. He got the horse quieted before the porch came down, and called for me to untie it. I started over, but as I got close it started to snort and paw the ground.

"Horse not like me," I said.

"He doesn't like Indians." Jack got down and untied the reins, then swung back into the saddle and took off at a wild gallop toward the windmill. I got my pony and rode after him.

By the time I caught up I saw Jack had tied a rope to one leg of the tower and looped it around Whitey's saddle horn. He was whaling away at the leg of the tower with a fence post and yelling "Pull, Whitey, pull!" The big horse wasn't moving at all, except to try to reach a clump of grass near the water hole. Jack took another mighty swing with the fence post, which broke in two and clattered off into some rocks. "Come here and help me with this thing!" he yelled. His white hat was rolling around in the dust and his mask had slipped down across his nose, but he didn't seem to notice. He grabbed up a big rock and began hammering on the heavy timbers of the tower.

I got down and watched him for a while. Splinters were flying each time he swung the rock, but it looked like it would take the better part of a week to knock it down that way. He paused to straighten the mask, and saw me watching him. "Well, don't just stand there," he said. "Either get a rock or see if you can get that horse to pull harder." I looked at Whitey, who was eating Jack's hat.

"Me no think this good idea," I said. But that seemed to spur him on.

"Go to it, boy!" Stumpy Morgan yelled from his porch. "Show the old man you got grit in yore craw!" He pulled a gun from his shirt and started shooting into the air. Whitey began to snort and dance around, making the rope lash around like a whip.

"Good boy!" Jack yelled. "Pull!"

The big horse wasn't pulling, but I could see his jumping around could cause trouble, so I started over to quiet him down. Jack's carrying on must have addled my brain, because I'd already forgotten that the horse didn't like me. I remembered when he took a couple of lunging strides away and hit the end of the rope with all his weight. Surprisingly, it held, though the tower gave a lurch and began to groan. Startled by the sound, Whitey bunched his massive muscles and lunged again.

This time the rope snapped, with an end whipping back like a snake on a hot rock. The big horse kept on going, and was out of sight over the hill in seconds. I heard the hoofbeats fading.

But I heard another sound, too. The tower was groaning even more, and I could see it was swaying. Jack was still smashing at the leg.

"Whooo,weee!" he yelled as the chips flew and the tower creaked and swayed. I ran to him and grabbed his arm, and we had just barely got clear when the whole thing began to go.

The tower fell the way things happen in a dream. A leg began to buckle near the bottom, creaking and crunching like a dead tree in a windstorm. The tower lurched. Then the cross-members gave way, and the other legs began to bend outward. The water pipe broke, sending a spout of water onto the dry ground. And then slowly, with great crashing and snapping of timber, the whole thing settled down on itself like a huge heron onto its nest. A cloud of dust rose around it.

As the dust blew away, we stood looking at a pile of lumber from which blades protruded like broken bones. A stranger, coming on the wreckage, would have been hard put to guess what it had been only a minute before.

Jack went to look for his hat in the rubble, and came back slapping the chewed-up remains of it against his leg. He was grinning. I could tell by the white teeth showing in the middle of the mud-streaked, dust-covered face. You could hardly even tell he had a mask on under the dirt.

Stumpy Morgan was whooping and yelling as he ran toward the fence. He stopped on the other side, but he was jumping up and down and waving his hat like a man standing in front of a stampede.

Jack turned toward Stumpy and waved his own tattered hat. "You see?" he yelled. "You tell Dulsie Jack Knight always keeps his word!"

He turned back to me, still grinning. "I guess that'll show my father what's what," he said. He looked around and saw that the white horse was out of sight, probably halfway back to the ranch by now. "I guess we'll have to ride double going home."

I mounted my pony and helped Jack up behind. As we started up the hill I could hear Stumpy Morgan whining. I couldn't make it all out, but the sum of it was, "How in hell am I gonna get water out of this well *now*?"

We rode back to the ranchhouse in silence. Finally, as we came in sight of the buildings, Jack said, "I guess my father will be pretty mad when he hears about this."

I had been trying not to think about that, so I didn't answer. I walked over to the breaking pen to watch some of the men work a new batch of mustangs while Jack went on to the barn to look for Whitey. Nobody was in any hurry to see Mr. Knight.

About an hour later, as it was getting toward dark, I saw a rider racing toward the house from the direction of Quit Well. As he jumped down and ran inside, I knew this day's trouble had not yet ended.

In a little while Mr. Knight came out on the porch and looked around. He saw me and waved for me to come up. I knew then I should have ridden on out to where Walker Clark and Two Moons were camping, but it was too late. I headed slowly toward the house.

When I reached the porch, Mr. Knight said, "Let's go in and

have a drink. I got a feelin' I ain't gonna like this a whole lot more than I did the stage robbery."

I followed him in and waited while he poured big slugs of whiskey into two glasses, then took mine and sat down in one of his big leather chairs.

He took a big gulp from his glass and said, "All right, now tell me what happened out at Quit Well."

I told him.

He gulped down the rest of his drink and poured another one. "Knocked it right down, huh?" He drank again, then sat staring into the empty glass. "So in two days he accidentally holds up a stage and then destroys a valuable windmill." He shook his head. "And there was that business out in Benton's Canyon, too. Oh, God yes, who will ever forget that."

We sat for a while without talking, then he looked at me as if he'd forgotten I was there. "Will you be sleepin' here tonight?" he asked.

I told him I meant to join my friends at their camp, then bring them back in with me in the morning to begin trail-branding the cattle.

"I see," he said. "Well, I'd take it kindly if you'd stop up here at the house for breakfast tomorrow, if you have the time. I want to think about all this tonight, and maybe I'll have something decided by morning."

I nodded and turned to go. As I went out the door I almost bumped into the Mexican girl, Elena, who served the meals. She was carrying a glass of milk. I figured that was the last thing Charles Knight was likely to drink tonight.

The next morning I left Walker Clark and Two Moons with the cattle out at the roundup corral and rode on in to the house. I found Charles Knight sipping coffee and looking like a man who had aged weeks since yesterday. He motioned me to a chair, and Elena immediately appeared with more coffee. It tasted good, but Mr. Knight kept making faces as he drank as if his cup contained poison. Finally he put the cup down and turned to me.

"How's the branding comin'?" he asked.

"We just started, but it should go fast."

"Fine, fine." He paused a while. "I guess I'm out a windmill, though."

I waited.

"You'll be leavin' soon then?" he said.

"In a day or two, I think. Soon as the branding's done."

He thought for a while again, as if what he had to say was hard to put into words. While he was thinking, we heard hoofbeats and neighing out in the lane, and he got up to look out the window. From where I was I could see Jack riding the big white horse up to the front of the house, making it rear up and paw the air, and then holding on for dear life.

Mr. Knight shook his head and turned back to me. "I want you to take Jack with you when you go," he said.

I must have looked surprised, because he said, "Hear me out and think about it, and whether you agree with what I'm askin' or not won't change my feelings about you one bit. But I've been up all night thinkin' about the way my life has been goin' lately, and I've had to come to some hard conclusions."

He came back to his seat and picked up the coffee cup again. As he stared into it for a while, I saw there was moisture in his eyes.

"Crazy Fox, the plain truth is I can't stand to look at him anymore. My own son." He gulped as if he had something caught in his throat. "Miz Knight ain't well, and I ain't gettin' any younger. I had wanted a son to follow me, but it's plain now that Jack will never do it."

There was nothing I could think of to say. A man's son should be the greatest pride of his life.

Charles Knight stood up and squared his shoulders. "I don't know if he's crazy or what, but I do know this: I can't let a masked fool ruin whatever's left of my life, and maybe even kill his mother with his commotions." His voice caught. "I just won't have it anymore."

I listened silently while he explained what he had in mind. He wanted me to get Jack to go along on the trail drive, and then somehow I was to keep him from ever coming back to Texas.

"Hell, just keep tellin' him Wes Hardin's right on up the road," he said. "And then keep hopin' he ain't."

His plan was simple. He would provide us with whatever money we needed for our expenses, plus extra money for me to spend any way I pleased. Or send it to my People, he added. I think he knew what was in my mind.

The system would also be simple. Whenever we reached a

town and needed money I was to wire his Austin bank in a code: "Aunt Matilda is dying in Abilene (or wherever). Need such-and-such for funeral." The bank would then have funds transferred to the biggest bank in that town, with instructions to give the money to me when I presented the return telegraph. It, too, would be code: "Deepest condolences. Give Aunt Matilda the best funeral you can afford."

It sounded a little strange to me, but I couldn't see why it wouldn't work. Unless someone else found out about the system and tried to play a trick, but I didn't see how that could happen unless I let it happen.

"And just to make certain, show the banker this when you go for the money." He reached into his pocket and pulled out something shiny and tossed it to me. It was a bullet made out of silver with the initials "CK" carved into it. "Old Sam Houston gave me that thing," he said. "Didn't vote for him, though."

I dropped the bullet into my pocket and spoke for the first time since he'd begun his strange plan. And I said the only thing I could think of to say.

"How much would I get?" I asked.

"How about a hundred a month, free and clear," he said.

Well, Children, what can I say. In those days that was a lot of money.

Chapter

3

*In which our heroes strike out for the
Indian Territory, recalling
earlier adventures with a longhorn herd.*

So I found myself heading up the Chisholm Trail, looking at the bony flanks and swaying backs of three hundred longhorns. I had Two Moons and Walker Clark riding swing and I was on drag, because Jack had sworn that if he couldn't ride point he'd go to Kansas by himself.

I had expected to have trouble persuading him to come along in the first place, but as it turned out I didn't have to bring it up at all. He did, after he overheard two cowboys talking one day near the corral. The two had been standing around there for some time, I had noticed, but when we walked past they suddenly started a loud discussion.

"Well, Hank, I hear the law has run that Hardin clean out of Texas," the first one said.

"You mean John Wesley Hardin, the outlaw?" asked the second in a voice that nearly broke from the strain of making it carry. "The one that killed a dozen men?"

"The very same, John Wesley Hardin," yelled the first. "They say he's headed up Kansas way. KANSAS." The last was nearly a shout, since we had gone past them by then. I hoped they had got a bonus for the wear and tear on their voices, if not for their acting ability.

Anyway, it worked. Jack had immediately decided to ride with us, and to continue on up to Kansas from there. He went off right away to tell his father about his decision, and by that evening he had packed up his gear.

41

We had crossed the Red and headed into the Indian Territory, crossing the Butterfield stage route without any problems. Now we were nearing the Canadian and still had had no trouble at all, but the responsibility for getting the herd through that outlaw-infested country was beginning to weigh on me, so I hired on two Choctaws we met on the trail. They were driving a small herd of beautiful horses they said they'd bought in Texas, though they didn't offer to show me the bill of sale.

Six men could ordinarily handle a herd twice that size, even with the horses added, but I had seen what Jack could do on a drive and felt I needed all the help I could get. However, as it turned out, I could almost have done it alone. In fact, of all the things I will tell in this story, none are as strange as that drive. Everything went easy all the way, with no problems to speak of. It was nothing like the first drive I'd been on, more than four years earlier.

That had been right after the war, when the longhorns were still running wild because the men had all been away fighting. Mr. Knight had first tried to send a herd to Sedalia, but that had been a disaster; the farmers and rustlers up around Baxter Springs got most of the herd. This time he had decided to look for a new trail around that area, but before he could make plans a rider had come in with the news that the railhead had been extended all the way out to the new town of Abilene, Kansas, and that the trail was safe the whole way.

"No trail is safe," Mr. Knight said, "but this way sounds better than the one to Missouri. We'll try it."

Ten ranchers from thereabouts agreed to make the drive with him, so ten outfits were riding the ranges rounding up the trail herd and branding any calves or even grown cattle that had been missed in earlier roundups. The idea was to put your brand on a calf that was with one of your cows, but once in a while some of the men would get mixed up and start branding every calf in sight. One man even tried for a while to use an "OK" brand, which worked pretty well as a running iron over Mr. Knight's "CK" brand. But Mr. Knight went over to visit him with a few of the hands, and the man decided to pick another brand to use after that. (It was said that the man had an OK brand on his own backside, but I never knew if that was so.)

Driving almost twenty-five hundred head to Kansas wasn't easy, especially longhorns. Do not think of the fat cows in your pastures now, Children, but try to picture a big, stringy, half-wild animal with horns that stuck out the width of a man's spread arms and got tangled in bush, trees, other cows, and sometimes people, if they were foolish enough to go among the herd on foot. They were in some ways the worst designed cows ever to eat grass, but for a long drive through rough country they were hard to beat. They were hard to eat, too, compared to the beef we have now when we can afford it. But their toughness was what got them over the long miles of the cattle trails.

It was hard, mean work, driving cattle, but most of us were young and the young get excited at the thought of new adventures. There were men from all the ranches that had cattle in the drive, and the trail boss was a man named Harvey Anderson, a professional drover who had worked with Mr. Knight before. Since the biggest number of cattle were from the CK Ranch, several hands were sent, including me. And part of the deal was that Jack Knight was to be Anderson's assistant.

Anderson almost quit then and there. He didn't mind taking an Indian along so much, but to have Jack right beside him all that long way was almost more than he cared to think about. Jack wasn't more than sixteen then, and it was before he'd started wearing his mask, but even so, some of his carrying-on had already begun to get around. But when you're Charles Knight, the biggest rancher in the area, and you've advanced the expenses for the drive, you tend to get your way. Besides, there weren't many Texas drives to work at that time, so Anderson stuck it out.

The first couple of days were spent trying to get those cattle to move off their home range. They had not been driven before, and some of them had probably never even seen a man before the roundup. They were not much interested in the adventure of life on the trail, and it was our job to persuade them to try it. We were riding hard most of the day and up most of the night trying to keep them bedded down in one big bunch.

Finally one day, after we had worn ourselves out chasing after bunches that kept breaking off and running the wrong way, Mr. Anderson called some of us over.

"See that big cow with the end busted off her horn?" he said. We all nodded. Every one of us had had to yell and kick at her at least once. "Well, I want one of you men to cut her out and drive her over behind those rocks there and shoot her."

"*What?*" Jack said. "That's a CK cow, and I don't see any reason to shoot a perfectly good—"

"The reason is I said to do it," Anderson said shortly.

Jack was still protesting as one of the men drove that cow off toward the rocks, and he didn't quit till we heard two shots from off that way.

We had a much easier time with the herd after that.

The herd usually traveled in a long, stretched-out line, walking along slowly and eating their way to the dinner table. Anderson's special bell cow, Elizabeth, was out in front, and the point men kept the herd following her. The swing riders were responsible for getting them back in line in case they forgot the reason for this trip and decided to head out elsewhere. Normally the green hands rode at the tail, and that would surely have included an Indian if I had not come from the Knight ranch. Not only was it hard to breathe in all that dust, but you had to contend with the laziest and stubbornnest of the cattle back there and keep them moving in directions opposite to where they wanted to go. As a CK rider I got a swing position and didn't have to eat dust all day.

It didn't take long for trail life to fall into a pattern, for men and horses and cattle. It was walk, walk, walk, with an occasional splash in a creek that got the dust off everything. Near the end of each day Anderson and Jack would ride ahead to pick a bedding ground that was open and level, with room enough for all the cows and with no ravines around in case of a stampede. The cook would pull his wagon around in front of the herd in the afternoon to make camp and get a start on the evening meal. The wrangler would usually take the remuda around the herd, too, because besides minding the horses he also helped the cook. Then the herd would reach the bedding ground, and if they'd had good feed and water that day a couple of the experienced hands could get them settled down easy.

Everyone took a turn at night watch, riding slowly and quietly around the herd, humming or singing and keeping an eye out for any signs of nervousness that might mean the beginnings of a stampede. Some said the singing helped soothe the cattle and others claimed it only helped soothe the men themselves, whose nerves were apt to get tight in those long dark nights. In some cases the singing was less soothing than in others, and after a couple of near runs Harvey Anderson had to ask Jack to stop doing it altogether.

Usually a few men would be enough for night herding, unless the cattle were hungry or thirsty and seemed restless. Then we'd all be up all night, and by morning every man in the crew would be red-eyed and mean enough to drink the chuck-wagon coffee without gagging. And on stormy nights it was even worse. All you could do then was hold your breath every time it thundered and pray the lightning wouldn't flash too bright.

After a few days out we picked up the Chisholm Trail, and a few days later we came to the Red River. Beyond was the Indian Territory. It would feel good to cross over into a land that was as much mine as theirs, at least for now.

We decided to make our night camp on the other side of the river, so we kept the cattle moving toward the crossing, with old Elizabeth clanking along in the lead. But when we got closer, we could see that the river was kind of high and brown looking, and running faster than Anderson liked. The cattle were milling around eating grass and drinking, but Anderson wasn't sure how the crossing would go. He was talking with a group of men up on a hill, chewing on a long blade of grass and watching the muddy water go by.

"What the hell, cows can swim, can't they?" Stumpy Morgan was saying when Jack and I rode up.

Anderson gave him a hard look. "You ever gone swimming in a fast current with twenty-five hundred of 'em?" he asked. "It can be a whole lot of laughs, specially if the danged fools get confused and commence swimming in circles. Most men would just as soon not be amongst them then."

"Well, we can't just sit here and look at this damn river forever," Stumpy said. "I don't have a whole passel of Mexicans and Indians and the Lord knows what-all workin' for *me,* and I got to get back to my place one of these days."

He was looking at Jack and me as he said it, and I could see that Jack was beginning to frown. "That little place won't fall to pieces without you," he said. "In fact, I hear Dulsie does all the work around there anyway, what little there is."

"That's a danged lie," Stumpy said. "Dulsie ain't even there now, and you know it."

"Where is she, Stumpy?" one of the others asked. "Makin' friends at the saloon in Cottonwood?"

Morgan's face got even redder. "I sent her off to school back East," he said.

The man hooted. "What's she studyin', new things to do in bed?"

"You son-of-a-bitch!" Stumpy yelled, his face purple. He put his hand on his gun but made no move to draw it. "I ought to shoot your ass off you for sayin' things like that about my little girl."

The man quit laughing and watched Morgan carefully to see if he really meant to use that gun, which looked like it had never been used for anything more dangerous than hammering fence nails.

About that time there was a thunderous explosion right next to me, and we all whirled to see Jack pointing a smoking gun into the air and looked madder than I'd ever seen him look. "By God, you'd better not ever talk that way about a lady again," he was yelling. "Next word you say about Dulsie, I'll shoot you dead."

We all stared at Jack as if we had never seen him before, and there was a long silence.

And then we all heard it at once. There was a low rumble from the herd, a little like distant thunder but closer. And in a moment the whole herd was off and running, right in the direction of the river.

"Goddamn," Anderson said softly. And then he kicked his horse and started down the hill, with all of us behind him riding as hard as we could.

We reached the river just as the first cattle went in, and we spread out on both sides to try to keep them swimming straight across. I saw right away that the water was deep and moving too fast for comfort, but I plunged in with the others and hung on as the horse swam wide of the churning mess of cattle.

The next few minutes will always be a blur in my memory, but it was mostly filled with screaming and neighing and bellowing and a few gunshots, until the guns got too wet to fire. The cattle somehow stayed headed across the river, even though we all drifted quite a distance downstream, and when it was finally over and we came out on the other bank, the cattle kept right on going in a flat-out, hell-for-leather stampede. Those of us who still had horses under us kept on after them, and in a few miles we managed to get a couple of riders out in front to start yelling and shooting off guns, trying to turn the lead animals.

It was going on toward night before they succeeded. Then, as suddenly as it had started, the stampede was all over, and the cattle were milling around in a wide circle panting and lowing and looking wide-eyed. But they were quieting down, and we began to relax a little.

That was when I discovered we had lost Jack.

I returned to the river and rode downstream, looking for him, hoping he had lost his horse, as he usually did, before the stampede really got going. About a half mile below the crossing his horse was calmly eating grass on the bank. I led the horse on down-stream, and in another few minutes I heard someone yelling. Out in the river about three horse lengths from shore a big rock stuck up from the water. Jack was sitting on it, clear in the rising moonlight. He saw me and waved.

"Why you no swim to shore?" I yelled.

"I would," he said, "but I never did learn how to swim."

I threw him a rope and he hung on while I pulled him in to the bank. And then, dripping but smiling, he got on his horse and we rode back to the herd.

"Actually," he said as we got close to where the men were pitching camp, "the crossing went a lot quicker than I had thought it would."

Everyone had come through the ordeal in good shape except the wrangler, little Bart Trembley. He was in one piece, but barely, because he had somehow got his leg broken up pretty bad. We found him not far from the river bank, stretched out near the overturned cookwagon, moaning and trying to hold back the tears.

Cookie found an unbroken lantern in the cookwagon and held it high while they tried to see how the leg was. "Looks like a bad 'un, boss," he said quietly.

Anderson nodded. "Bart, I doubt we can do much here in the dark," he told the boy. He motioned a couple of the men forward. "Let's get him in the wagon and try to make him com-fortable till daylight. Some of you men get that damned wagon right side up and make a place for him."

After Trembley was settled in the wagon, Cookie moved it up nearer the herd and made up a pot of coffee. We took turns having a quick cup, waiting for sun-up. No one was going to sleep that day.

When the sun came up you could see cows everywhere. Most of them were still in one place where they'd been turned last night, but a lot of them had slipped by us and run off all over. There weren't any ravines or gulches holding dead or trapped cows, but there was a hell of a lot of space stretched out there and we could see dots moving all the way to the horizon. Getting them back was not going to be an easy job. One by one the men got fresh horses from Harry Gonzales, the new wrangler, and started the long day's work.

Bart Trembley was in such pain even Cookie had stopped yelling at him. He'd kicked and fussed at the boy ever since we'd left

Texas, but now he tried to sooth the moaning youngster with a wet cloth and hot coffee. "Don't fret so, Bartie," he kept saying. "Anderson's gonna get you fixed up just fine."

Anderson wasn't so sure. When he got a good look at the leg in daylight he knew he couldn't set those jagged ends of exposed bones. And Cookie wasn't about to try it either. "My medicine box ain't fer things this bad," he said when Anderson suggested it.

They wrapped Bart back up in blankets and moved off to talk. Anderson saw Jack standing around and motioned him over. "Jack, we've got to get a doctor for this kid, and I'd like for you to do it."

"Me? Look, Harvey, I've got to see the CK cattle get rounded up. Send one of the—"

"The men are so tired they're about to drop, and we've wore out nearly every horse we've got already. But that horse your daddy gave you is fresh, and it's the fastest one we've got."

"But where am I ever going to find a doctor out here?"

Whenever Harvey talked to Jack, he spoke slowly and quietly like a man working hard to keep his temper down. "According to my map we ought to be fairly near a town called Muddy Creek, maybe ten miles or so off thataway. You fetch whoever does their doctoring and tell him we'll pay him for the trip."

Jack stood there digging his boot into the ground as if trying to think of a good reason why he shouldn't go. But he finally went to get his horse without further argument. As he rode off I thought Harvey was right to send him. His horse was the strongest and freshest, and besides, with him gone the work would get along quicker.

Before nightfall we'd both know he'd made a bad choice.

In the late afternoon two riders came in, Jack and a stranger carrying a leather bag. When they got down, Harvey pointed to where Bart Trembley lay snoring. It had taken all the whiskey supply we had to keep him numb through the whole day, but he had finally gone to sleep. He might have been green about cows, but he sure had passed his marks at drinking.

While the doctor was working on that leg, Harvey asked Jack how the trip had gone.

"Fine. Just fine. Seems like a nice little town. Found the doctor at home napping, and we rode right out. I did have a slight argument with a fellow on the way in, but it didn't—"

Just then the doctor yelled for some hot water and some help in holding Bart down, so Harvey left without hearing the rest of Jack's story.

Later he didn't have to ask about the fellow in the argument, because the man came riding into camp on a mule that looked almost as mean and ornery as the rider. And neither one of them was interested in friendly conversation.

"Who heads up this here outfit?" the man demanded. The afternoon sun was behind him so it was hard to see, but it wasn't hard to hear the anger in his voice. Even his handlebar mustache looked stiff and unbending.

Harvey walked over from helping the doctor and said, "I do. What can I do for you?"

"You can explain how come you're crossing my land with all them cows without paying the toll."

"Toll? What in blue hell are you talkin' about, whoever you are?"

"I'm John Halden, that's who. And this here's my land."

"In the Territory? I doubt that. Anyway, since when does a man have to pay to walk through this part of the country? I never paid before."

"Since I got the range rights, since cows trample down fields, since those damned Texas cows use the water holes and spread tick fever, and since some jackass cowpoke from this outfit interfered with me this afternoon and caused a no-account farmhand to steal my money and my horse." He was nearly out of breath when he finished all that, but he wasn't out of anger by any means. He looked around and spotted Jack edging around the cookwagon. "I don't know who that damn fool is," he said, pointing his finger at Jack, "but if I was you I'd fire him, cause he's gonna cost you a nickel a head to get through the valley."

Harvey's glance followed that pointing finger and ended up on Jack. He winced like a man with a toothache. "Look, mister," he said quietly to the man on the mule, "I don't know what happened between you two and I don't much care, but I'll tell you here and now there ain't no way I'm gonna pay out that kind of money. Hell, that's over a hundred dollars, and that's robbery."

"Not around here it ain't. And up this way Texans are liable to find things mighty rough if they don't heed the law." Even then the Territory was beginning to fill up with ne'er-do-wells and shirttail farmers who usually had a reason for leaving wherever it was they had left.

"What law are you talking about?" Anderson said, still speaking in the same quiet tone he used with Jack.

"My law," the man said.

Anderson shook his head sadly. "Mister, why don't you get down off that critter and have some coffee and let's see if we can't get this straightened out before somebody gets hurt."

"No thankee. Me and my men are camped back over that ridge, so you can expect me back early in the morning to collect my toll." He turned the mule and rode off.

Harvey stood there staring after the mule for a while, until he noticed the doctor standing beside him. "Listen, Doc, who in the hell is that anyway?"

"Don't know. Some say he comes from back Ohio way. Moved in about six months back with a wife and a horse and a mule, and the whole shebang looks like it hasn't had a good meal since Christmas. I think he's got a hired hand, too, if you can believe that. Probably that's the army he's got waitin' over the ridge. Lessen the hired hand is the one who stole his horse. Called him Andy I heard. The hired hand, that is. Don't recall what he called the horse."

Harvey shook his head. "We lost cows in that stampede, we got a kid with a busted leg, I got a mess of cowboys here that ain't worth soap, and now I got a crazy nester pestering me." He stared at the disappearing mule for a while and then turned back to the doctor. "Why don't you stay the night," he said. "You can look at the kid again in the morning before you leave."

"Okay. I think he'll be all right till you reach Abilene. He probably won't make the trip home with you, but he'll still have two legs anyway. And he almost didn't." He headed toward the cookwagon and the smell of beans. "Any whiskey around here?" he asked the men who were eating. His face got mighty sad when they told him no.

Harvey looked around and saw Jack. He motioned him over, and I could see a vein standing out in his neck even though he was smiling.

"Harvey, I can explain all this," Jack said.

"I'd appreciate that," Anderson said. "If I'm gonna have to kill that crazy farmer I'd at least like to know why."

"That's the thing, Harvey, he's crazy. I tried to reason with him."

"Uh-huh. Tell me about it."

"Well, I was riding along toward Muddy Creek and minding my own business when I heard someone screaming. It sounded like a woman in trouble, so I followed the noise. Anyone would have done that, Harvey."

Harvey nodded and waited.

"What I found was that man beating on a young boy," Jack went on. "They were out in a pasture not far from a shack, and that man was whopping the boy across the bare back with a belt and the boy was really yelling. So I rode up and told the man to stop hitting on someone who couldn't defend himself. Anyone would have done that, too."

Harvey waited.

"So then Halden tells me it's none of my business, that it's a matter between him and his hired hand, and that I was trespassing on his property."

"You were," Anderson said. "And maybe he had good reason to whip the boy."

"Oh no, Harvey. The Knights of Texas don't take kindly to people beating on defenseless youngsters like that and will always try to make them see their error."

"Did it look like he was killing this kid?"

"Well, no, but—"

"So you butted into a private matter. Then what happened?"

"Well, this Halden says the boy was supposed to be minding some sheep but he let them wander off. And the boy says he *was* minding the sheep and that the real reason Halden is mad is because he asked for his wages—nine months' worth at six dollars a month. And Halden says he doesn't owe him that much because he bought the boy a pair of shoes and paid for the doctor when he was sick."

Anderson was staring at the ground now and taking deep breaths.

"Should I go on, Harvey?" Jack asked.

Anderson nodded.

"Well, I felt it was my duty to point out that the shoes had been worn on the job, so he had got his money's worth there. And the way he was beating on the boy it was no wonder he had to have a doctor. So it seemed to me like they were even and that Halden ought to pay him his wages."

"Oh, God," Harvey said softly.

"Halden said he was nearly broke and couldn't pay the boy,

but the boy broke in and said there was a box of money hid under a floorboard in the house and that he had seen it through the windows one night."

Every man had stopped eating and was straining to hear what Jack was saying.

Anderson said, "I've got a feeling there's more."

"Yes," Jack said. "I felt there was only one fair way to settle the thing, so I told the boy to run to the house and bring back the money box. He came back with it, and I counted the money and found there was close to a hundred dollars there. So he wasn't telling the truth about not being able to pay the boy, now was he?"

Harvey just waved his hand to go on.

"The boy said he was owed for nine months at six dollars a month and the man hadn't disputed that, so I counted out the sixty-four dollars and gave it to the boy."

"Fifty-four," Anderson said.

"What?"

"Never mind, it doesn't matter. Is there much more to this?"

"No, that's about all. I gave the rest of the money back to Halden and told him he ought to feel better now that he had done right by the boy. And I rode on into town."

"Oh, God," Anderson said again.

"What's the matter? Something else must have happened after I left to get Halden so riled up, but I don't see where I did anything wrong."

"Somebody stole his horse, for one thing."

"Well, it wasn't me," Jack said righteously.

"Oh, God," said Harvey Anderson.

Next morning Halden rode back in, and Anderson talked with him off away from the camp. In a minute Halden rode off at a fast clip, kicking the mule so hard its ears were flat back on its neck and its hind feet were flying all over.

We broke camp and formed up the herd, and started off toward Abilene again. About noon Halden came riding out from some trees with his guns blazing. He almost got shot down by every hand on that side of the herd, but Harvey yelled for them to hold their fire. Halden fired a few times more and rode off.

The next day he came tearing over a hill and started shooting up a stump. This time no one touched a gun, and we just watched the performance. On the third day we returned his fire, but shot over his head. No one wanted to put a bullet in the best laugh we'd had since we'd left Texas.

That day we found about a dozen sheep following the herd. Anderson called for a couple of us to help him drive them back to where Halden was camped. "I sure as hell don't want the mangy things hangin' around our cows," he said, with his nose wrinkled.

We got pretty close to Halden's camp, but then he saw us and started yelling and shooting and scared the sheep so bad they bolted right past us and headed back for the herd again.

We had mutton for close to a week.

The old man made one more early-morning run and finally managed to shoot a cow. The last we saw of him he was standing over the carcass pumping one shot after another into it and yelling, "That'll show you who means business, dammit!"

We kept riding and herding, and every day was pretty much the same as the one before. Up early for breakfast, then in the saddle. Get the lead cows headed in the direction Anderson had decided on for the day, and the herd strung out behind. A break for a noon feed and then back on the trail till after sunset, when the evening camp was made. In a good day you could make ten miles. It seemed like we had been on this trail forever.

Then one day, as if to give us a break from the monotony, we were met by a hunting party of Kiowas.

There were only five or six men, and some of them seemed pretty young for serious hunting. They looked like they'd had a bad winter, and they were still having trouble finding enough game to feed their people. They didn't want to fight, but they did ask, in sign language, if they could have a couple of beeves. They waved back over the hills, indicating that their village was not far away.

Harvey Anderson knew the reputation of hungry Kiowas, and he wasn't about to risk any kind of trouble over a few head, even if the loss came partly out of his own pocket. He told a couple of the men to cut out some of the older cattle who were straggling behind and slowing up the herd anyway.

Just then Jack rode up to see what was going on. When he saw the Kiowas he said, "Harvey, just see you don't give those dirty Apaches any CK cows. Our cows are going to Kansas, not into the cookfires of every blankethead who sits down in our path."

Harvey looked quickly at the Kiowas, but they showed no signs of understanding. He turned back to Jack, obviously fighting against a need to yell. "Look, our agreement says I handle the expenses, and paying a couple of cows to these folks is like paying a toll, and that damn well comes to an expense. And they're Kiowas, anyway."

Jack turned to me. "Mr. Fox, please make a note in that book my father gave me that I protested giving in to this bunch. I want him to know who was looking out for Knight interests and who wasn't." He looked at the impassive Kiowas. "And who cares what kind of savages they are."

Stumpy Morgan hooted. "Hell, Jack, if you hate savages so much how come you got one keepin' your ledger book?"

Jack looked surprised. "Mr. Fox is no savage. Besides, he works for us, and I want him to learn how a ledger ought to be kept."

"Cow piles," Morgan said.

"This jawbone session ain't gettin' us to Kansas," Harvey said. "You two plan to keep at it till these Indians' friends come along, or what?"

Three men were assigned to deliver the five scrawny old cows to the Kiowas, who were waiting up on the hill while we cut them out of the herd. Jack insisted on going, and I went because I was an Indian and therefore less likely to get them upset. Stumpy Morgan was the third.

The Kiowas watched expressionlessly as we drove the sorry-looking cattle up the hill. Then the oldest motioned for two of his friends to drive them on toward the village, but he and two others stayed and stared at the three of us. Finally, in sign language, he asked what I was doing with this smelly bunch of white faces. I answered that one of them was the son of a man who had done me a favor, and that I would return to my People as soon as I had repaid the debt. It was partly true, I thought. After all, if Mr. Knight hadn't been the one in charge when I drove that wagon in that day, I could just as easily be with Turning Smith and Eagle Flies in the home of the Great Spirit.

"What's all this hand-waving about?" Jack said impatiently.

I saw the Kiowas go suddenly rigid, and looked around to see what was the matter. I saw fast enough. Jack had his hand on the butt of his gun.

"Get hand off gun," I said as quietly as I could.

"Why should I?" he said. "There's only three of them now."

"Because me want keep hair," I said patiently, watching the Kiowas. "May be hundred more right over hill."

He looked stubborn for a minute, but then took his hand off his gun. I let out the breath I'd been holding. "Let's go now," I said.

Before I could turn my horse one of the Kiowas said, *"¿El hombre, es amigo de usted?"*

"Si, es mi amigo," I said. *"¿Porque?"*

"¿Es muy loco, no?"

I smiled and said, *"Es niño a dios."* I touched Jack's arm. *"¿Loco?"* I shrugged. *"Quien sabe. Es mi amigo."*

The Kiowa nodded. He said his name was Pony Man and that I was welcome in his lodge any time, but not to bring any Texans. Then he and the others whirled their horses and galloped off over the hills to where I knew his wigwams waited. There would be good friends there, and this night there would be beef over the cookfires. I wished I could be among them.

"What was all that Indian talk about?" Jack asked as they disappeared over the hill. "They trying to threaten us?"

"No, they ask why Indian ride with you. Me say you friend."

He looked a little surprised, and then he smiled happily. "Really?" he said. "Then you can be my keensobby too."

"My what?"

"Your keensobby. You know, that's friend in Indian talk, isn't it?"

For a minute I couldn't figure out what he meant, and then it came to me. I smiled at him. "That right," I said. *"Quien sabe."*

Stumpy Morgan was laughing, but he quit when we both looked hard at him. "Well, let's get back to the herd," he said. "Keensobbies."

That had been the last bit of excitement on that drive. The rest of the way was riding and eating and sleeping, all the way to Abilene. Just like the drive we were on now, heading north with a much smaller herd and only a handful of men: Jack and myself, and the two Choctaws and my Cherokee friends. And we had only half as far to go.

Looking back, I've often wondered if I was being lulled in those weeks on the trail. Perhaps if things had not gone so well I might have had second thoughts then about the bargain I'd made, and maybe I would have gone back to my People right then, without the money they could use so well. But Fate willed that nothing happen to breed doubts in my mind.

Two Moons and Walker Clark had gotten used to Jack and his mask quickly, and even the Choctaws seemed to take it as a thing of little importance. They never even asked about the mask. Were we not in Indian Territory, after all, where outlaws were far more plentiful than lawmen? If I didn't ask about their horses, they were willing to accept the man on point.

Even Jack was on his best behavior, and he made no disastrous mistakes. After a while it began to seem that I had no worries at all.

Chapter

4

---

*In which we deliver the cattle to
the Cherokee Nation,
and seek Wes Hardin in Abilene.*

We neared the Cherokee capital, Tahlequah, in early May, and I began to relax for the first time in many weeks. We had been met by some young boys from town while we were still a day out, right after we'd forded the Arkansas River. Some of them stayed to help on the last leg of the drive, while the Choctaws went on their way.

We bedded the cattle the last time within sight of the big white house George Murrell had built just south of town. It was one of the few houses of any size that had survived the war, and some said that was because Murrell was a white man, even though he had married one of John Ross's nieces and lived most of his life with the Cherokee. But he had gone off to war, too, and had not come home again.

Next morning we moved the herd out for the last time, heading past Murrell's mansion and on toward town, where my uncle lived. The area had been pretty well burned out during the war, but new houses were going up everywhere, it seemed.

In a little while we passed the Female Seminary with its high red-brick columns, and Jack gaped at it in disbelief.

"That looks like a school," he said. "What's a big thing like that doing here?"

"Educating Cherokee girls," I told him, and couldn't resist adding, "We have a better one for boys."

Joe Creole met us in a pasture south of town, and began his inspection of the herd. He directed his men to cut out some of the older ones and move them to another field, then rode back toward the little knoll where Jack and I were waiting. Jack had been watching him with a look of utter amazement. Finally he turned to me and said, "I can't believe that man is really an Indian."

I tried not to laugh as Joe rode up. He had been my uncle's slave, but now he was a foreman and was married to John Two-Bears' daughter. "Look purty good, Crazy Fox," he said. "Get some good Cherokee grass in their bellies and they'll be fine."

I smiled. "Even a Texas longhorn will grow fat on our grass," I said.

We left Joe Creole with the herd and rode on into town, past the new Capitol building, which had been completed a short time before I left, to replace the building destroyed in the war. It was a big, two-story red-brick structure, and not far from it stood another, slightly smaller brick building that housed the Supreme Court of the Cherokee Nation. Jack stared at the structures.

My uncle lived just north of town, so we rode on through without stopping at the newspaper office, where he often worked on articles for the *Cherokee Advocate*. Two Moons and Walker Clark had ridden in with us, but as we came into town Walker Clark had begun to ride a little faster and Two Moons had started to laugh. "Your bride may have grown old and ugly while we were away," he said. Walker Clark glanced at him and kicked his horse into a trot. "Better at least wash before you go in," Two Moons yelled after him, laughing harder. "She may not wish to sleep with a man who smells like cow piles."

Jack had not understood, of course, since they had spoken in Cherokee, but he wouldn't have listened anyway. He was still trying to comprehend the big houses and the black foreman and the signs of civilization he had not expected.

As we turned into the lane that led to my uncle's house Jack's eyes grew even wider. The house was almost as big as the Murrell place, a two-story white building in a style my uncle said was common where they used to live in Georgia. I had always admired the tall columns that formed a wide verandah across the whole front of the house, but Jack's look was something beyond admiration. This was a long way from the tepees he had associated with Indians. I could see he was having a hard time taking it all in.

We unsaddled our horses at the barn and turned them over to Georgia Pete, the old black man who tended my uncle's stables. "Come, Jack. We go meet my mother," I said.

"Lordy, boy, your momma's not here," Pete said. "After your aunt died and you went off to Texas again, she said she missed her folks and she went off to be with them."

"When did she go, Pete?"

" 'Bout two weeks back, I think it was. Maybe three."

As we headed back toward the house I was sad that I wouldn't see my mother, and I wondered why she had gone without me. I hurried, planning to ask my uncle about it, but when we got inside, Mabrie, the cook, said he had gone down to the newspaper office. She told us water was hot for baths any time we wanted, and asked if we would like partridge for dinner. "One of the men brought in a whole mess of 'em this afternoon," she said. She was gone before I could answer.

As we went to take our baths, Jack was shaking his head and muttering. I caught "female seminary" and "black foreman" and "newspaper" and "partridges," but couldn't quite make out the rest. While we were getting out of our filthy trail clothes, he turned to me and his face was lit by a smile of understanding. "I get it," he said. "This is all some kind of a joke, isn't it?"

By the time my uncle got home we were shiny clean, waiting on the cool verandah for dinner to be served. He came up onto the porch and shook hands with Jack, then gave me a hug. He seemed pleased to see us, but his smile wasn't as bright as it had been before my aunt's death. Mabrie brought us a pitcher of cool water and we all sat down to talk. It was very warm for May, and as we sipped the water we could smell the wild plum blossoms and hear mockingbirds off in the trees. Finally I asked about my mother.

He looked a bit grim. "She went to join her People," he said. "Or what's left of them."

"You mean back up in Kansas," I said.

"No, they're out in the Territory now, on a reservation with the Shawnees." He shook his head. "I guess she didn't want to worry you, but your People lost everything they had in Kansas. They got cheated out of their allotments, and your mother's land was lost along with the rest. They were removed out with the Shawnee People, and we hear they're having a bad time of it out there."

"In the Territory?" I said. "But she's never been there before. Surely she didn't go out there alone, did she?"

"No, one of her young cousins came to visit, and when he

told how bad it was for your People she decided to go back and see if she could help. She and the boy left with a wagonload of supplies about two weeks ago. They should be there by now."

If they made it, I thought sadly. I thought of my frail mother driving through that wild country with only a young boy to protect her, and my heart grew as heavy as a stone. "I must go to her soon," was all I could say.

My uncle nodded. He looked at Jack, who had wandered away while we were talking and was now standing in front of one of the columns, kicking it with his booted foot. His clothes were clean now, but the black mask was still grimed with weeks of trail dust. It was the only one he had, so he couldn't risk washing it.

"Jack's father is Charles Knight of the CK Ranch, where I worked before," I explained to my uncle. "He sold us three hundred head at a good price, and Jack came along to help with the drive."

He nodded again. "The Council will be over to inspect them before the week is out," he said.

And then Mabrie called us all in to dinner.

We stayed around my uncle's house for several days, and during the whole time not one person mentioned Jack's appearance. I began to suspect that Walker Clark had told of his dream, that everyone knew about my "raccoon." Jack's ability to understand only "Indian" English had drawn no comments; it was as if they had decided he was touched by the Great Spirit, and therefore anything he did was all right.

But after we had said good-bye to my uncle and my friends, I began to get edgy again. We were heading north, and up that way they wouldn't have heard about the dream. I tried to think up answers to the questions I knew could be coming.

The only answer I could come up with was to steal Jack's mask. I waited for a good chance, and one day while he was splashing around in a stream I got my opportunity. "Come on in," he yelled at me. "If you'd wash more often, people would stop remarking on your Indian smell."

"Me gather wood," I yelled back, quickly pocketing the mask from on top the pile of clothes he'd left on a rock. While I was hunting wood I put the mask under a pile of cow dung. If he found it there, maybe people would be remarking on his white smell.

He spent most of the morning looking for it.

Finally he gave up and sat down by the cookfire with a very

woeful countenance. "I can't believe this," he said. "If you didn't take it, then who did?"

"Me no have mask," I said innocently. "Me make fire." Since I was turning a rabbit over the fire at that very moment, my alibi stood up.

He sighed. "Well, we'll just have to head for the nearest town so I can replace it," he said. Then he brightened a little. "Actually, it might be nice to have one made by a real seamstress."

The next morning we broke camp. We had decided to head toward Wichita, since Jack was determined to replace the mask or not to go on at all. He looked different without it, I realized as I caught myself staring at him. In fact, after riding in the sun and wind so long with the mask on, he now looked like he was wearing a white mask instead of the black one.

He caught me staring and said, "You're right. I can't ride into Wichita like this. Wes Hardin might be there for all we know." He got a chunk of charred wood from the fire and went to work, and when we finally got mounted he was wearing a somewhat smeary black mustache and the heaviest eyebrows I'd ever seen.

I had been in Wichita once, before the white man's war, and I knew that the Wichitas I had seen then had been removed down into the Nations and had been mostly forgotten, except for their name. Now it was more famous for Jesse Chisholm and his trail, which was really nothing more than two deep wagon ruts he'd put in prairie mud back in 1865. There was talk now about the railhead at Newton being extended on down to here. Instead of grass lodges along the river, a town sprawled at the river's edge and was beginning to spread out into the prairie. There was a hotel for cowboys and traveling drummers, and enough saloons to keep them all in a permanent stupor. But no bank to get money from Texas for my mother.

We took a room at the Munger House while Jack went to find someone in the mask-making business. That seemed harmless enough, so I went to the livery barn to repair a worn saddle girth. About midday he returned looking pleased.

"Well, I found someone," he said. "Not only has she agreed to make me a mask, but she does laundry too. I left all my dirty things and she promised to have everything done by tomorrow."

I sighed. I couldn't keep stealing the masks forever, so I'd have to think of some other way to handle the whole business.

The next morning we headed for the east bank of the Little

Arkansas River and stopped at a log cabin that had a sign over the door: "City Laundry." Jack knocked, and in a minute a little boy peeked around the corner of the cabin and motioned for us to come out back.

We followed him and soon found ourselves walking into a big cloud of steam. There were big wooden tubs standing around, and as we watched, a woman came across the yard lugging a pail of scalding hot water and poured it into one of the tubs. The young boy was standing up on a block of wood, stirring the contents of the tub with a large wooden paddle. Another boy, even smaller, was wielding a similar paddle at another tub.

The woman put down her bucket and headed toward us. As she came through the steamy yard she pulled a mask out of her pocket and held it up to her face. "Boo," she said to the smallest boy as she passed.

She handed it to Jack. "How do you like it?" she asked. "I had to cut up an old hat, but I didn't mind. It was the one I wore to my husband's funeral, and I just got sad every time I looked at it anyway."

Jack tried it on. "It's just fine, Mrs. McCarty," he said.

I thought it had looked better on the woman.

"Hey, mister, how come you wanna wear a mask?" the larger of the boys asked.

"Now, Henry, don't ask questions," the woman told him. "You know that ain't polite."

We stayed there through most of the afternoon while Mrs. McCarty finished cleaning up Jack's clothes. He spent the time explaining about Wes Hardin and his vow to find him, and the two boys listened with their mouths open as Jack described how he would draw on Hardin and gun him down. "If he refuses to surrender, I mean," he added.

The bigger boy, the one called Henry, was almost hypnotized by Jack's gun. Finally he asked timidly if he could shoot it once.

"Sure," Jack said. "In fact, I'll teach you how."

I went along to try to keep Jack from shooting up Wichita. We found some whiskey bottles in a ditch and set them up on fence posts. Jack squared off and then jerked out his gun.

The first shot knocked a limb off a tree over our heads.

"Actually, it's much better if you aim," he explained. He took careful aim at one of the bottles and fired. Nothing happened. He emptied the gun and reloaded, and finally hit one of the bottles.

63

"See," he said. "With practice you can do that too." He handed the gun to the boy and told him how to cock the hammer and aim with both hands.

The boy fired and a bottle splattered. He fired again and more glass flew. On the fourth shot he missed, and Jack took the gun back. "Not bad," he said. "Keep at it, and you'll get better."*

After we left Mrs. McCarty's I began to get edgy about Jack's mask, and the stares we were getting as we rode through town. Jack insisted on going into the general store for some supplies, and nothing I could say would stop him so I went along.

As we walked through the door the proprietor threw his hands up and started yelling. "Don't shoot me, mister," he said. "I got my hands up, like you can see, and I only got about five dollars in the till but you can take that. Just don't kill me."

Jack looked surprised, and then he started to launch into his Wes Hardin story again so I stepped up in front of him. "Don't mind him," I said in a whisper. "He's got a bad war wound across his face and he's embarrassed to have people see it."

The man looked at me as if I was playing some kind of trick, but then he saw that Jack was more interested in canned peaches than in gunplay so he put his hands down. He shook his head. "Injun, that just about beats all. I'll tell you, though, your friend better take to wearing bandages or something, or one day someone's gonna plug him and ask questions later."

I knew he was right.

"Anyways, he don't look to be no match for Hardin," the man added. "He was through here last week, and I saw him shoot three bottles off that fence out yonder with three shots so quick you could hardly hear where one left off and t'other began."

Jack put down the peaches and came over. "Where is he now?" he asked.

"Up in Abilene, I expect. Least that's where he said he was headin'."

We left for Abilene the next morning.

As we rode north, I found myself remembering Abilene and

*Readers might be interested to know that Mrs. Catherine McCarty, a widow from New York State who lived in Wichita for only a short time, has a unique place in Western history. Her son, Henry, later became much better known as William H. Bonney, alias "Billy the Kid."

looking forward to seeing the town again. The last time I'd been there was more than four years ago, at the end of that first big drive after the war. It had been a raw, new town then, but it had looked like the Promised Land to us. By then we were all so sick of trail life that we would have cheered a swamp, so long as it had a saloon in it. And Abilene was strong on saloons, even back then. There were freight wagons all over, unloading lumber for the new buildings Joseph McCoy was putting up, but here and there you could still see the old log buildings he hadn't knocked down yet. Everywhere there was hammering and bustling. A place called Drovers' Cottage was getting its last coat of paint, but not far away a bar was still doing business in a tent.

It was said that McCoy had bought the whole place for five dollars an acre that year, and had then talked the railroads into extending the line to the new town. They'd just started shipping cattle in September, but he'd had riders out in all directions trying to intercept herds and direct them to Abilene. It was beginning to work, but the herds coming in were still such big events the few residents of the town would come out and cheer you through the streets.

It had been a very friendly town, and to keep it that way the saloon owners had all got together and were offering every drover one free drink in each establishment. There was a saloon on practically every corner, so this meant enough free liquor per man to flatten a horse. Most of the men took full advantage of the hospitality. (Oh, Children, men love whiskey and have lost their money and their lives under its spell. Stay away from the bottle. Stay with peyote.)

Indians weren't supposed to be sold whiskey, but I have never met a bartender yet who wouldn't serve me if conditions were right and I had the money. And during my first stay in Abilene the conditions were right, because right away I had met a Eastern newspaper writer named Stanley who was trying to get an objective Indian opinion on the peace commission he'd just been covering. So I was drinking in important company, judging from the reactions of the saloon keepers. (Actually, since he was spending a lot of money in their places, they probably wouldn't have cared if he'd been drinking with a monkey.)

The first day I spent with him he insisted we drink in one of the most jam-packed gambling halls. We finally worked our way through the crowd to the bar, and at last managed to buy two drinks.

And then, just as I started to lift my glass, a prairie dog ran right over my arm. I just missed hitting it by inches.

"Hey, you, Injun," the bartender yelled. "Don't do that again if you want to drink here. You can buy one of those if you want, but don't hit Myrtle."

Buy a prairie dog? I couldn't believe what I was hearing. Probably if I had ever made a list of everything I might ever have even possibly wanted to buy, prairie dogs would have been pretty near to the bottom. The prairie was full of them, digging their tunnels all over and making babies by the thousand. Many a good horse had broken a leg stepping into one of their holes. Why would anyone want one inside his house?

Stanley was leaning over to see down the bar, where the prairie dog was drinking out of someone's glass. "You expect to sell very many of those?" he asked.

"Sure," the bartender said. "Tourists will all want souvenirs, won't they? I've got a whole room full of them out back."

The prairie dog was heading back our way, and Stanley was getting his pencil ready to write. "You expect a lot of tourists, do you?" he asked.

I didn't mind getting free drinks for telling a reporter what I thought about white men's peace commissions, but that didn't mean I had to sit there and watch him interview a prairie dog. I went outside to get some air.

Jack was sitting on a bench, using a piece of lumber as a desk and writing away. "What Jack do?" I asked him.

"I'm writing out my impressions of the West for Mr. Stanley. I thought I'd save him some trouble and get my thoughts down on paper directly."

I began to think this wasn't going to be a very good day. Sharing my drink with a prairie dog, listening to some crazy man plan to get rich selling the filthy things, and now watching Jack try to write Mr. Stanley's stories for him. And to cap it all, I saw Stumpy Morgan and a couple of the men coming down the street, yelling insults at some black workmen as they came. I considered going back inside to talk some more with the prairie dog.

Just then the three men passed a house with an upstairs porch, and some girls in what looked like underclothes leaned over the railing and started yelling invitations for them to come up and visit. The cowboys stopped to consider whether or not to accept the invitations, and while they were talking it over Morgan suddenly got real red in the face and started cussing like a man who'd just found a snake in his bedroll. The men looked up and saw what Stumpy had just seen, and both of them started whooping. "Whoooo-eee!" one of them yelled. "Just look where old Stumpy sent his little girl to school." Morgan gave the man a shove which landed him in a water trough, but he never missed a lick in his whooping.

Morgan pushed his way past the jeering cowboys and disappeared into the building. By now a good-sized crowd had collected.

Jack looked up from his writing to see what all the commotion was about, and caught a glimpse of flouncing petticoats on the balcony just before one of the girls was jerked inside. "Say, didn't that girl look a lot like Dulsie?" he asked.

"Somewhat," I said.

There must have been a back door, because Stumpy Morgan never did come out the front through that throng of jeering and cackling men. In fact, he left town on the stage that same day.

By the fourth day, Harvey Anderson had made a deal for the cattle and had paid the men off. Since there was yet no bank in town, he put the rest of the money in the hotel safe until he could figure out how to get it back to Texas to settle his notes. Everyone had been talking about the drover and his two friends who had been ambushed a while back (some claimed the bushwhackers were of The People) on their homeward trip. Their twenty thousand dollars had been left alone amongst their scalped bodies, but that didn't reassure anyone very much.

Harvey didn't feel too easy about the hotel strongbox either, so he hired two mean-looking men to sit in the lobby and guard the safe. The hotel manager kept watching the two men watching the safe, and he didn't feel very easy either. There was more money in it than any of them was ever likely to see in a lifetime, and even the free drinks that were brought over every hour from the saloon couldn't have wiped that out of their minds entirely.

The next morning I was up early, strolling along Front Street and wondering how to pass the time till the saloons got going for the day. I walked by an old black man standing next to a buckboard, and his face looked somehow familiar. I turned back for another look. This time I saw that his eyes were misty and blinking.

"Hello," I said. "Are you from Texas?"

"Yassuh. I works on the Broken Wheel Ranch, down near Nacogdoches."

Now I remembered where I had seen that black face before. About a year ago, I had gone down the Camino Real with Mr. Knight to keep him company while he talked business with Mr. Harry Wilson of the Broken Wheel. He had been trying to convince Mr. Wilson to sell a couple of his prize bulls to the CK Ranch.

"Is that herd in the far pen Broken Wheel stock?"

"Yassuh. We brought 'em in last week. Sold 'em off to a man from Chicago."

"Good looking cattle." I started to walk on, and said, "You tell Mr. Wilson that Mr. Knight is still interested in those bulls."

"Can't do that," he said.

I stopped and turned around.

"Nawsuh, I reckon Mr. Wilson ain't gonna sell nobody no cattle now," he said. I noticed then that he was crying, and looked toward where he was pointing in the back of the wagon. For the first time I realized what was back there—a coffin.

I stared at the coffin and then back at the sad black face. "You mean—?" I waved my hand at the coffin.

"Yassuh. He in there all right. He sent our outfit on back down home three days ago, and him and me was supposed to go on to St. Louis for a visit." He pulled out a large white cloth and blew his nose into it. "We was headin' for the station to git on that train, and first thing I knows Mr. Wilson jest plain falls down dead in the street." He shook his head, thinking about it. "Jest falls right down like a tree," he said.

"Are you heading out to the cemetery?" I asked.

"Nawsuh!" the black man said emphatically. "I ain't gonna have these low-down cowboys ridin' their horses over Mr. Wilson and peein' on his headstone. I'se takin' him home to Texas, where he's got a real purty spot all picked out for his buryin'."

I stared at him, not willing to believe my own ears. The Broken Wheel was beyond the CK Ranch, and it would surely take him several weeks to get there. An idea was beginning to take shape in my mind, so I asked him to wait for me for a little while. I went looking for Harvey Anderson, and found him sitting on the hotel porch, looking into the lobby where the hotel clerk was watching the two tough customers watching the safe. Anderson didn't look happy.

I sat down and said,"Harvey, I've maybe got your problem solved."

"You mean the mon—" He stopped and nodded toward the safe.

"Yes. I was just talking to—"

"Hold it," Anderson said. "If you've got any kind of a plan I don't want to hear it here." The street was already getting crowded even this early in the day. People of all shapes and sizes, speaking dozens of languages, were pouring into the West from all over the world. Foreign accents were as common as bad food, and greed was more common than both of them. "Let's stand in the middle of the street and talk."

When we were out of everyone's earshot I said, "Listen, Harvey, this will maybe sound kind of strange, but hear me out."

"I'm listening, ain't I?"

"That was the Broken Wheel outfit we were following in last week. Man called Wilson; Mr. Knight knows him. Or he did know him, anyway. Wilson sold his herd and sent his people on home several days ago, but he stayed on."

"All right, but what's that got to do—"

"Wait. Wilson died right here in this street, and a man who works for him is planning to take the body all the way back to Texas. On a buckboard. Alone." I pointed to where the black man still stood by his loaded wagon. While we watched, a couple of men started by the wagon, got a whiff of what was in it, and made a circle around it.

"See," I said. "Already people are backing off from that coffin. Think what it will be like when he's been on the road for a few days. And he's got to go all the way to Texas with that."

Harvey seemed puzzled. "I can see how he's apt to be hard to get near after a while, but I still don't see—" He stopped and began to smile. But then he looked serious again. "Maybe that would discourage bushwhackers," he said, "but what about those scalp-huntin' redski—" he caught himself and remembered who he was talking to. "I mean, would that stop Indians?" he said.

"My People would think he was crazy," I said. "Besides, they don't think black men are quite as bad as white men anyway."

He grinned. "Okay, I guess I deserved that. Why don't we go have a talk with your friend."

We arranged to meet the black man and his wagon outside of

town that night, and then Harvey rubbed his hands together and said, "Crazy Fox, let's you and me get a couple of bottles and go visit with those two birds guarding that money for me."

We spent the whole afternoon visiting with the two guards and passing a bottle around, and by nightfall the two men were in no shape to notice if their pants caught fire. Harvey got the money sacks from the safe and we wrapped them up in old newspapers.

We found the black man sitting on his buckboard under a big cottonwood about a half mile out of town. We tied our horses and took the money bags over to the wagon.

"Are you sure you won't let me pay you for this?" Anderson asked the black man again.

"Nawsuh," he said. "Mr. Wilson often spoke well of Mr. Knight, and I know he'd want to do a friend one last favor if he could."

We opened the coffin, put the money bags in carefully next to the late Harry Wilson, and nailed the lid back on securely.

"Well, I thank you kindly," Harvey said. "And I sure do wish you a good journey. I'll have someone meet the wagon before you reach home and take the money off your hands. Mr. Knight will surely be grateful for this."

The black man clicked the horse into motion. "Mr. Harry and me been together a long time now, so I reckon I'd better be takin' him on home."

We watched the buckboard disappear down the dark road, and finally Harvey said, "That is damn sure gonna be a very lonely trip."

He turned to me a minute later and said, "Well, Crazy Fox, let's get back to town and give those two men hell for drinkin' on the job. And then let's me and you have one last hooraw before we head back to Texas ourselves."

We went back to that gambling hall where the prairie dogs were up for sale, but tonight Myrtle must have gone to bed early because we got to drink our drinks without sharing them. And we got to drink quite a few of them. In fact, I was even beginning to feel friendly about prairie dogs after a while, so when Jack came in it took me a couple of minutes to realize what was different about him.

"Well I'll be a jackrabbit's ass," Harvey said.

Jack might not always have been really bright, but he sure was beautiful that night. I don't know how or where he had found them, but he was wearing pants and shirt made out of pure white deerskin, and black boots polished till they sparkled in the lantern light. He was so shiny you could hardly bear to look at him.

Slowly the saloon got silent, as everyone took in the splendid sight. Jack smiled and clapped his black gloved hands together. "Pretty clothes, aren't they, Mr. Fox?" He motioned to the bartender for a drink. "Now what I want to get is a white horse," he said. "A pure white one."

By the time we left town the next day people were pointing Jack out to one another and talking about something "that man in white" had said to them. Like I said, he shone.

And when he finally got back to the CK Ranch and Mr. Knight had a good long look at Jack, I can tell you that he was pretty astonished too. But I guess he got used to the white outfit after a while, because Jack had been wearing nothing else since that time four years ago. And I guess after he added the mask, the white clothes didn't look so bad. Or at least you didn't notice them so much.

The nearer we got to town, the more I looked forward to seeing the place again. I wondered if they were still selling prairie dogs in that saloon. If Myrtle was around, I might even buy her a drink, I was feeling so good about the whole thing.

Of course, I had no way of knowing then how different this trip to Abilene would be. If I had, I would most likely have voted to pass it by.

Chapter
5

*In which we go to the races in Abilene,
meet its infamous marshal,
and head once again for the Territory.*

As we rode in, I saw right off that Abilene had gotten a lot bigger and a whole lot louder in four years. The saloons lined the streets, packed day and night with the five thousand cowboys said to be in town that summer. And there seemed to be almost enough girls to go around. They were hanging off every porch and out of nearly every window.

One thing that was a surprise to me was the number of chuck wagons standing around town. The outfits that were holding cattle out on the ranges had brought the wagons into town to feed their men, since there weren't nearly enough eating places for so many people. Not that the cowboys were all that interested in eating, with all the gambling and whiskey and women the town had to offer.

And whenever there was a lull in the noise made by the people, you could hear the cows. Some said there were hundreds of thousands of them waiting to be shipped out, in the holding pens and spread out all over the countryside. I don't know who counted them all, but I do know there was a constant hum in the air from lowing cattle. And the wind that blew in from the prairie could make your eyes water.

We found a room in one of the hotels, which was remarkable in itself. It may have been that the mask confused the man behind the desk, because he started the same old business with his hands in the air when we came into the lobby.

Desperately looking for something to say, my eye hit on a big poster stuck on the front of the counter. It said that a man named Hawkins was offering a hundred dollars to anyone who could beat his "pure Arabian steed" in a horse race.

I stepped around Jack and started talking quickly. "I want you to meet the Mysterious Masked Rider," I said. "He's come to race that man Hawkins, and anyone else who thinks he has a fast horse."

The hands came down. "Yeah?" he said. "Boy, wait'll ol' Hawk hears about this."

"We'll need a room," I said. "Unless you'd rather the Mysterious Masked Rider stayed somewhere else, of course."

"No sirree," he said. "You just go right on up to room fourteen, in the back. It's the best one we got."

I thanked him and waved for Jack to follow me. He left the potted palm he had been inspecting and came along. "You know, I don't recall ever seeing a tree like that before," he said.

By the time we got cleaned up and went to find some supper I had almost forgotten the story I'd made up for the desk clerk. I guess he hadn't, though, because there was a small crowd collecting in the lobby when we came down the stairs.

"There he is, Hawk!" the clerk yelled, waving his arms.

"I see him, Lloyd. Just keep your pants on." The man called Hawk stared hard at Jack, and then said, "What's all this shit about a Mysterious Masked Rider anyway?"

"What?" Jack said.

"Me explain later, Jack," I told him. Then I turned to the man called Hawk, who was twirling a big mustache and looking as if he'd just struck gold. "Maybe we can arrange something later," I began. "We're really just in town for a good time—"

"Horse crap," he said. "You told Lloyd you were gonna beat my Ay-rab horse, and all these fellas heard about it. What's the matter, you turnin' yella?"

Jack was looking from Hawkins to me in confusion. "I don't understand," he said.

"Course you don't," Hawkins said. "You come ridin' into town on some crow-bait nag, talkin' big about beatin' the fastest horse in Kansas, and now you don't know what we're talkin' about. How about that, boys?"

Everyone started laughing, and I stood there thinking as fast as I could of how to talk us out of this. But before I could say anything I heard Jack. He sounded angry.

"Crow-bait nag? Whitey? What do you mean?" His voice was

getting high and edgy. "There isn't a horse anywhere that can beat Whitey when he feels like running. Tell them, Crazy Fox."

The men were still laughing. "When's he gonna feel like runnin'?" one of them asked. "About next Christmas?"

Hawkins held up a hand for quiet. "Here's what I think," he said. "I think I'm gonna be out on the edge of town tomorrow at noon ready to race somebody, and I think these fellas here are gonna be hidin' under a bed somewheres."

"You think I'm afraid to race you?" Jack said angrily. "Well, we'll see about that. Make a note of this, Crazy Fox. Noon tomorrow at the edge of town." He turned back to Hawkins. "Which edge?" he asked.

"You just ask anybody," Hawkins said. He turned to the others. "Let's go get a drink, fellas, and see who's bettin' on this here Mysterious Masked Rider tomorrow." They all trooped out whooping with laughter.

Jack stared after them, then turned to look at me.

I could only think of one thing to say. "Me sorry," I told him.

"Oh, that's all right," he said. "Whitey needs some exercise anyway."

The next morning I was up early and waiting at the telegraph office when it opened. I sent the agreed-on wire to Mr. Knight's bank asking for two hundred dollars. Then I went to the general store to buy some paper and a pencil while I was waiting for an answer to my telegram.

The proprietor had put up a poster asking everyone to sign where they were from. While I was waiting for him to finish with another customer I counted signatures from twenty-seven states and thirteen foreign countries. And the permanent population of that town probably wasn't more than a thousand. I put my own address down as the Cherokee Nation, bringing the number of foreign countries to fourteen.

The answering wire came in an hour or so, and I took it to the bank. I was a little nervous about this, since it was the first time I'd tried this system and wasn't sure how it would work. I was clutching Mr. Knight's silver bullet in my hand.

I needn't have worried. Not only had the banker already received the instructions by telegraph, but he even remembered me from four years ago. He had been a hotel clerk then, and the business with the men guarding the safe and the trick we'd pulled had gotten pretty well known after we had gone.

"Always glad to be of service to men like Charles Knight," he told me as he counted out the money. "Now you come in again, you hear?"

I went to find Jack. It was nearly eleven o'clock, and I figured it was time to either get Whitey ready or find a place to hide. Jack was not at the hotel.

I found him at the livery stable, grooming Whitey.

"Hello," he said when he saw me. "I wanted Whitey to look good for his run today. I think this is going to be fun."

"Me hope so," I said.

We saddled up both horses and rode down to the end of town where we could see a big crowd collecting. A way cleared for us as people saw Jack in his mask, and I could see that there was a big open space beyond the last buildings where no cattle pens had been built yet. There had been a herd bedded there the night before, but the men had moved it this morning to clear room for the races.

Hawkins was waiting. His horse was a smaller, almost delicate-looking animal, and it was pawing the ground and snorting nervously. He saw us and yelled over, "Is that what we're racin' against today? Looks like it ought to be pullin' a plow, don't it boys?"

I saw Jack stiffen. "Whitey's a wild stallion," he said.

"Sure he is," Hawkins yelled. "Well, let's get to it."

There was a man who was the official starter, and he explained the rules. When he dropped his white handkerchief the race was on. The horses were to run around a big cottonwood off about two hundred yards or so, and they were to finish up back where they started. "First one in wins all bets," the starter finished.

While they were getting lined up several men offered bets, and I took a few of them, writing them down on slips of paper. I didn't know how much I had bet because I hadn't had time to count, but it seemed that everyone was sure Hawkins' horse would win.

At last they got lined up right, and the man let the handkerchief fall. "Git a-goin'!" someone yelled at the top of his lungs.

Hawkins' horse did, zipping off as if it did this kind of thing all the time and knew just what was expected of it. Whitey wasted several seconds rearing and pawing the air, but then he took off too, his big muscles flashing in the sunlight as he flew after the little Arabian horse. I just hoped Jack wouldn't fall off.

He didn't. As they rounded the tree he cut short and came out in front of the other horse, and started back in the lead. Then he started trying to look back to see where the other horse had gone to, and while he was doing that the Arabian passed him again.

I could see Jack kicking Whitey hard, and again the big muscles rippled and bunched and the big horse speeded up. He crossed the finish line about a foot ahead of the Arabian.

The first thing Hawkins yelled was "Foul! He cut in front of me out at that tree. You all saw it."

Everyone started yelling at once then, but the starter finally got things quiet. "I don't know of any rule about how you got to go around that tree," he said. "So this here masked feller wins, and bets pay off accordingly."

"I want another chance," Hawkins was yelling. "He can't beat me again and he knows it. Next time I won't let him pull a stunt like that."

"Oh, come on," Jack said. "Fair is fair, and I won. Don't be a bad sport."

"Bad sport is it!" It looked like Hawkins was about to burst several blood vessels in his face. "You know damn well you cheated. Your goddamn plow horse could never beat Phantom fair and you know it. You and your damn-fool mask."

I could see that Jack was stiffening again. "All right." he said. "We'll see about that. Just let these horses rest up a few minutes and I'll give you a second chance. But then that's all of it."

"It'll be all of *you*, goddammit," Hawkins yelled.

While they rubbed the horses down and argued, I counted up our winnings. I was amazed to find we had won almost three hundred dollars. I should have been counting the bets as they were made, I realized, because if we had lost I wouldn't have had enough to pay up.

It seemed that the bettors weren't convinced, and many of them believed that Whitey had cheated. This time I did count, and stopped when I'd put down four hundred dollars. I figured we'd have to have something to live off of if he lost.

They got the horses cooled off and lined up again, but then nobody could find the starter. There was more argument about that, and then a fellow yelled, "Hell, I'll start them." He was a medium-sized man wearing kind of ragged-looking overalls, and I figured he couldn't be more than eighteen or so. But everybody seemed to listen when he talked.

He didn't have a handkerchief, so he pulled out his gun and said, "Take your marks!" And then he fired off a shot, and Whitey took off as if he'd got the bullet right in his backside.

This time it was a different race. Jack reached the tree about three horse lengths ahead of the other horse, and it was all he could do to get Whitey to make the turn and head back. He looked like he wanted to continue on back to Texas. But Jack did get him to swing wide around the tree, while the Arabian cut close and took the lead.

He didn't keep it long, though. Whitey must have been getting the hang of this racing business, because when he saw the other horse out in front of him he really turned on the speed. About halfway back he flew past the Arabian, and when he hit the finish line he had gained back most of the three-length lead he'd had out at the tree.

When Hawkins was in and the horses were stopped, someone yelled, "What was that about cheatin' by cuttin' that corner, Hawk?"

Hawkins glared around him. "Shit," was all he said.

I collected our bets, except for one man who admitted he didn't have the fifty dollars to pay up. "I've got a herd outside town," he explained, "but so far I haven't been able to get in to sell them. I'm really sorry about this."

"How many head you got?" I asked him.

"Oh, nigh to five hundred," he said. "And if the price keeps droppin' they ain't gonna be worth sand by the time I get them sold."

I thought quickly. Cattle were bringing ten dollars a head then, but he was right about the price dropping. It was going down every day, now that so many cattle were coming to market.

"I'll tell you what," I said. "I'll take a hundred head off your hands at half the current price and we'll call it square."

"You got a deal," he said. "I never welched on a bet in my life, but this time it just seemed like a sure thing. I'm glad I can pay up."

We arranged for me to come out the next day to pick out the cattle I'd be taking. "I don't see how you're gonna get 'em sold," he said. "But then t'aint none of my business neither."

I went to find Jack.

I found him in the Alamo saloon, buying whiskey for the house. "Have a drink," he yelled as he saw me. "I won a hundred dollars, did you know that?" He told the bartender to set 'em up again.

He was some kind of hero, it seemed. No one else had ever

beat Hawkins' expensive Arabian horse, and since nobody liked Hawkins very much they were all happy to see him bested. They didn't even seem to notice the mask anymore.

I had meant to tell Jack about the bets we had won, but more and more people kept coming in for free drinks, so I decided to wait a while before giving him more money to throw around. Even with the one unpaid bet from the cattleman, I had almost nine hundred dollars in my pocket. And there were better uses for it than buying drinks for every cowboy in Abilene, which looked like what was happening. The bar was getting packed with men as the word got around.

Jack's hundred dollars ran out just in time. One more round of drinks would have put him under a table. I persuaded him to come outside for some air, and he waved good-bye to all his friends and staggered out with me.

We headed back toward the hotel, with Jack weaving from one side of the boardwalk to the other and barely missing two ladies who were coming out of the dry goods store.

"I'm awsufly sorry," he said, bowing deeply to the ladies. As he straightened up he lost his balance again and lurched back right into a smaller man who was trying to get past. It was the same young fellow who had started the second horse race, I saw. He looked downright shabby, like a sodbuster's kid, but he was wearing guns tied down at both hips.

He pushed Jack away. "Better watch who you're bumpin', fella," he said.

"What?" Jack said, blinking.

The young man stepped back. "I said don't go pushin' people around," he said. "You may be a hot pistol when it comes to horse racin' but you don't own this sidewalk."

Jack was still blinking in confusion, and now he took a step forward and started to put his hand out. "Say, now—" he began.

The young man moved back a step and went into a half crouch, his hand near the butt of his gun. "Mister, you back off or you're a dead man," he said.

Jack stopped and looked twice as confused. I watched, not knowing what to do and afraid to make a move.

Just then a voice boomed behind the young man. "Now what's goin' on here?" it asked. The voice had the sound of one that usually got answers, so we all turned around at once.

"You know there's no gunplay in this town," the man said. He was as tall as Jack but had a good deal more beef on him. He also had on a big frock coat, pulled back, and two guns stuck in his belt. His hair was light colored and hung down past his shoulders, and he had a real mean look on his face. I hadn't seen the famous marshal of Abilene before, but I knew this had to be Wild Bill Hickok.

I took Jack's arm and moved him back, away from Hickok and the young man, who were standing about three feet apart and glaring at each other. Neither reached for a gun, but both looked ready to if anyone sneezed.

"Now, Little Arkansaw, I'll have to ask you to hand over your guns," Hickok said to the smaller man.

The small fellow stared a minute longer, then slowly took the guns out of their holsters and held them out by the barrels. Hickok looked relieved, I thought, as he reached out to take them.

Then, just before he had his hands on them, something happened almost too quick to follow. The young fellow suddenly flipped both guns over in the air and caught them by the butts, and before you could blink he had thumbed the hammers back and was pointing them straight at Hickok. I had heard of that trick called the "road agent's switch," but I had never seen anyone actually do it.

Hickok looked surprised. He stared at the guns for a long while, as if he was trying to figure out what came next. Then he looked at the young man's face and broke into a smile. "You know you'd never make it out of town," he said.

He was right. Already a crowd was gathering, and two men wearing stars had come out of it and were approaching cautiously.

"Now why don't you just put them guns back in their holsters and let's you and me go have a drink and talk this over," he told the young man.

The smaller man looked undecided for a minute, but then he looked at the deputies up the street and put the guns away.

Hickok threw his arm around the young fellow's shoulder and led him into the Alamo, laughing like they were the best of friends.

Jack was still standing there blinking. "What?" he said.

"Never mind," I told him. "We go hotel. Gettum sleep." It was not even dark yet, but I figured sleep was about all Jack could handle right then.

As we walked away I heard one man talking to another one, and what he said nearly stopped me in my tracks. "I thought ol' Bill was a-gonna git it that time," he cackled. "That Wes Hardin is one mean little hombre, ain't he?"

I looked quickly at Jack, but he hadn't heard a word.

Jack slept for close to fifteen hours, and woke up as frisky as a colt. "I must have had too many drinks," he said. "I don't remember, though. Let's go get some breakfast."

I was no longer nervous about the mask, since everyone now knew about the horse races and they all seemed to accept the whole business as pretty normal. But I had something else to worry about, now. Suppose someone pointed out Wes Hardin to Jack?

All the eating places were packed, but when people saw Jack they insisted on making room for us. They were still chuckling about Hawkins and his fancy horse. "The danged thing ain't worth beans for work," one of them said. "What's ol' Hawk gonna do with it now, you reckon?"

We ordered flapjacks and a pot of coffee. While we waited I stared out the window, thinking of how to tell Jack about the bet money and the cattle deal.

While I was staring I became aware of a commotion of some kind, with people collecting and voices raised. And then I saw the marshal standing in the street in front of the Bull's Head saloon, the place run by Ben Thompson and Phil Coe. "You git on out here, Phil," Hickok yelled.

Coe came out. He was a tall man of considerable bulk, and he was not wearing a gun. "What do you want?" he asked the marshal. "You're not here to pester us about that sign again, are you?"

The sign was a painting of a bull that covered most of the building's front. The bull was particularly well fixed for servicing cows, and I had heard talk that some of the people in town had been complaining about it. But up till then Coe and Thompson had refused to change it.

"No, I ain't here to pester you," Hickok said. "I'm here to change the damned thing once and for all." He waved to some men who were carrying paint cans and brushes. "You boys get on with it now, and if anyone bothers you he'll answer to me." He patted the shotgun he was cradling in his arms.

Coe went back inside, and in a matter of minutes the bull became a steer. The men cleaned up their mess and walked off, with Hickok following them.

Our flapjacks and coffee came, and while we ate I explained about the bets and the cattle.

He looked puzzled. "It's nice about the money," he said.

"But what do we want with a hundred head of cattle? We can't even get them into town to sell them, I hear."

"No want sellum," I told him. I explained about the bad times my People were having down in the Territory, and told him I wanted the cattle for them. "Me not ask Jack drive cattle," I said. "Half bet money yours. But me need five hundred for cows. You take rest."

He smiled. "No, the money is yours. I didn't even know about the betting." He looked sober. "I'd even be glad to help you drive the cattle down to your people, if only I didn't have to track down Wes Hardin."

I looked around us quickly, and sure enough someone had overheard. I held my breath as a man at the next table leaned over and said, "You lookin' for Hardin?"

"I am," Jack said. "Do you know if he's in town?"

"Was," the man said. "Rode out last night, I hear. Had some ruckus down at the Trail's End café and shot a feller and skedaddled."

"Do you know which way he went?"

"No. Prob'ly headin' for the border is my guess."

Jack turned back to me. "Which way is that reservation?"

"South," I said. "Down in the Territory."

He nodded. "Looks like we'll be riding together a while yet," he said.

We packed up our gear and rode out of town that morning. It took us most of the day to locate the man whose cattle I'd agreed to buy, but we finally found him.

"We agreed on five dollars a head, didn't we?" I asked him.

"We did. They're goin' for ten in town, but a deal is a deal. Let's cut out your hundred head."

I let him mix in a few old cows and a couple of runty-looking ones, to make him feel better about the price. And when he'd made out the bill of sale I counted out the five hundred dollars and handed it over.

"Thankee kindly," he said. "I expect I'll be lucky to get that much for the rest of this herd, if I ever get into town at all. I don't know what you figure to do with your hundred, but I surely wish you luck."

We camped nearby, taking turns riding watch through the night, and the next morning we formed up our little herd and headed south.

Again, we got the cows through with almost no trouble.

The closest we came to it was in a little town called Prairie Station, where Jack insisted on riding in for supplies and nearly got himself shot. But he managed to convince the storekeeper there that he was not an outlaw, and before he was finished, as he told me later, he had the man believing he was hot on the trail of Wes Hardin.

"And do you know, Hardin had passed through not hours before," he said. "He stopped to ask about some fellow named Bideno, but no one there had heard of the man so Hardin rode on out south. We're on his trail for sure."

I would just as soon not have heard that. Still, traveling with a herd of cattle is a lot slower than traveling alone, so I figured we'd be unlikely to catch up with Hardin any time soon.

I was right. We met a couple of other herds heading north as we traveled toward the Shawnee reservation where my People were now living. Each time we asked about Hardin, but no one had seen him.

At last we came to the land of the Shawnees, and we were directed to the area where my People now lived. As we rode into their village the People came out of their wigwams to stare at Jack and the cattle.

We came at last to my mother's wigwam, and I saw her standing outside, her hand over her eyes to see better. I got down off my horse and went to her.

"I've brought you some cattle," I said.

She recognized me at last and smiled. As we clasped each other in greeting she said, "I knew you would come." Then she held me at arm's length and said, "You are getting as big as a buffalo. It must be the white-face food." Then she saw Jack sitting on Whitey, staring around him, and she gave me a questioning look.

"He is my friend," I said. "I will explain about the mask later, but first let us get some food that's fit to eat."

I motioned for Jack to get down and come inside the wigwam with us, but he said he would rather wait outside. I followed my mother in and sat down on some skins to explain where I had been, and why Jack was traveling with me.

As I talked I watched her, and there was a sadness in my heart as I saw how the years and the hard times had marked her. There was a stoop in her shoulders, and her face had lines it had not had before. She was growing old in this strange place, old and alone.

Chapter

6

In which we leave The People
and return to Abilene, to get fleeced
by a beautiful woman.

"Our People first saw the white man more than two hundred years ago, when we lived near the great waters in the north. The white man came with a new religion to take the place of our old beliefs, and he came with wars that lost us our homelands. We were sent from our ancient lands to places called Iowa and Kansas, and then when the white man needed those lands we were sent from those places too. And now some of us are here, on land set aside for us in this Indian Territory. We hope this will now be our home for all time. We are not a powerful People and cannot make war, as some of our brothers still do. So we have given up our lands and our lives to the white faces, and can now only hope to live as the Great Spirit directs."

I heard those words as I sat before an evening campfire under a starry sky. They were spoken by an old man of the tribe, and his face was sad as he told of our People's troubles. I looked at my mother and saw that her eyes glistened with tears as she heard his words. There was nothing I could do to change the past, and perhaps I could not change the future very much either, but at least Charles Knight's money might help.

There was much that money might do. No one here was as well off as those who lived in the Cherokee Nation, but our People were working hard with what they had. They got little help from the Indian agent, who had too many side ventures to give much time to their problems and who would eat well whether The People did or not. But most of my People were willing to take what they could get, if only the land would at last be theirs.

As the old man finished speaking there was a sudden rain, and we all went to our wigwams. Jack had chosen to sleep outside, but he joined my mother and me to keep dry. He had not taken to the ways of our People, nor vice versa, though my mother tried to make him welcome.

As we sat on skins and talked, Jack was silent. Finally he said, "I'm getting as wet in here as I would outside. Might as well go back out and check on Whitey." He left.

I realized that he was right about getting wet. The wigwam was not well made, and water leaked in at many points. I decided to fix it, and told my mother so.

"That would be good," she said. "It should be made better before the cold of winter comes."

"Winter? Surely you do not plan to stay here all winter, do you? You'll be returning to the Cherokees."

She looked surprised. "Why would I return there? My sister is gone, and there are none of my People there now. This is where I belong. I am at home here, and perhaps I can help."

I realized that she could not be persuaded to leave, and that set me to thinking. The money I could send would be of more help, I knew, than I could be if I stayed with her. On the other hand, with no man she would be much alone, and would have to depend on my young cousins for many things. But they were hardly more than children. I went to sleep that night thinking about the problem.

When I woke the next morning I knew the money was more important than my presence. But before I left again I could at least build her a cabin against the winter winds. The wigwams of our People were shelter enough if built right and tended to, but for a woman whose years were growing shorter a more solid building would be best. I went to tell Jack my plan.

At first he was delighted, because he said he knew all about carpentry and would teach me the proper way to construct a building. But then he remembered about Hardin. I assured him that with both of us working the cabin would go fast, and then I could ride with him on his manhunt. He agreed, and we began.

We cut trees of the right size and stripped away their branches and bark. Then we borrowed some tools from the Indian agent and went to work, smoothing and notching them to fit at the corners and around the door and window frames. We cut smaller trees for the roof poles and lashed them to the walls, then began to cut the blocks of sod and place them on the roof.

The days went quickly and the cabin grew. My mother, who had at first scoffed at the notion, now came to look at it with a smile of pride. Others of the village came too, to watch and sometimes to help for a while. But mostly Jack and I worked alone.

And then Jack slipped while placing a sod block on the roof. He landed on the ground howling with pain. He had sprained an ankle. My mother made him a poultice, but the ankle still puffed up. Soon he had to give up walking and sit below as he offered advice on the work. I tried to be sympathetic with his pain, but there were times when I wished that poultice covered his mouth instead of his ankle.

As the swelling receded he took to hobbling around the village, offering advice to all who would listen. Few understood enough English to follow, but he threw in enough sign language to get his meaning across. Pretty soon people were ducking out of sight when they saw him limping in their direction.

Then one day the cabin was done, and we went to help my mother move her few belongings into it. Jack was still hobbling, but he tried hard to pick up one end of my mother's trunk. "What's in this thing," he said, "rocks?"

"Winter clothes, herbs for healing, other things of our family. My mother Indian woman, strong. We carry trunk."

He nodded and picked up some smaller things in his free hand, and in a few minutes we had my mother settled in her new home. The look of pride on her face made it all worthwhile.

The next day Jack's foot had swollen again, and he was hobbling around complaining steadily. I told him I'd have my mother make something up for the swelling as soon as she came back from a visit.

I didn't have a chance. When she came back she brought with her some of the older people of the village, so they could admire her new cabin. They were much impressed, and we took them inside to show them how the shutters worked to keep out the cold.

And immediately we were all struck speechless. Because there was Jack, pawing through the contents of my mother's trunk. He saw us and stopped. "I was looking for some salve," he said. "I couldn't find any. There were some dried plants of some kind, and I did find that little leather bag." He pointed to the pouch on the floor, its contents strewn around it. "There was nothing in it but some bear claws and stuff, and most of it is rotting away anyway."

I could see the stricken looks on the faces of my mother's friends, so I told him to wait outside. My voice must have had an edge to it, because he went quickly. I turned back to my mother, who was staring in utter disbelief at the mess on the floor.

"Why would he do such a thing?" she said softly. "Does he hate our People so much?"

I tried to explain that Jack would not have known the importance of the medicine bag, whose contents were a kind of history of good events in our clan. It was a misunderstanding, I told her lamely.

She shook her head. "Perhaps," she said. "But it has seemed to me, and to others in the village, that your friend has little interest in our ways or our beliefs. Even if he had known, it might not have mattered to him."

The others left and she began to pick up the pieces one by one and replace them in the bag. I knew that their power had been diminished in her mind, and in the minds of the others of our clan who had seen. I also knew that Jack could not stay here any longer, if there was to be a good feeling in the village. He had been accepted because he was my friend and a guest of our People, but he was no longer welcome here.

I told my mother this. She was silent. I told her that Jack and I would be leaving the next day. She looked up at me in surprise. "But why must you go?" she asked. "This is your home now. These are your People."

I talked for some time, explaining about Mr. Knight and the debt I owed him. She listened, but she seemed not to comprehend. I said I had made a promise, and that I felt bound to keep my word.

She shook her head. "I do not understand," she said. "Surely you do not owe this man your whole life."

I thought about that, and for the first time I saw that I had entered into an agreement that really had no end. As long as Jack lived and as long as Mr. Knight wished him to stay out of Texas, I would be chained to him by the money. And by my promise.

I explained about the money to my mother, and told her how it could be used to help our People. I gave her most of what was left of our horse-race winnings.

She took the money and listened, and then said what I had said to Mr. Knight back in Texas. "How much will you get?" she asked.

"A hundred dollars a month, and all my expenses," I told her.

She looked at the remains of the medicine bag and then

looked out the door, to where Jack stood waiting. And then she looked back at me.

"It is not enough," she said.

Next morning, as we prepared to ride out, I wondered if I would ever see this peaceful village again. This would be my home, if I was ever to have a home.

When we were ready, there was some argument about which direction we should take. Jack wanted to ride south, into Texas and down to the border, on the trail of Wes Hardin. I argued that Texas was a big place, and Mexico was even bigger. Without a trail to follow we could ride around for years and not find Hardin or anyone who knew him.

We compromised and rode east, on the theory that we would probably cross Hardin's trail that way, and then could follow where it led. If we had not heard by the time we reached the borders of the Cherokee Nation, Jack could head south if he chose and I would visit my uncle for a while. I was not happy with this arrangement, but at least it gave me time to think of some other way to keep Jack from returning to Texas.

As it turned out, the problem solved itself when we had been riding for only three or four days. We met a party of Texans heading south, and as soon as I had managed to explain about Jack's old battle wounds again we were invited to share their evening meal.

Jack, of course, began talking about Hardin at once, telling how he was prepared to track the outlaw all the way across Mexico if he had to.

"Mexico? Hell, Hardin ain't in Mexico," one of the men said. "He's right back in Abilene, or leastways he was back in July, when we was through there. He was struttin' around like a rooster and gettin' free drinks and what-all from damn near every Texan in the town."

"Free drinks? Why?" Jack was thoroughly confused.

"Didn't you hear? He tracked down and shot that Bideno fella who killed ol' Billy Coran, and he's a big hero now. Even Hickok is leavin' him alone."

The next morning we headed back to Abilene once again.

Some birds were already beginning to fly south by the time we rode back into Kansas, and the biggest part of the cattle boom was over. Some said as many as half a million head had been driven to

Abilene so far that year. What the Eastern buyers couldn't handle had been driven on north to Wyoming and Montana. Whatever the reason, the smell of cow dung was not nearly as strong as it had been in the summer.

The town was still plenty lively, though, with enough cowboys still around to keep thirty saloons in business and the girls occupied. There was a county fair going on, which had brought a lot of farm people into town. They stomped around glaring at the Texans, but the cowboys didn't seem to care. They didn't even care all that much about the notices posted all over town by the Dickinson County Farmers' Protective Association warning drovers to seek another market for their cattle, though the notices did get ripped down pretty regularly. Mostly, though, the cowboys were getting ready for their annual fall custom they called "the roundup," which consisted mainly of trying to rope the town's businessmen and take them into saloons, where the victims had to buy free drinks.

And just in case all that wasn't enough to keep people occupied, a circus was also in town, set up in a vacant space next to the Drovers' Cottage. Posters were up all over the place.

Jack stopped to read one of them outside the hotel, and I went on in. There was a different clerk, so I started to revive my Mysterious Masked Rider story.

"Oh, you folks must be from the circus," the clerk said as he saw Jack coming through the door. "We've got some other folks from there stayin' here. Miz Thatcher and her daughter have rooms upstairs, in fact."

"Oh, good," I said. "We'll feel right at home, then."

I hustled Jack upstairs before he could begin to carry on about going to see the circus.

Again I was up early and off to the telegraph office to send my coded wire to Mr. Knight's bank in Austin. Then I returned to the hotel and got Jack, and we went out for some more of those flapjacks we'd both remembered.

There were few people in the café, and no one seemed to remember Jack or the horse races. But it didn't matter, since everyone simply assumed we were circus folks, who evidently were a pretty strange looking lot on the whole. And no one seemed to know anything about Wes Hardin, to my relief.

"He was in town a while back, I know," an old man said. "Don't recollect seein' him lately, though." He turned to the fat woman who ran the place. "You seen Wes Hardin around lately, Cora?"

"No, and I ain't lookin' for him neither," the woman said shortly. "I wish to hell they'd chase all that Texas riff-raff out of town, and that fancy marshal along with them."

That seemed to end the discussion.

After breakfast I left Jack sitting on the porch of the hotel and went back to the telegraph office. I passed some cowboys pulling Jake Karatosky, a merchant I had done business with, into the Applejack saloon, where he'd be made to treat the crowd. I was tempted, but I thought I'd better get my money affairs in order before I got caught up in roundup drinking going on all over town.

The answering wire was there, and I took it to the bank just as I had before. This time I wasn't worried at all.

I should have been. The manager who had remembered me was away on a trip back East, and the young man who was filling in for him was completely confused. He had received the instructions, but it seemed that they were just too much for him.

"I can't just hand over five hundred dollars to an Indian I've never even seen before, and I don't care how many silver bullets you show me. You could have got that anywhere." He shook his head. "No, this is just too irregular. I could lose my job over a thing like this."

I tried to explain about Jack Knight, but all that got me was an even more suspicious look. "If you're traveling with Mr. Knight's son as you say you are, why doesn't he come in and transact this business himself?"

I thought of the kind of sensation Jack might cause in a bank and dropped that fast. But by now no amount of telegrams or identifying watch fobs was going to sway the young assistant manager. "I'm sorry," he said. "Mr. Cooper will be back in a few days, and if he wants to take this kind of risk it's his responsibility. I just don't have that authority."

I was stumped. And at that moment, while I was standing there trying to come up with another argument, I saw a familiar figure walking by. It was Dulsie Morgan, but now she was dressed in clothes that would have done the mayor's wife proud. And her shirt-waist was even buttoned all the way up to her neck.

I went out and called her.

She turned and squinted at me in the sunlight, and then broke into a big smile. "Well for mercy's sake," she said. "What are you doin' in Abilene?"

"Jack and I just rode in yesterday," I said. "He's back at the hotel while I do some business in this bank. Or try to, anyway. I don't seem to be getting very far, though."

When I had explained the problem, she insisted on going back inside with me and telling that young man a thing or two. Which she did, in language more ladylike than I had ever heard her use before.

He was dazzled and even more confused, but he finally concluded that he would have to at least make a show of doing something "to please the lady." He promised to telegraph Mr. Cooper for instructions.

It was better than nothing, so I agreed to check back with him tomorrow and see what instructions he got. Dulsie and I walked back outside.

"Well, hell, I tried," she said. "If you need me tomorrow you can find me over at the Alamo, probably. I've been dealing Faro there some nights, when my boyfriend is busy. He used to own a saloon but he sold out and mostly plays cards now." She thought a minute. "I'd love to see Jackie," she said then, "but I'm not sure how Phil would take to him, especially if he's still wearin' that silly mask."

I told her he was, and promised I'd try to keep Jack out of her boyfriend's way while we were in town. And I thanked her again for her help with the young bank manager. "He really seemed to want to please you," I said.

She laughed. "He was kinda carryin' on, wasn't he." She waved and started to walk away. Then she stopped and turned. "Listen, you tell Jackie I'm real sorry about his momma passin' on," she said.

"When did that happen?"

"Oh, I guess about a month ago, maybe. You mean you-all didn't know?"

"No, we've been traveling," I told her.

She nodded. "Then I reckon you don't know about the wedding, neither," she said.

"Whose wedding?"

"Why, Mr. Knight's," she said. "His wife wasn't hardly in the ground before he up and married that girl, Elena. I heard she was always follerin' him around him like a shadow."

I remembered the Mexican girl Elena, pretty and quietly seeing to the needs of an older man. I hoped she would give him some happiness in his later years. He deserved it.

Dulsie went on toward the Alamo, and I started back to the hotel, wondering if I should tell Jack. I decided to wait a while. I figured Mr. Knight didn't need Jack back in his life just then.

Jack was not at the hotel. He was not at the livery stable, either, and Whitey was gone too. I began to get worried. Had someone set him off after Hardin in that brief time? Would he have gone without even telling me?

I asked around, and finally someone said they'd seen him riding through town. Where I found him was at the circus, watching a bareback rider practice.

"Isn't that amazing, Crazy Fox? That lady can ride that big horse around standing up on its back on one foot. Even you Tontos can't do that, I'll bet."

I sighed "No, me guess not," I said. "You want go eat?"

"In a little while," he said. "You know, a man came over and tried to buy Whitey just before you got here. Said he'd be a natural for their Cowboys and Indians act. He even said I could probably get a job with the circus, playing an outlaw. In fact, he thought I *was* an outlaw until I explained." He smiled at the man's ignorance. "You know, I bet you could play an Indian in their show," he added.

The lady finished her fancy riding and went inside the tent, so we left to stable Whitey and find a place to eat. It was the middle of the afternoon by then, and the cafés were half empty. We ate quickly and walked back outside to sit in chairs on the hotel porch and watch the world go by.

Jack kept watching the crowd for a familiar face, so he could ask about Hardin, but we saw no one we knew for the next hour. He began to kick at the chair leg and hum, and finally he took out his gun and began to clean it. His gun gleamed most of the time, since he was convinced that if he kept it really polished up it would shoot better when he needed it to. I remembered the worn, dull-looking guns Hardin had worn that day he'd faced Hickok.

He rubbed and rubbed on the gun, then held it out in front of him and pulled the trigger.

I nearly jumped out of my chair, but the gun only clicked. "What you do?" I said. "You shoot gun, Hickok arrest you."

"Oh, I don't plan to shoot it. That's just the empty chamber I keep under the hammer." He peered at the gun. "Now which one is it?" he wondered, turning the cylinder.

I suggested he put it away, still worrying about Hickok's order that no guns were to be fired in Abilene under penalty of arrest. But he kept on fiddling with it, a stubborn look on his face.

Then suddenly the look changed to one of surprise, and then to a smile of happiness. "Look, Crazy Fox, it's Dulsie," he said. He stood up and began to wave his arms. "Hey, Dulsie, over here!"

I looked up, and he was right. It was Dulsie, strolling along in front of the Alamo on the arm of a very large man who could only be Phil Coe. She was wearing one of her "uniforms," and I couldn't help thinking how helpful the man in the bank would have been if he'd seen her dressed like this. I'd probably have the money in my pocket right now.

Jack was still yelling and waving his arms, and I saw Dulsie point at him. And then I saw something else, and a cold wind blew down my back. Coe had pushed Dulsie out of the way and was poised with his hand on his gun.

I looked quickly at Jack, and saw why. The hand he was waving was holding his gun. I reached up to grab his hand, but I was too late. He stepped down off the porch and started toward Dulsie, the gun still in his hand, forgotten.

Coe drew a gun and fired, and the bullet sang past and took a chunk out of the corner of the building. I leaped off the porch and grabbed Jack, who was standing there with a frozen smile on his face. I pulled him back up on the porch.

People were running every which way, trying to get out of the line of fire and into buildings. Coe was still standing with his gun aimed, waiting for return fire, but I was between him and Jack.

Just then the doors of the Alamo banged open so hard they sounded like gunshots. Coe whirled that way, and saw Hickok in the doorway. He still held his gun.

"Who fired that shot?" Hickok roared. Jack started to open his mouth but I pulled his mask down across it before he could speak.

"I said who fired that shot?" Hickok yelled again, and his voice sounded as mean as a wounded cougar. Coe still stood there, as if he had turned to stone. But Jack was struggling to right his mask, and trying to pick up the gun he'd dropped. He found it and brought it up, waving it as if to show that his gun hadn't been the one that fired.

Coe looked from Hickok to Jack and started to swing his gun back our way. Dulsie screamed, "No, don't shoot!" and as she yelled, Coe whirled again and fired at Hickok. I saw the marshal's frock coat jump out behind him as the bullet went through.

Hickok pulled his gun and fired twice, all in a motion like the blink of an eye, and Coe flopped over backward and landed in the dust, twitching like a fish on a line. The street was so quiet you could hear breathing.

Suddenly a man ran out of the alley next to the Alamo behind Hickok, a gun in his hand. Jack yelled "Look out, Hickok!" and Hickok spun around and fired again in that same blurred motion. The man flew backward into the alley and landed on his back. You could see his legs twitching.

What I had also seen, just before Hickok had fired, was that the second man had been wearing a badge on his shirt. Hickok had just killed his own deputy.* I figured it was time to get lost in the crowd, so I pulled Jack through the door of the hotel.

The clerk was coming out of a back room, and he asked if those were gunshots he'd just heard out front.

"Might have been," I said. "Kind of hard to tell in all that confusion."

I got Jack up to the room and persuaded him to stay there for a while until I found out what was happening. He argued at first, claiming that he hadn't done anything wrong and surely the marshal could see that. But I pointed out that he might get Dulsie into trouble if he started explaining, and at last he agreed to wait till I had scouted around.

That was a night to remember in Abilene. Wild Bill Hickok sure earned his name that night, if there had been any doubt of it before. He roared around from one saloon to the next, smashing bottles and furniture and roaring that he'd find the blankety-blank who'd caused him to fire at his friend, and when he found the blankety-blank he would personally shoot off his manhood, for starters. He didn't give anyone much chance to talk, so no one so far

*The deputy's name was Mike Williams, and this incident took place on October 5, 1871.

had told him about the masked man, but I knew it was only a matter of time till someone did. And when that happened Jack had better not be handy.

I went looking for Dulsie, and finally found her in a room upstairs over the Alamo. She was afraid to go out. "Hell, he killed Phil without givin' him a chance," she said. "And he'd kill me too, from what I hear. Some say he doesn't like women much anyway, and if he thinks I had anything to do with what happened . . ."

I agreed she should stay in the room tonight, but I figured that by morning Hickok would have run out of steam and would be sleeping it off somewhere. He'd emptied a few bottles before he smashed them, I'd heard.

I didn't really think Hickok would shoot a woman no matter how worked up he got. It just wouldn't look good. But he might scare Dulsie to the point where she'd begin talking about Jack, and there was no doubt about whether he would shoot Jack, or worse. I explained to Dulsie that Jack and I would have to leave town for a few days, until this all blew over. I asked her to check on the money at the bank for me, and gave her the telegram and the silver bullet to show the manager. I said we'd be back to pick up the money soon.

She said she would do it if she ever got up the nerve to leave this room again, and I left her trying to pour whiskey into a glass with a hand that shook so bad she ended up pouring half of it onto the table.

I went back to the hotel for Jack, and told him the news I had just learned. "Hickok go loco," I said. "Scare everyone, many leave town. Hardin ride out hours ago, head west."

"Well why didn't you say so right away," he said impatiently. "That's more important than this business with Hickok." He shook his head in annoyance. "I don't see how I'll ever get this job done without up-to-date information," he said.

We got our horses saddled up and headed out of town without having to answer any questions. As we rode out Texas Street I could still hear yelling and glass smashing over on Railroad. I wondered which would run out first, Hickok's fury or Abilene's windows. The street got darker by the minute, as Hickok shot out the fancy new oil lamps with their big reflectors.

We camped about a mile outside town that night. Next morning I picked up a single trail and convinced Jack it had to be Wes Hardin's. "One man ride west," I said. "We follow?"

"Of course we'll follow," he said impatiently.

We followed the tracks for three days, until they ended at a small stream where a drunken cowboy was lying amidst a mess of empty bottles. His horse was wandering free, grazing, and I could see more bottles poking out of the saddlebags. This fellow had planned on a long drunk.

Jack peered at the man. Then he shook his head. "I just can't believe this is Wes Hardin," he said at last. "I think we've got the wrong man. This fellow smells so bad even his horse won't come near him."

"Name's Josh," the man in the creek said, raising his head a little. "Have a drink." His head splashed back into the water.

"See," Jack said. "I think your information was wrong. I doubt that Hardin ever left Abilene. He's not the sort to run off from a fight, I hear."

"We go back?" I asked.

"Of course. We'll never find him out here, even if he did leave. We'll go back and get better information."

I agreed. The money should be there by now, and we would need it before we could move on anywhere. I borrowed one of the cowboy's whiskey bottles from his saddlebag and we pitched camp a little way upwind from him. We slept very well.

The next day we started back to town, to ask around about Hardin (Jack's plan) and pick up the money (mine). We made it back in two days, since we had no trail to follow.

When we rode in I went to look for Dulsie, and couldn't find her at the Alamo, or anyone who knew where she was living. Then I went to the bank, and was told that the beautiful lady had indeed picked up my money the very next day after I'd been in.

I went all over town looking and asking questions, but Dulsie had disappeared as if she had jumped in a hole and pulled it in after her.

And so had our five hundred dollars.

Chapter

*In which we travel to the
Dakota Territory, meet the Boy General,
and one of us travels on alone, toward
a confrontation in Dodge City.*

Jack had been right about the circus. They hired us on just as they were leaving Abilene, and we traveled with them for quite a while. It was a small show, nothing like the kind of thing P.T. Barnum put on, with knee-high colonels and live whales. But people took what they could get out in the smaller western towns, and most seemed to enjoy the show. It was not a bad life, on the whole, traveling from town to town with three meals guaranteed and a chance to see new places. And it gave Jack a chance to ask everyone about Hardin, which pleased him even though every new story he heard seemed to contradict something else he'd heard before. Hardin had been everywhere and done everything, it seemed, but everyone had a different theory of where he was now.

I waited a long time before I told Jack about his mother's death, pretending I had just heard about it from someone in one of the audiences. By then several months had passed, but I said I would understand if he felt he had to go home to be with his father and his new stepmother.

"New what?" he said. "You mean father has married again?"

I told him about Elena, but he just shook his head in bewilderment. "Is she the one who was always scrubbing that hallway?" he asked. "I never could keep them straight."

"So, Jack go home?" I asked. "Forgettum Hardin?"

His face took on that stubborn look it got whenever anyone suggested he give up his quest. "No, I won't forget Hardin," he said. "I can't help my mother now, and it seems like my father has his own ideas about family anyway. Besides, my mother would understand about duty, even if my father doesn't."

There were more jobs around a circus than there were people to do them, so everyone had more than one job. Jack took care of the horses between shows, and during each performance he wandered through the audience wearing a sign that said "Buy your auto-graphed portraits of Mrs. Thatcher from the Mystery Man of the West." At first he'd objected to the sign, but Mrs. Thatcher had said it was either that or get rid of the mask. And since she was the star attraction and also the owner of the show, even Jack learned not to argue with her. Besides, every person who bought a picture of her in her pretty costume, standing atop her favorite gray with one leg held high in the air, also got to tell his version of the John Wesley Hardin story to the Mystery Man. It slowed up Jack's progress through the crowd some, but he seemed to sell enough pictures to keep the management happy. And I helped, whenever the crowds were too big or too talky.

My main job was selling tickets, in a booth outside the big tent. Mrs. Thatcher had produced a war bonnet someone had won in a Kansas City poker game, but I flatly refused to wear it. We had a fairly heated discussion (she was not an easy person to say no to), which I settled by informing her that she might be risking a Co-manche attack if someone from a different tribe wore that sacred bonnet. She eyed me suspiciously but put it away, and I kept hoping no Comanches ever showed up to be questioned about it. I had a strong hunch the thing had been made back East somewhere, for sale to tourists.

As a compromise I agreed to her second idea, which was a sign next to the ticket booth informing everyone that I was a descendant of Sacajawea and Charbonneau, who had guided the Lewis and Clark expedition. She figured that if enough people showed interest, maybe we could work it into one of the pageants. Hardly anyone did, though, and no one ever questioned the claim.

Circuses then didn't have very good reputations, and when we hit a town we were usually greeted with about equal parts of interest and suspicion. Housewives didn't hang out their wash while we were around for fear we'd be wearing it when we pulled out. And when a farm family came in for the show, they left a hired hand behind, shotgun loaded, to make certain their livestock didn't run off to join the circus.

It is true that some circuses were not much more than a camp for the cappers, grafters, shell artists and clothesline thieves who posed as roustabouts in between cheating or robbing the public. The performers were usually a cut above, but not always. And even those who were mostly honest had a hard time getting their wages from owners who thought nothing of charging fines for everything from losing a button to losing a whole costume at poker. Mrs. Thatcher's outfit was on the up and up, but how was a town to know?

It was this mistrust of circus people that caused our trouble in that little town in Missouri. It's true that what happened might have stirred up a certain amount of trouble anywhere, but friendly neighbors would probably have worked it out without so much fuss.

The thing began because of Jack's belief that horses as well as people benefited from sunshine and fresh air. He decided, on his own, to take all the circus horses for what he called an "outing" in a pasture outside town, one that conveniently had a fence around it so they wouldn't wander off. There were even some horses already there, so ours would have company, he figured. Well, he was right on several counts. The horses were glad of the company, and Whitey certainly benefited from the outing by re-discovering some interests no one had thought about.

It was one of those spring afternoons when the earth seems to be singing, so I had decided to take a stroll myself. When I reached the meadow outside town, wild flowers were everywhere, birds were singing in all the trees, and two boys were throwing stones at a white-clad figure that was trying to disappear in the short grass.

I jumped over the fence and ran toward a little knoll where Jack was trying to hide. A rock just missed my head as I hit the ground beside him.

"What happen?" I asked, trying to peek through the grass at the two boys, who were gathering up new ammunition. I ducked down as they began to throw again.

"Just help me get Whitey out of here," Jack said. "I'll explain it later. Ow!" A rock bounced off his knee and looped away toward a cherry tree in full bloom, beneath which Whitey was astride a black mare in a world of his own. He was working away with great energy, totally oblivious to the yells of a third boy and the rocks that were bouncing off his silvery flanks.

Jack whistled. "Come on, Whitey!" he yelled. Another rock came whizzing past us as the boys got our range.

"Me no think Whitey come now," I said. "But me think we go, or get heads busted."

I stood up, waving my arms in what I hoped was a gesture of peace. "Let's talk about this," I yelled at the boys.

"Talk, shit!" the nearest one yelled back. "That's a prize mare that danged hayburner of yourn is a-ruinin', and if you don't make him stop I'm gonna get the sheriff to run you and your whole damn circus out of town." He remembered the rock he was holding and whanged it at me for emphasis.

I ducked and stood up again. "You know we can't stop him till he's fin—" Another boulder came at me and I flopped down again.

"And all them others is eatin' up private property, too," the boy yelled as more rocks flew. These missed, so I sneaked another peek and saw that both boys were circling wide around us and heading toward the third boy, and Whitey. They all threw rocks at him for a while then, though he seemed unaware of all the commotion.

At last he finished and reared up with a high whinny. The boys scattered in all directions, but Whitey just came down on all fours and pranced away across the pasture with the black mare following behind. Whitey whinnied again, as if to confirm that life in the sunshine was truly all Jack had claimed it was. The three boys ran after the two horses, stopping to grab up more rocks along the way.

Jack and I edged our way back toward the rest of the circus horses, who had been gulping down grass all this time without any interest in all the ruckus going on around them. "We gettum horses," I said to Jack. "Whitey come after us."

But Whitey was already coming, galloping merrily along toward the herd as if something had just occurred to him. We could hear him snorting and whinnying halfway across the pasture.

"Stop him!" I yelled at Jack. "He stampede herd!"

Jack ran toward Whitey, and when they met they both did quick little dance steps from side to side. Then Whitey lunged sideways and streaked around Jack.

Then it was my turn. I didn't get in front of him but paced myself alongside those rippling muscles. Just before he got past me I dived for his neck and held on. Startled, he slowed for a second, and I managed to get my footing and swing up onto his back.

"Gettum horses back to tent," I shouted as Whitey sprang and leaped and plunged all around the springtime meadow. I grabbed two handfuls of mane and hung on desperately, wondering how long my body could stand the crashing, twisting, jarring leaps of that monster. He seemed to fly into the air facing north, twist and flail around for several minutes, and then come down, stiff-legged and iron-spined, facing the opposite direction. And then off again, lunging and leaping like a bronc on its first ride, but twice as big and three times as mean as any bronc I'd ever ridden.

On one of our circles I saw that Jack had got the rest of the herd out of the meadow and headed down the road back into town. I began to look for a soft place to land. Whitey, however, had other ideas. He was running full speed toward that cherry tree again, and for a minute I thought he'd crash headlong into it. Then I saw what he must have remembered—the branches were low on one side, and there was no way I could avoid getting scraped off, or worse.

I let go of the mane and rolled over the side just before we reached the tree, landing flat on my back in the grass. Whitey stopped and looked back at me, then gave a snort and raced away across the meadow toward the road. He soared over the gate in an effortless leap and headed back toward town after the herd.

I lay there for a while, enjoying the smell of cherry blossoms and hoping Jack had got the horses back before Whitey caught up. It was the only time I had ever been on that horse's back, or ever would be. We had a mutual understanding from then on: If I would never try that again, he would try to ignore my existence as much as possible.

I got up and started the walk back to town. There may have been a couple of bones somewhere in my body that didn't hurt, but I doubt it.

That afternoon was to be the first try at a Rose Garland, a complicated thing involving twelve horses in a kind of equine quadrille that was to be the new show opener. Jack had been putting Whitey through the paces for weeks and pestering Mrs. Thatcher to give them a chance at it, but she had been doubtful. Besides, they had twelve horses and riders already trained for such things, and they didn't need another one.

But as the music began, one horse was acting up, dancing around and refusing to get into the Entree line. As the rider jerked at the reins the horse reared, snorting and lashing about with its hooves. The other horses were beginning to toss their heads and roll their eyes too.

"I don't think that horse is ready, Mrs. Thatcher," Jack said. He didn't volunteer that Whitey had caught up with them on the return walk that afternoon and driven this mare out of the line and all over the countryside before we could catch them. I felt an explanation probably wouldn't help much at that moment myself, in fact.

"Pshaw," she said, dodging the flailing hooves. "Oh, all right, get Whitey in place." She jumped up on her gray and moved to the head of the line.

I knew Jack was getting what every performer hopes for—the big break. I ran quickly to the ticket booth and told Willie I'd take his turn on the tent crew if he'd run things for me for a while. Then I ran back in just as the horses galloped into the ring.

Things were going just fine. Jack had drilled Whitey well, and the big horse pranced through the intricate steps as if he'd always done them. They trotted around the ring, then all turned nose in toward the center and sidestepped in a kind of pinwheel effect, then went up on their hind legs in unison.

That was when a stranger ran out of the audience and pulled Jack right down off Whitey's back into the sawdust.

Jack was rolling around, trying to straighten his mask and spitting out sawdust mixed with who knows what. The stranger was jumping about and kicking at him from all sides.

"I knew I'd find you again someday, you bastard!" The stranger was yelling loud enough to be heard above the neighing and the cheers of the audience. "I'm a-gonna kick the shit out of you!"

Jack was trying to get up, but the stranger was pummeling him around the head and shoulders so fast he couldn't keep his balance. And he couldn't see what was happening because of the slipping mask.

"Don't act like you don't know me," the stranger was shouting. "It's me, Andrew, the feller whose life you damn nigh ruint." He punched Jack's nose and laughed wildly. "That's what that old sheepherder gave me after you left." He swung again, but missed. "You was the one that caused me to turn into a horse thief, you bastard!"

I started to run to help Jack, but about then I saw something that stopped me in my tracks. Whitey had been reared up on his hind legs during the whole thing, but just then he turned slightly, lined himself up with Mrs. Thatcher's gray mare next to him in the garland, and came down squarely astride her flanks.

Mrs. Thatcher sailed gracefully through the air and landed next to Jack in the sawdust.

Andrew took one more kick at Jack and then saw me coming toward him. He turned and ran into the audience.

I stopped next to where Jack and Mrs. Thatcher were sitting, covered with sawdust, and joined them in watching while Whitey put on a show with the gray mare that drew more cheers than any Entree ever had or probably ever will.

It was a long and vigorous performance. Jack was still waiting for Whitey to finish when I left to pack up our gear.

So we drifted north.

We worked here and there at one thing or another, and finally ended up working cattle again, this time for the Western Enterprise Company with headquarters at the Circle J. Every now and then a newcomer would be startled to see Jack riding line with his mask on, but most people seemed to think his lopsided notion of how to catch an outlaw was harmless enough and left him alone.

After we'd been there a couple of years, the Circle J sent around three hundred head up to Fort Abraham Lincoln in the Dakota Territory. Since the drive was not very long and the number of cows small, only two men were needed to handle it. Tom Harris, the foreman, looked us all over at breakfast and made his choice.

"Hell, those Army boys up there could probably use a good laugh," he said. "Besides, who knows, maybe your Hardin has went and joined up."

If I had known who those cows were for I wouldn't have driven them a mile. But I didn't know, so we finished gathering up the herd, and a couple of days later we were on the trail once again.

The whole fort was bustling with activity when we arrived, and we soon found out why. They were preparing for an expedition into the Black Hills, to be led by that killer of children, George Armstrong Custer. The three hundred cows were to feed his men in the field.

Once we had delivered the cattle we were free to go, and I was ready to leave right away. But Jack would not hear of it. "I can't go without at least seeing Custer," he said. "I may never be this close to a great man again."

A great man? This was the slaughterer of Black Kettle and his People, which had made him a hero to some, I suppose. Black Kettle had just missed being killed at Sand Creek, but at Washita Custer had come in with the morning sun, bringing death for breakfast. The general claimed to have killed a hundred and three warriors that day, though the Cheyenne claimed he was a liar as well as a killer of women and children—sixteen women and nine children, by their count, but only thirteen warriors. But however you counted the dead, it was a morning no one of The People would ever forget, or forgive.

I wanted nothing to do with such a man, but Jack insisted on asking everyone where to find his hero. Finally we were told that Custer should be returning soon from his morning hunt.

In a little while he did ride in, sitting ramrod straight on a big bay horse with a bunch of odd-looking dogs trailing in his wake. He wore fringed buckskins with a red neck scarf and a gray hat, and with that long yellow hair and thick mustache you could hardly miss him. He rode right into Jack's heart.

"Look how he sits that horse," Jack said in a voice filled with awe. "I tell you, that man was born to ride. And look at those dogs. That's a foxhound there, and I think that big one's called a stag-hound."

I suppose the scene was impressive, or would have been if I hadn't known who the man was. "All right, we see-um Custer. We go now."

But we didn't. Jack couldn't tear himself away from so much greatness, so we hung around the sutler's watching the preparations. Many troopers were off on two-week marches, we learned, to toughen them for the expedition. And meanwhile over a hundred wagons had to be fitted, new guns had to be ordered, and feed had to be procured for all the animals. "Do you know how much feed we gotta carry for nine hundred mules and a thousand horses?" Sergeant Miller asked as he drank Jack's whiskey at the sutler's bar.

"Well, let's see," Jack said. "If each horse eats about—"

The sergeant stared at Jack's look of pained concentration, then rolled his eyes heavenward. "Never mind, just believe me that it's one big shitload of corn," he said. He finished the whiskey and started to leave.

"Wait," Jack said. He had paid for the whiskey, and he was determined to get more for his money than a report on feed suppies. "Do you think we could go along? I know you're taking some news-paper men, and I once collaborated with Stanley on a story down in Kansas."

Miller gave Jack a long, hard look. "I reckon you're pullin' my leg," he said finally. "Because number one I ain't the one that hires on people for this damn-fool business, and number two I wouldn't recommend nobody I ain't never seen his face. Drink or no drink." He stalked away, but turned at the door. "I thankee anyway," he said politely.

We'd been there close to a week by then, and I knew they'd be expecting us back at the Circle J. We weren't carrying the herd money (the bookkeepers and bankers must have taken care of that), but we were still on salary. The Circle J had a policy of wanting to know where their hired hands were, and why.

"Jack, we go back or we lose-um jobs," I told him.

"I suppose so," he said, watching the bustle of preparation. "It's just that I wouldn't even mind not looking for Hardin for a while if I could go on this glorious expedition with General Custer."

"Glorious! Expedition not even legal! Treaty of '68—"

He waved his hand. "That's only paper, Crazy Fox. And treaties are renegotiated all the time."

"Treaty not renegotiated!" Only paper, indeed. "No new treaty made!"

He was not listening. "Just think," he said dreamily. "The whole country will be talking about it and reading about it. Men who can command the attention of the nation don't come along every day. General Custer will go down in history, you mark my words."

I gave up talking. "We not go with Custer, so no use talk. We leave in morning." I walked away, leaving him staring toward Custer's tent with a look like a hungry dog.

The army sounded reveille long before sunup, and once the bugles started it was hard to go back to sleep. So we were up and mounted before daybreak. But not soon enough.

"Hey, you there!" someone was yelling.

We turned and watched as a figure strode toward us. As he neared, I recognized the buckskins and red neck scarf.

"My God, Crazy Fox," Jack whispered. "It's him."

"Can you play an instrument?" Custer asked as he got nearer.

Jack looked all around, then back at Custer. "You mean me? Play? Instrument?"

"Of course I mean you." He looked up at Jack, head cocked. "But first maybe you'd better explain that mask."

Jack looked at me, Custer looked at Jack, and I looked at the lantern at the sutler's. This was one time I wasn't going to help out. Let Jack tell his Hardin story. We'd be sure to leave 'em laughing, as the clowns said.

Jack stammered, began to say something about his wound, stopped. Then he cleared his throat and charged ahead into his real story, his quest.

Custer listened intently, and when Jack was finished he said, "Remarkable."

Well, maybe the General and I agreed on one thing at least.

"Truly remarkable to find a man who knows what honor is in these tawdry days," Custer went on. "Sir, I commend you to your quest." He swept his hat off and bowed.

"But sir, you were asking if I play . . . ?"

"No, I cannot turn you from your mission for a mere favor to me," he said. "I couldn't ask it now."

Jack jumped down off Whitey and removed his own hat. "Oh, sir, please ask."

"Well, one of my musicians' mounts stepped in a gopher hole and had to be shot, so we're short one white horse. I'd rather not go into the field one short, so I thought perhaps you might care to fill in. Or sell me your horse, if you don't play."

"I'd be honored to sell him to *you,* sir," Jack said. "But the thing is, he bites. Even whites. I'm the only one who can ride him." He stopped, unwilling to give up the chance to please Custer. "I don't play too well, except for the tambourine. I'm pretty good on that." He saw that wasn't doing the trick, so he added, "I'm sure I could learn, though, and by the time this marvelous expedition leaves I would not embarrass you or the Seventh Cavalry, or the country."

Custer knew when he had found a true believer. He smiled and clasped Jack by the shoulders. "Yes, this will truly be a marvelous expedition, and we'll see that the whole country feels about it as we do. Sergeant Hawkins will issue you an instrument and temporary papers. Glad to have you with us, man." He clapped Jack's shoulder and turned to leave.

"But General Custer, sir," Jack said. "What about my friend here? I'm sure he could learn to play an instrument too."

Custer turned and looked at me for the first time. "This man is an Indian," he announced. I heard in my mind the screams of the dying on the Washita. "No, that wouldn't do," he said. "But you can ask Lieutenant Wallace if he needs another scout." He strode away across the busy compound.

Jack stared after him until he was gone in the gray dawn light, then turned to me. "He's just like I thought he'd be," he said. "Come on, let's go see this Wallace about you."

"No."

"What?"

"No. Me no work for Custer."

"But why not? You'll get a chance to work with that Charley Reynolds. And you'll get to watch a true American hero in action."

"Custer not hero. Him murder good People." I turned my horse and started away.

"But that was war," Jack said. I kept on going. "My God, Crazy Fox, you can't leave me here alone," he called. I stopped, waited. "I mean, you're the only one I know well besides General Custer, and he'll probably be too busy to do much entertaining."

I turned and looked at him, standing there next to Whitey with a plaintive look somehow showing through the mask. It was true that we'd been riding together for three years, and I was beginning to get used to his company. It wasn't the money now, because ever since Dulsie had skipped from Abilene with the five hundred dollars and that silver bullet I had not been able to bring myself to wire the Austin bank. I remembered how much trouble I'd had even with the bullet, and somehow explaining the loss seemed too much to bite off. So Jack and I had lived like other drifters, working here and there and managing to keep ourselves fed. But always before I had found the jobs and made the arrangements. This was the first time Jack had come up with work for us, and now I was turning it down.

I felt bad, but I knew I would feel even worse if I went along with this. I shook my head. "Me sorry, but no work for Custer," I said. "Me go back Circle J, wait for you there."

"All right for you," Jack said. "You're just mad because he asked me first." He punched Whitey in the side and nearly got his arm bit off.

I turned and started away again.

"At least stay till the expedition leaves," Jack called. *"Please."*

I decided to give him that, at least. So we hitched the horses and went to look for breakfast.

On July 2nd the expedition was at last ready to leave, and I got my first real notion of its size. I didn't actually count them, but it was said that close to twelve hundred people would move out in that line, along with all the animals Sergeant Miller had mentioned and over a hundred wagons carrying supplies and grain. There were newspapermen, guides, almost fifty Indian scouts and at least fifty children from the Santee Sioux Indian School who were going along to assist the scouts. It was a kind of learn-on-the-job program someone in the government had dreamed up, and all those little boys had been outfitted at some considerable cost.

They also had a paleontologist, a botanist, a photographer, an engineer, a geologist and President Grant's son, Fred. And a band, mounted on matching white horses, tootling a tune someone told me was an Irish jig. One of the musicians wore a mask, and I thought I heard some odd notes in the tune, but on the whole the sight was impressive.

The procession formed and began to move out, with Custer and his wife in the lead, followed by Fred Grant and the group of scientists, with the band behind them playing full blast.

It was a stirring sight, and I almost got on my horse to gallop off after them. I even had a job waiting, tending bar for the sutler during the encampments. The notion of being probably the only Indian bartender in the West appealed to me, and I had wavered in my refusal to go along. But then we heard a talk one evening by the "Boy General." He boasted that the Seventh Cavalry could wipe out the whole Sioux nation if they gave the expedition any trouble. That decided it for me.

I watched while the ambulances passed and then the artillery, the cavalry and the infantry, the remuda and the cattle. At the end was the sutler's wagon, followed by a group of civilians, including some miners.

Didn't I mention the miners before? You see, Children, the true purpose of this expedition was not the mapping of unknown territory. It was a search for gold in the sacred hills of the Sioux.

I rode back toward the Circle J, but by the time I had reached the White River crossing, one day's ride from the bunkhouse, I had changed my mind. I knew Jack would be on that expedition for at least a couple of months, and I had not seen my mother in three years. I sent a letter of explanation along to Harris by way of a stage driver, and I rode on south, toward Kansas and the Indian Territory.

Jack had vowed to write many letters along the way, and had

suggested that I save them all in case he decided to allow them to be published later, as part of the historical record. But I knew they would be slow to reach the Circle J, and I figured Harris would save them for me anyway. (He did, and I have put them in here according to when they were written, to give an idea of what was happening to Jack as well as to me during our time apart.)

I decided that night riding was still the safest way for an Indian to travel alone, so I rode mainly in the darkness and looked for a place to hole up when the sun was high. And in a couple of weeks I knew I had reached Kansas.

Dear Mr. Fox:

We made about fourteen miles the first day and had to make a fireless camp due to lack of anything to burn. There was grass and water for the animals, but no hot coffee for us weary humans. (I bet you're eating Mrs. Harris's wonderful flapjacks as you read this!) But those of us who have reports to write had to labor late anyway, tired and hungry.

But most days it is better. Reveille sounds at 2:30 A.M. and we all turn out for some boiled Rio coffee and hardtack. (Sugar helps a little, but that coffee still makes my eyes water.) Then pack your gear, load up your horse, and head out for another day of adventure. (The officers have a slightly different routine, as their larger tents require several hands to take down so they have breakfast while the privates do that. Their breakfasts smell somewhat different, too, though so far I haven't been invited to share them.)

I was sorry to see Mrs. Custer turn back after the first day, as I do think a lady's presence lends graciousness to the social life of a group. Also, I haven't made too many friends, since my job keeps me pretty busy (my new job, that is). Besides, men who call names are not going to be friends of mine.

> Your stalwart friend,
> Mr. Jack Knight, Esq.

As I neared Dodge City I became aware of more and more activity going on around me as I looked out from my daytime hiding places. All day long the air was filled with the sounds of rifle fire, and sometimes I could identify the resounding boom of the Sharps .50. It seemed like most of Dodge City's population was swarming all over the prairie shooting at buffalo. And I didn't see very many of those left, I realized.

I needed supplies, but now I began to wonder how wise it would be to go into Dodge. And I began to realize something else, too: All the time I had been "taking care"of Jack, he had been doing the same thing in a way for me. Mask and all, he was a white man, and he had been my pass to worlds not traveled much by lone Indians in those days.

A couple of miles from Dodge I found a shallow cave at the base of a rise and holed up for the day. The shooting had driven most of the game away, and even if I had found a rabbit I was afraid to make a fire to cook it. I ate the last bite out of my pack and knew that tomorrow I'd have to make a decision: It was Dodge City or an empty stomach.

I drifted off to sleep, not knowing that the decision was about to be made for me.

Dear Crazy Fox:

Today we camped by a small stream the Indians call Chanta Peta, though the water is so bad that even the horses didn't want to drink it at first. A couple of them have been bit by rattlesnakes, and the grasshoppers are so thick the horses crunch them like shale as you ride along. I know you have expressed admiration for the Sioux, but I doubt their intelligence in wanting to hold onto land as ugly as this.

I've asked the journalists who are traveling with us for advice on my writings, and have been advised to try for the "human interest" side of our experiences. So I am now alert for such stories, such as the one that concerns one of our guides. He carries with him some books containing colored pictures of animals, and he also happens to be a very good hunter. He noticed that the Indians were giving him strange looks and talking in whispers, and wondered what that was about. Well, he found out. It seems they had decided that the scout was casting some kind of magic spell over the animals by using the pictures in the books. They were discussing killing him so his magic would be gone and there would be more animals for the Indians. I think the aborigines (as Mr. Grinnell calls them) with their childlike ways will provide many human interest stories, don't you?

I forgot to tell you about my new job, now that I am no longer playing in the band (I knew Whitey would cause problems there, and no one can say I didn't warn them). I am now in charge of two things called chronometers, which I have to carry very carefully in baskets. It is very important that they not be jarred. Sergeant

Becker comes around every so often to look at them and make notes.

Well, while you're eating those incredible flapjacks of Mrs. Harris's, I hope you'll think of your old friend crossing the alkali flats with only stagnant water to drink.

Your thirsty friend,
Jack Knight, Esq.

"Hey, Pa, come lookie here," someone was yelling.

I snapped awake and found myself looking right down the barrel of an ancient rifle. It was bigger than the boy holding it.

"Hey, Pa, I got me a Injun," the boy yelled.

I started to sit up, but the boy jabbed the gun at me and said, "You better hold still, Injun, or I'll blow a hole right through that dirty red hide of yourn." I decided to wait for his pa.

In a few seconds a battered wagon came creaking up and a small man in worn-out clothes jumped down. "What ya got, Sonny?" he asked. Then he saw me, and his eyes lit up in a way that chilled my heart. He took the gun from the boy and motioned for me to come out of the cave. "Good work, Sonny," he said. "If we cain't make nothin' off'n bufflers, maybe we can git somethin' for this Injun's hide. Let's git him tied up and load him in the wagon, so's we can take him to the fort."

"Mister, I don't know what you're talking about," I said. "I'm just passing through trying to reach my mother before she dies." I thought that had a sad ring to it, and might touch their hearts.

"You don't say," the old man said. "Well, Injun, I reckon your mama's not a-gonna see you in this life. Git that rope, Sonny."

So I rode into Fort Dodge in the back of a bouncing wagon, tied hand and foot with a filthy bandanna stuffed in my mouth. My horse clopped along behind. I remembered that horse-thieving Kiowa from years ago, and began to feel better toward him.

Dear C.F.

Well, I haven't seen any buffalo since we left the fort. Mr. Grinnell says there are probably some left in the interior of the Black Hills, but he's from New York and doesn't have the true eye that we Westerners have. I mentioned this to him yesterday as we watched the General's dogs run down a fox kit. They got him in a very short time.

Have asked Mr. Illingworth to take my picture, but he says he's too busy right now. He says it is hard for him to work and carry on an intelligent conversation at the same time. I have never been bothered by that particular problem. He usually disappears early in the morning, climbing high up on a hill with all his heavy equipment so he can be ready when we all ride by below. Then he has to develop his plates inside some black canvases he rigs up, and then get everything back down safe and unbroken. I've offered to help, but he prefers to do things alone.

I'll ask him about the picture again tomorrow, if I see him. But I may not, since I have a new job now, carrying messages for the General and some of the others. I'm sure they all understood that I never meant to drop those chronometers, though. It's just that snakes are scary.

Your weary friend,
J.K.

The wagon rattled into the fort, but no one paid any attention to it, or to me. Maybe such sights were common in those days, or maybe no one wanted to argue with a gun-toting buffalo hunter over a tied-up Indian. (Later I learned that people had had so much Indian trouble hereabouts, that they were in no mood to help out any of my People, whether they had done anything wrong or not.)

The wagon stopped in front of a building with a HEAD-QUARTERS sign over it. The boy's father jumped down and went in. I heard loud voices inside, and then the door opened and the voices came out. "By God, I'd think you fellers would be glad to pay somethin' for bringin' in the varmint that murdered poor Warren," the hunter said.

"You don't have any proof this Indian murdered Warren," another voice said. A stocky, red-faced captain leaned over the tailgate to peer at me. "Fact is, we don't even know that Warren was shot by Indians at all. With all you people out there banging away at everything that moves, likely Warren got between somebody and a buffalo."

"Huh. And I reckon that danged buffalo scalped him, too. Is that what you're sayin'?"

"Mr. Snelling, what I'm saying is that this Indian isn't wanted by us, so far as I know. And this command doesn't buy Indians suspected of crimes against the settlers anyway. But I can hold him in the stockade till we find out his business if you want. I doubt that he's from any of the local tribes, but he may be wanted somewhere else."

"No, thankee. He's mine, and I'll just take him on into Dodge and see if anyone there thinks different."

The captain looked at Snelling with distaste. "Have you asked him what his story is?" he said.

"Who? The Injun? Who in tunket cares what his story is? Listen, cap'n, I found him and I mean to keep him till I see what he's worth, and you can't stop me."

"Now wait just a goddamned min—"

"Good morning, Captain," said a third voice from a little distance.

The captain snatched his hat off and turned beet red. "Ah, good morning to you, miss. You're looking prettier than summer sunshine, as always."

"Why thank you," said the lilting voice. "Is the major in?"

"He's always in to you, miss." The captain moved aside to let her pass, and I got my first look at the yellow-gold hair and green eyes I remembered so well. I thrashed around and grunted as loud as I could through the gag.

"Well I'll declare," Dulsie said. "Captain, I believe you've got a friend of mine hog-tied in this here wagon." She stepped closer and gave me a wink. "In fact, this gentleman is a business partner of mine."

The captain stared at me in confusion. "You don't say," he said. "Business partner?"

"Yes sirree," Dulsie said. "I don't know why he's tied up like that, but I can surely vouch for him one hundred percent. Let's just get him untied so you can hear his explanation." She started to tug at the ropes on my feet.

Snelling came to life. "Now you just hold on there, Miss Dulsie," he said. "This here man's my prisoner, and I mean to take him in for the reward."

"Reward? There ain't no reward for him. But I'm willing you should have something for all your pains." Dulsie was digging in her little red satin pouch, and came up with some coins. "Would twenty dollars be right, you think?"

Snelling eyed the coins hungrily. "Well, I don't know now . . ."

Dulsie led him away a few steps and whispered something into his ear. His face lit up like a rainbow and he had me untied before I knew what was happening.

"But Pa," the boy protested. "What about the reward? Don't I git half of what you git?"

"Shut up and git in that wagon," Snelling said. "Hell, you wouldn't know what to do with it anyway."

Dear Crazy,

I went out on an excursion with some of the "bug hunters" the other day, and they dug up a bone they said was the lower jawbone of a rhinoceros. I doubt it, though. There aren't any of those animals around here. ("Bug hunters" is what we men call the scientists, by the way.)

A little farther on we passed an Indian burial platform, and I noticed that some swallows had built a nest underneath the scaffold out of the Indian's hair. (Mr. Grinnell says he has seen this before, but I don't know where he would have seen such a thing back in New York.) Do you think this will make a "human interest" item?

A soldier died and some of the men are very upset, claiming it was negligence on the part of our doctor. They hold the opinion that Dr. Williams was drunk on the night in question, but I personally don't believe it. Williams is much too concerned with his health to indulge in alcohol. He has frequent colds and has to sniff chloroform all the time to ease the discomfort.

On the 25th of July we came to a place so beautiful that the General named it Floral Valley, and even the hardest teamster picked flowers for his cap. We marched up and down and played several songs that someone told me were called "How So Fair Something" and "The Mocking Bird." (Did I tell you that they are letting me play in the band again? Even after what happened. But I guess they realized I couldn't help it that Whitey doesn't like drums.)

Some Indians came to talk to the General the next day, but I haven't heard what it was all about.

Your lonesome friend,
Jack

I had entered Fort Dodge trussed up in a nester's wagon. I left it in a shiny black buggy pulled by a high-stepping dapple-gray, with the prettiest white woman in Kansas by my side. And as we drove into Dodge City, I explained what had happened and where Jack was.

"Riding with Custer!" she said. "Lordy, now there's a pair." She shook her head. "Still, I'm kinda sorry not to see Jackie after so long. Especially since I'm not sure how long I'll stay on here."

She explained that times were bad in Dodge, and money was scarce. That's why there were so many people out on the prairie, trying to make some money on buffalo hides. "Hell, there's whole families out there a-bangin' away at everything, none of them knowin' the first thing about huntin' buffalo or about much of anything except tryin' to feed too many with too little. That's probably how that man Warren got killed, though his friends tried to lay it on Indians. You can't blame poor old Snelling for tryin' to make something, I guess."

"Sure, what's one Indian more or less," I said.

"Ah, now, don't take on," she said. She poked me in the ribs. "Hell, you got more meat on you than Snelling's whole family put together. He'll scratch his whole life and never have much of anything."

"Whereas I'm a rich man," I said.

She gave me a quick look and changed the subject.

We rode into Dodge and down Front Street, which had grown up around the railroad tracks, like in most railhead cattle towns. In fact, Dodge looked a good deal like Abilene, except for the big piles of buffalo bones stacked up all along the street, waiting for shipment. They were bringing $2.50 a ton here at the railhead, I learned later, and $14 a ton back East, where they were used for fertilizer and in making bone china.

Dulsie pulled the buggy up in front of the Long Branch, one of the first saloons in the four blocks of false-fronted buildings. She gave a nickel to a gawky kid and handed him the reins, then said. "Well, come on in. It ain't home, but it'll do."

Inside it looked like a hundred other saloons I'd been in— men, whiskey, sawdust, sour smells, and rooms upstairs, where the girls were probably resting up for the evening trade. Dulsie motioned me into a seat and said, "I'll have Joe send over a bottle, and if you'll set still there I'll find you something to eat." She saw the solid row of open mouths at the bar and frowned. "Okay, you yahoos," she said loudly. "Anybody that ever wants to be friendly with Dulsie Morgan again had better say howdy to my old friend from Texas here."

That got me a few mumbled howdies and a row of backs turned toward me.

Well, it wasn't really a rousing welcome to Dodge, but I'd settle for it.

Crazy,

Have you ever panned for gold? It's interesting, but it gets boring fairly quickly. But I did borrow some pans from a man named Ross and tried my hand at it. And I found what he called "color" the second or third try. I guess that's almost as interesting as gold, from his reaction.

A more interesting thing, though, is a game called "base ball" that the men were playing. It's too complicated to explain to you, but I joined in the game we played the other day here in Custer Park. After we'd played awhile I was given the most important job of all, keeping the "bat" clean so the "hitters" wouldn't get their hands dirty when they swung at the ball. Maybe I'll teach you and the other men the game when we meet again at the Circle J.

Everybody's shooting things. The General shot a bear, and several of the men shot deer today. And on August 19 a lot of horses had to be shot because they were completely worn out.

Sometimes I feel almost worn out too, but I hope nobody gets the notion to shoot me, ha ha.

Your venturesome friend,

Jack

I got fed, had a bath, and spent most of the day talking with Dulsie. She told me about Mr. Knight and about his new young son. We reminisced about the past, recalling the windmill and speculating on where John Wesley Hardin might actually be.

What we never talked about was the $500 she had stolen from me in Abilene. And no matter how kindly I was feeling toward her after the business with Snelling, I felt I had to bring it up. I was almost broke, and I wanted money to take to my mother.

Finally, after trying for hours to find some way to turn the conversation in that direction, I simply blurted it out.

"Dulsie, why did you steal our money?" I asked her.

"Well now, I don't know as *steal* is a nice word to use. *Borrow* sounds much better." She pushed her coffee cup away and got up to pace around her elegantly furnished parlor above the saloon. "But I'm glad you finally brought it up, anyway. I couldn't seem to find a way to talk about it."

She fiddled with a stray curl of hair, frowning. "You got to understand that I was scared to death that night in Abilene. I figured Hickok would come after me sooner or later, me bein' Coe's girl and all, so I packed a bag and hid at a friend's across town. In the mornin'

I knew I had to hightail it out of there, and your money was the only cash I could lay my hands on fast."

She stopped in front of me. "I did try to find you later, you know. But your trail was as cold as yesterday's grits."

"We were with the circus," I said.

"No foolin'? No wonder I couldn't find you." She laughed. "Hell, all that time I thought you were punchin' cows, and instead you were punchin' elephants. Who'd of thought it."

I waited.

"Anyways, I did spend your money. That is, I invested it. I own part of this saloon, along with some other people. And I own two other buildings on Front Street. It ain't a whole lot, but it's something."

She went to a dresser and took out a box. From the box she took a little key. She went across the room and kicked at a spot on the floor, and one side of a picture flew away from the wall. She pulled another box out of the dark hole behind the picture and unlocked that, then took out an envelope tied with a pink ribbon and handed it to me.

"It's all there," she said. "Once I'd made it back I put it away and vowed never to touch it. It's yours now, and I thank you and Jackie kindly for the use of it."

I hefted the heavy envelope and thought of my mother's face when I put it in her hands. Then I remembered something else.

"What about the silver bullet?" I asked Dulsie.

"I lost that in a poker game last year when things were kinda tight. I didn't touch your money, but I thought I had a hand good enough to risk that blamed bullet. I tried to buy it back later on, but the no-account had lost it in another game over to Newton. I'm sorry."

What could I say? I had the money and my life, and I was feeling too good about everything to hold a grudge. "It's all right," I told her. "It wasn't important."

I decided to ride on south the next day, to the place my People now called home, down in the Territory. I said good-bye to Dulsie in the empty saloon early that morning.

"Will you try to make Jackie write?" she asked me.

I said I would.

"And if I move on I'll send my new address to the Circle J, all right? We've got to keep track of one another, you know."

I smiled and promised to send her our address too, if we moved on.

There was moisture in the deep green eyes, and she put a hand on my arm and tiptoed to kiss me on the cheek. "You take care now, you hear?" she said softly. And then she ran back upstairs.

Even though she was a white woman and not of my world, Children, I felt a heavy sadness in my heart as I rode out of Dodge.

Again I rode at night, but after I'd gotten three days out of Dodge I saw few people, and had an uneventful trip into the Territory. After a while I rode day and night, stopping only to rest the horse. I felt an urgency inside me I could not explain, and drove myself and the horse to the outmost point of endurance.

When I reached the reservation I rode straight to my mother's cabin. It still stood, and I was pleased that it had kept my mother warm.

But it was my cousin's wife who came to the door, and when she saw me she covered her face.

I knew I was too late.

Dear Crazy,

Well, the trip is over, after 883 miles (according to those chronometers and odometers and what all, if you can believe them). I am very tired, and will be glad to get back to the Circle J. But knowing this great man, General Custer, has been an experience no one could forget.

One of the problems with greatness is that others are always ready to besmirch one's reputation. So if you have heard those rumors about the drunkenness of the Seventh Cavalry, I can tell you it isn't so. The General tolerates no drunkenness. That champagne dinner was held while he was out hunting.

Just last night I happened to pass the General's campfire, and eventually I was asked to join the party there. I wish you could have been here to hear his stories about the campaigns against the Cheyenne and Arapahoe. You would have gained a better understanding of the situation I'm sure. His description of the battle on the Washita was particularly stirring.

I will be happy to see my old friend again, and have much to tell you. I have written to my father down in Texas, so he will know that I am well, and that I continue to live for duty and honor.

Hoping to see you soon,
Jack

P.S. Please keep these letters in good condition, since they will probably be much prized by Eastern publications hungry for a first-hand account of this historic expedition.

P.P.S. There seems to be some interest in the gold we found, too. Perhaps that will make those publications even more interested, particularly since I was the one who found it.*

---

*Evidently Jack was not aware—and Crazy Fox does not see fit to tell us—that the discovery of gold in the Black Hills was the cause of the bloody Sioux wars that followed.

Chapter

8

My cousin opened a box and showed me what remained of the money I had left with my mother three years before—fifteen dollars. She had spent it carefully, buying little for herself and as much as she could for others in need. She had invested some of the money in farm equipment, bought from the Indian agent. The fields were more prosperous now, and The People were eating better.

"Your mother did the best she could," Sharp Nose said. "The money has made life better for The People."

"Often I had wished I could send more," I told him. I took the envelope from inside my shirt and handed it to him. "My heart is heavy because I shall not see my mother again, but maybe some of the sadness will leave me if I can help my People."

Sharp Nose untied the pink ribbon and handed it to his wife. Then he put the envelope in the box where the other one had been kept. He did not open it, but instead looked deeply into my eyes. "Even though you do not live among The People, your name is much honored around our campfires."

We walked outside, among the wigwams where the quiet children stood watching us. I could see that the needs of my People were still great, and I remembered the words of the old man when I was here last. Well, The People still had the land and maybe they would keep it, but it was not enough. They needed more.

"When I was a small boy I sat around the campfires and listened to the tales of our greatness," I said to Sharp Nose. "Then I dreamed that those days would return. But now I know they will not. And we can expect help from no one but ourselves."

"You will stay, then?" Sharp Nose asked.

I looked back toward the cabin Jack and I had built. "No, my cousin. My mother's house is yours now. I can do more for The People out there, in the white man's world."

I wasn't sure that was true, but I knew I had to try, at least. So the next day I rode away from the reservation again, and headed for Abilene. That was where the system had worked best, so that was the place to see if it would work again. I had to get money for my People. And maybe a little for Jack and me, too.

Abilene was a different town. The farmers had won back in '72, and the Texas trail herds had sought a different market. The cowboys had moved on down the line, to Ellsworth and Dodge City. Now the air was filled with farm talk and the creak of wagon wheels.

For my purposes the change was all to the good. I only wanted to get into the telegraph office and the bank as quickly as possible and ride out again.

I had worried about the missing silver bullet, but I could have saved myself the trouble. I never got that far.

I sent my wire and very quickly got my reply. It was short and right to the point: "CHARLES KNIGHT DECEASED STOP ARRANGEMENT DISCONTINUED."

That was all. Nothing about when he had died or how, nothing about a will, nothing about the ranch or any of the Knight holdings. Surely Jack had been left the ranch. Or had he? Could the old man have died without ever deciding what to do about Jack?

Whatever had happened in Texas, one thing was certain: There'd be no more money to bury Aunt Matilda.

I headed for the Circle J, thinking about Mr. Charles Knight, a man I had admired in spite of his skin color. He was the first white man I had ever met—and to speak straight, I haven't met very many since—who really seemed not to see the color of any man's skin. He hired men of all kinds on his ranch, and I never heard a bad word pass his lips that had to do with their color. Many bad words passed his lips when work was not done right, but they were handed out evenly to everyone. He was as good a man as I have ever known.

But he must have had something to atone for, or else why had the Great Spirit given him Jack?

When I got back to the Circle J bunkhouse, Jack was already there, and from the looks on the faces around the place I guessed that he had come back filled with tales of Custer's glory. The very mention of anything to do with that expedition could just about empty the room.

I kept looking for the right moment to tell Jack about his father, but we were either working at different jobs or surrounded by the whole crew, and it was hard to find a quiet moment to break the news. Then, a couple of days later, the mail came in on Bucking Bill's supply wagon, and the problem was solved for me.

There were letters from Dulsie for both of us. I opened mine quickly, and inside was another envelope addressed to me, along with a note from Dulsie. I opened the second envelope and took out a piece of paper with the "CK" brand in the upper corner.

Dear Crazy Fox:
    The bank in Austin hasn't heard from you for a spell, which leads me to think something may have happened to foul up the arrangements. I hope you'll let me know, so we can get things untangled. I know you will always be a good friend, to me and to Jack.
    I have written to him too, but I don't think there's any need for you fellows to come home. Not if Jack's still afflicted with that craziness about Hardin. But I've told him, and I'm telling you now, that Judge Gannon holds important papers concerning you both.
    A day doesn't pass but what I think about you and thank the Almighty for your friendship.

                                                Charles Knight

Dulsie's note was just as brief. She said she had received the two letters not long before she'd heard the news about Mr. Knight's death. She hadn't known when Jack and I would be back at the Circle J, but she hoped we'd get them eventually. I put both letters away and went to find Jack.

He was leaning against the corral fence staring at the papers in his hand. He handed me one of them.

To my son, Jack Knight:
    I hope this letter reaches you wherever you are now. Stumpy Morgan was over recently with some complaint or other, and he mentioned that Dulsie had written a while back and had said something about seeing you. So I got her address and am hoping she will see to it that you get this.
    As you may know, after your sainted mother died I took me a

new wife, Elena Gonzales. She is a good woman, and she has blessed me with a son which we have named Charles Junior. He is just a little thing now, but already he shows traces of the best of both our peoples.

However, all the news ain't good. Of all things, after a hard life in the saddle, I went and fell down on the waxed floor of the hallway and busted a hip. And it ain't mending like it should. Fact is, I been feeling generally pretty poorly since then, and have been kept in my bed a good part of the time.

I had hoped you would give up on Hardin and come home, but now I doubt that you will find me here if you do come. So, if I don't see you again, honor your mother and remember a father who did the best he could.

I have left a letter for you with Judge Gannon. It will explain the arrangements I have made for the ranch, and for Elena and Charles Jr. and you.

> Your loving father
> Charles Knight

I looked up and saw tears in his eyes.

"My father's dead," he said.

"Me know. Me get letters too."

"What should I do?" he asked. "I can't go home till I've found Hardin. Not after the way everybody talked. Knight is a proud name in Texas. My father—" he broke off and turned away. "I'm the only one left now," he said.

"You forgettum baby," I reminded him.

He stared at me. "My God, Crazy Fox, that baby's half Mexican. What do they know about honor?"

After much debate with himself, Jack finally wrote to Judge Gannon. He asked the judge to hire an honest, hardworking manager to run the ranch until he could return. He explained that he would come back now but his duty lay clear before him. He was honor-bound to find Hardin, the dastardly villain who had . . . etc. etc.

Well, the judge got one paragraph about the ranch and close to ten pages about duty and honor.

Ranch life went on, with a lot of hard work and a little time off for visits to town. During one of those visits Jack came across a picture of Hardin in a newspaper and tore it out. "The man looks kind of familiar somehow," he told me. "Or maybe it's just that evil puts a stamp on a man that the trained eye can recognize."

He decided to have some wanted posters printed up, to simplify his hunt for Hardin, which even he had to admit had just about run out of steam. He found a little printing shop that could do up some flyers, but there was no way to print the newspaper picture so Jack drew one of his own. The result was a face that looked like a cross between a buffalo and a Gila monster. It might not have resembled Hardin much, but it sure did look mean. And in the following weeks that face got to be familiar to everyone, staring down from every building and wagon and tree for miles around.

In whatever spare time he had left, he kept up a one-sided correspondence with several Eastern newspapers and book publishers about his "Journals." When the mail came he would put the perfumed letter from Dulsie aside until he was certain there was nothing from an interested publisher. But the letters from Dulsie kept coming regularly, and still from Dodge I noticed, though she often talked about moving on.

Jack got on the wrong side of one person or another from time to time, but mostly people left him alone with his posters and fancy stories. We ate our bean pies and sourdough, worked, and lived in the only world that seemed real now, in the bunkhouse scented with manure and old boots and tobacco and plastered with pictures from catalogs and magazines. We plowed firebreaks in the summer, rode fence in the winter, and led the branding in the spring and fall.

We might have stayed on forever if it hadn't been for the mange—on the cows, that is, not on us.

The way you treated the mange was by soaking the infected parts with coal oil, and it was a stinking, messy job. We had been at it most of one morning when I noticed that Jack was sloshing the coal oil around pretty carelessly.

"We treatum cows, not give-um baths," I told him.

He was more careful for a time, but then his attention wandered and before long he was splashing it all over the place again.

I started to caution him, but I was too late. Before I could say anything he had splattered half a bucketful on one cow and a good part of it went in her eyes. She let out a terrible bellow and took off like someone had shoved a hot poker up her behind. I made a grab for the cow but missed, and someone else yelled and jumped at her too, but all he did was confuse her and send her flying right into the cookfire. She blazed up like a torch and ran bellowing into another cow Jack had sloshed. In seconds there were blazing cows zigzagging all over the field, setting one another afire.

When it was over there were eight charred carcasses in the field, and half the men had burns someplace or other. Tom Harris looked like he was about to go up in flames himself as he stared at Jack.

"All right," he said finally. "That is the goddamned last and final straw. You draw your wages and get the hell off this ranch by sundown."

As we were packing our gear, Bucking Bill's supply wagon arrived with the mail, and the men came in to see what they'd got. What Jack got was a letter from Dulsie—or rather a charred piece of a letter.

"What happened to this?" he asked Bill.

"Looks like it was delivered by one of them cows," someone said, and laughed. A couple of the other men laughed, but not many. It was still too soon for the blazing cattle to become a bunkhouse legend, though that would no doubt come later.

Bill explained that the mail bag had been put down too near a cookstove in the stage office, and half the Territory mail had gone up in smoke. "Hell, you're lucky to get part of a letter. Most folks didn't even get that."

It was hard to make any sense of the letter, but it seemed like she was leaving Dodge for a while, for some reason. Part of a line read "You can reach me in . . . . . . wood until the end of summer." The fire had burned a hole right through the address.

We got our gear and started to saddle the horses, but Whitey began to act up. He pranced around and nipped Jack's arm as the saddle went on his back. It slid off on the ground.

"He needs a run," Jack said as he picked the saddle up for another try.

"He needs a fence rail up side his head," someone else said. "I seen a horse like that out in Deadwood. Feller finally shot the damn fool."

Jacked pulled the saddle blanket out of the watering trough and tried to wring some of the water out of it.

"What kind of a place is Deadwood?" someone else asked. "I hear folks out there will steal yore boots whilst yer a-walkin' in 'em."

"Or shoot you for yore dust," the first man said. "Hell of a place. I left as quick as I could turn around."

Jack had been listening with a look of great interest. He got Dulsie's letter out and pointed to the burnt address. "See?" he said. "Where it's burnt, there? I bet that was Deadwood. Sure, that's the kind of place she would go, where exciting things are happening. She always was an adventurous girl."

Lots of towns end with "wood," but I figured he just might be right. There was gold being found out that way, and where there was money being made you might very well find Dulsie helping the men find ways to spend it. Besides, what did we have to lose? We had to go somewhere, and one town was as good as another.

We could have ridden almost due west to Deadwood, but that would have taken us through some Sioux country best not traveled without plenty of company. So we swung to the south of the Bad Lands until we crossed the trail that ran north from Fort Laramie. We camped there until a couple of wagons filled with men came by heading up the Platte and joined them, after the usual questions about Jack's mask and the hard looks about the color of his friend's skin.

In a few days we caught up with a wagon train. Our party camped with them that night, then moved out ahead of the train in the morning into a blinding rain that turned the ground into gummy alkali mud. It built up on the wagon wheels until you had to stop and knock it off, and then within minutes the wheels were clogged with it again.

The drinking water wasn't fit to drink, the gnats swarmed around you and got into everything (including your mouth if you were foolish enough to open it), and the land got more grim looking every mile. By and large it was not a pleasant trip, especially since we were all aware that the Sioux might appear at any moment to show their displeasure with the whole gold-seeking business. So when we met a wagon heading south, and the men in it reported no Indian problems on the trail ahead of us, we all breathed a bit easier. Even me. The only sign we ever saw of the Sioux was some fresh pony tracks in the mud where we crossed the trail someone said led into the Red Cloud agency. But I had a constant feeling that they were not far away. And that we were trespassing on their land.

One day we rode into a fair-sized town called Custer City, and Jack stared in amazement. "Look, Crazy Fox, that's French

Creek," he said, pointing toward a stream. "That's where I found the first gold. There was no town here then, of course."

We drove through the deserted streets and past a thousand or so houses in which no one now lived. The news of a richer lode at Deadwood had emptied the town. In gold mining it was a quick birth and a quicker death.

Muck and mire and lousy food, and sleeping on rocky ground that turned into more muck and mire while you slept. That was the trail to Deadwood, but it was the road to gold and twenty-five thousand had traveled it ahead of us. It was Abilene all over again, except that it was gold instead of cattle that had built the string of towns up and down the gulch.

Deadwood itself was about in the middle of the string, its one street filled with saloons and brothels. The piney hillsides behind it were dotted with shacks where the miners tried to get some sleep when they weren't working their locations. A creek of dirty sludge flowed through the town toward the Belle Fourche River. As I looked at the bustle of activity on the main street it suddenly seemed possible that Jack might be right, that Dulsie might have come here. She had a nose for money, and I could see where capital might pay off in Deadwood. In fact, one place called the Green Front was so big it ran from number 591 to number 601 on Main Street. That kind of thing might appeal to Dulsie, as an investment.

The town was filling up fast, because the next day was the Fourth of July and miners were pouring in from miles around for the festivities. We ended up sleeping under a wagon, with Jack complaining steadily.

"I wish we'd had time to look for Dulsie," he said. "I'll bet she'd know where to find a bed."

That would have been the best bet in town.

July 4, 1876. Gunfire, horse racing, yelling, drinking, fighting and whoring—that's how Americans celebrated their independence. By nightfall some would be richer, some would be busted, and all of them would be drunk, or working hard at it. But first came the contests.

To begin there was a competition to see who could rope a calf fastest. This was something everybody who worked cattle had to do, so Jack and I decided to enter.

The man who took our dollar entry fee looked skeptical. "What the hell's the mask fer?" he asked Jack. "You ashamed of runnin' with an Injun?" He spat tobacco juice on his left boot, then stared at me. "Fact is, this feller's hair might be worth some money to somebody. We got a bounty on redskin scalps here, and one kind of Injun's as good as another."

Jack opened his mouth to explain and I opened mine to protest, but before either of us got started somebody behind us said, "Hell, Jud, I know about these here fellers. This one's the Mystery Man of the West and t'other's some kind of fancy damned Injun with a name that'd break your jaw. They used to sell pictures with some circus I saw."

"No kiddin'? Mystery Man, huh?" He took Jack's dollar and held his hand out for mine.

"Actually, it's really the name we used for horse racing," I told him.

"Yeah? Well, now, that's right interestin'. So happens I won the St. Louis Rides two years runnin'. Might be we can do some business, Injun."

"Maybe later," Jack said. "First, though, please note down there that I rope in the name of Dulsie Morgan."

"Dulsie?" Jud spat on his right boot. "That's a damn queer name for a man."

"No, she is the lady of my life, and I dedicate this deed to her."

Jud nearly swallowed his tobacco laughing.

The way it went was that they had several fair-sized calves in a little pen, and they'd let one out into the street at a time. The cowboy whose turn it was had to ride after the calf and get his rope on it, then snub the rope to his saddle horn and jump down to hogtie the calf just like we did for branding. There veren't too many working cowponies in the town, but men had entered riding anything that even looked like a horse. (One man entered riding a mule, in fact, but the critter flat-out refused to chase the calf and just trotted along down the street with the man kicking and cussing at it so loud he scared the calf into running twice as fast. It took several minutes to catch it and bring it back.)

The first cowboy chased the calf all the way past the Green Front before he got his rope on it, and the next man missed his toss altogether and had to run his calf all the way out of town. Then came the man with the mule, and by then the crowd was in a good mood for Jack.

"Go to it, Mysterious!" somebody yelled as Jack and Whitey went tearing off after the calf. They caught it fairly quickly and Jack even got his rope on it the first try. But he always had been forgetful, and this time he forgot to snub the rope to the saddle horn. When the calf hit the end of the rope Jack had a good hold on his end of it, so the result was a flying dismount flat on his chest in the dust. The crowd seemed to like the performance, but Jack took a long time getting up.

On my turn I thought I had done pretty well, getting the rope on before we'd gone more than halfway down the street and getting all four feet tied on the second try. But then a black cowboy had his turn, amidst jeers and insults from the crowd. He was got up in some pretty fine clothes, featuring chaps with conchos all over them and fancy tooled boots, but the crowd hooted anyway. He just smiled and held his rope like an old friend.

When the calf was let out the black man took off right with it and had the rope over its head before the thing had taken more than three or four jumps. The calf was down and tied so fast some people were still hooting while the others had started cheering. The man's name was Nat Love, somebody told me, and it seemed that no matter how people felt about his color, most of them had to admire his skill with a rope.

The next contest was sharp-shooting, and Nat Love won that one hands down, shooting three bottles out of the air all at one time with a staghorn-handled .44. No one else could even get two.

By the end of the morning everybody knew who the black fellow was, and somebody had started calling him Deadwood Nat.

Jud was still trying to get a horse race set up, but by then nearly everyone had headed for the saloons for a noon drink. Gold pokes were changing hands like money, and when one sourdough spilled some dust on the floor the other oldtimers nearly died laughing as the greenhorns tried to pick it up off the rough planks.

The noon break had gone on for a couple of hours when the black man came in, and everybody wanted to buy a drink for Deadwood Nat.

One miner reeled up to him and showed yellow teeth in a big grin. "Say, I was talkin' to Maizie over to the Green Front, and she swears it's true that all you niggers has got dicks like a stallion." Cheers went up all around.

And that is how Deadwood Dick got his name.*

Horse races couldn't be held that afternoon because the only ones who weren't drunk were the horses. Jud challenged the "Mystery Man," but when he tried to get on his horse he fell right over the other side into the dust and just lay there laughing.

We slept under the wagon again that night, but we swore that the next day would be spent finding Dulsie.

The next day Jack forgot about Dulsie when a rider came in with some news. Custer and five troops of the Seventh Cavalry had been wiped out by an army of Sioux and Cheyennes at a place called Little Big Horn. Jack headed back to the bars to mourn for his hero, and I went up to the cemetery above town to think. I remembered the arrogant Boy General in his buckskins and yellow hair, riding out in front of that incredible expedition into the sacred Black Hills of the Sioux. He had opened these hills to the white man, greedy for gold and filled with hatred for the Indians whose land they plundered. And now, farther west, Sitting Bull had evened the score.

I thought about Custer, his band playing "Garry Owen" as he brought death on the Washita. Had the band played a gay tune at the Little Big Horn, as the Sioux and Cheyenne gave back the death Custer had handed out so freely? Jack thought him a great man, and mourned.

I found I was not sad.

In Deadwood most people made a living by mining or gambling. You needed a grubstake to mine, and not too many people thereabouts were eager to back "Mysterious," as Jack was now called, or an Indian. So we spent our dwindling money carefully and spent our time riding up and down the gulch looking for Dulsie. In Gayville we found a couple of days of work, but no Dulsie; in Lead we raced Whitey and won, but prices in the gold towns were so high that our winnings were soon gone. We worked at a Chinese laundry for a while. But still no one had seen Dulsie, or Hardin either.

By the time we got back to Deadwood, Jack was feeling pretty low. "I can't get any work done on my memoirs of General Custer this way," he said. "I just can't understand where Dulsie could have gone."

*We have left this anecdote in lest we be accused of bowdlerism, but we must point out that it is as dubious as it is vulgar.

"Maybe she not—" The words jammed in my throat like dry corn bread. Because up ahead I had seen an unmistakable figure standing in front of a tent, hands on hips, frock coat pushed back to show the guns on his thighs. Hickok looked much the same as he had that time in Abilene, except that now he seemed to be squinting as if the light hurt his eyes.

I pushed Jack through the nearest doorway, which turned out to be a saloon.

"What are you doing?" Jack asked. "I'm not thirsty."

"Just see-um Hickok on street. Me no like. May be he still mad about Abilene."

"Oh, surely not. And after I explain that I was really trying to help—"

"May not get chance. Him shoot quick."

Jack considered that. "Well, maybe this isn't the best time," he said. "What do you think we should do?"

"Me think you not wear mask here."

He straightened his back and prepared to lecture me, but I cut him off. "Hickok remember that."

He thought about that. "Maybe I could get a different color mask?" he suggested.

I shook my head. "Me think of something," I told him.

Outside a miner staggered by wearing glasses, though they didn't seem to improve his vision too much. As he collided with a porch post and sat down hard, the glasses dropped off in the mud. He didn't notice. After a few tries he pulled himself up and went reeling across the street and into a saloon to steady his nerves.

I went out to pick up the glasses, then took them back inside to where a coal oil lamp burned in the back of the saloon. A few seconds over the chimney smoked them nicely. Jack put them on and walked straight into a wall.

"You gettum used to glasses," I told him, leading him outside.

We stayed as far away from that tent as possible the rest of the day. As we ate dinner that night, I asked about Wild Bill. I learned he was not a lawman here. In fact, he was playing poker every night in the saloon at Number Ten.

If Hickok was staying, it seemed like a good idea for us to leave town. Besides, we had found no trace of Dulsie, and the money was running out fast.

As we were leaving the restaurant, a husky young fellow with the look of a Texas cowhand stepped up to me. "Hey, Injun, where's that fella they call 'Mysterious'? Somebody said you ride with him, and I'm lookin' to challenge that big horse of his'n."

"Oh, I don't think—" I started. But Jack broke in.

"I'm the man you want," he said, extending his hand. "I guess you wouldn't recognize me without my mask. And it's hard to see in here anyway. But I'm the Mysterious Rider, and I'll be happy to race your horse."

"How about tomorrow morning? It's Sunday, and a lot of men will be in town. We can get some bets up. Hell, I been hearin' about you and that white horse ever since we took a herd into Kansas. But I can beat you."

"We'll see about that tomorrow," Jack said as I led him outside.

Sunday was a fine clear day, and the sun shone down on bleary-eyed miners and pale-skinned gamblers alike. It also shone on Preacher Smith, who stood on a crate in the street sermonizing at a great rate. He got to a part about the "scarlet women of this modern Sodom" just as someone let fly with a bottle. He ducked it without breaking stride and tore on into some really fine words such as fornication and degradation, but I noticed that his eyes darted about constantly. In his line of work vigilance was the thing.

Another bottle flew by him and he paused to point a finger at a girl in a doorway. "God has always loved you, Jane," he shouted, "and so have half the men in Deadwood."

Several men hooted and the woman called Jane let out a string of curses that could've singed the hair off a buffalo. It didn't deter the Reverend, though. He was a man of some grit, and he spread salvation up and down the gulch, until someone killed him that summer on the road to Crook City.

Word of the horse race had gone around, it seemed, and a good-sized crowd had collected in the street. Jud was there, from the calf-roping, ready to challenge the winner. "I'll let you Texicans tire each other out and then I'll show you some horse racing," he told us, passing a bottle around.

"Shit, us Texans was racin' horses afore you folks had learned which end had teeth in it." It was the stocky fellow, leading a nervous-looking bay. "You ready, Mysterious?"

Whitey was prancing around and snorting. By now he'd done

this so often he had gotten the hang of it. He was raring to go, maybe thinking of the lumps of sugar I always had for him when he finished. I had to give them to him on a board to keep from losing fingers, but he had grown pretty fond of the custom and looked forward to it.

They were just about to line the horses up when Hickok arrived. He said hello to the woman they called Jane and then came over to look at the horses. "Who's gonna start this race?" he asked the crowd.

"I reckon you are, Bill," somebody said.

Hickok pulled his gun and held it up, but before he could pull the trigger, Rev. Smith was there exhorting him to cease doing the devil's work.

"Hell, I don't believe the Lord has located Deadwood yet," Jane said. She pushed the preacher into a puddle.

Hickok fired his gun and the horses took off down the town's only street. At the end they turned around and came galloping back right through the crowd. Whitey was several yards ahead and stayed there to the finish line.

I went around collecting our bets while Jack was shaking hands with the man he had beat and telling him what a healthy sport horse racing was.

"Ain't all that healthy for me, I reckon," the stocky young man was saying when I came up. He handed me the money we'd won. "In fact, if I don't find some better way to make some money, old Sam Bass ain't never gonna show his face in Texas again."*

I noticed that Hickok was staring hard at Jack, with a puzzled look on his face. "Seems like I know you from somewheres," he said. "Can't think where it was, though. Hays City? Abilene?"

"Well, now, Mr. Hickok," Jack said, "as a matter of fact . . ."

"I believe it was Abilene," Hickok said. "Right around the time some damned fool caused me to shoot my own deputy." His jaw clenched and his face looked mean. "I lost my job because of that," he said to Jane. "And I never did get to shoot the son of a bitch who caused it, neither."

Jack was looking a little green by then.

Hickok peered at him again. "Abilene, you say?"

Jack gulped and adjusted his smoky glasses. "Actually, we

---

*Sam Bass and some of his friends were in Deadwood in the summer of 1876. After losing herd money that wasn't theirs, they turned to train robbery as a livelihood.

probably met when I was working with Mrs. Thatcher's circus," he said nervously. "I mean Mrs. Hickok's, that is, only she wasn't Mrs. Hickok yet then but was still Mrs. Thatcher, as I guess you know, being her husband now."

Hickok stared at him. "You worked for Mrs. Thatch— I mean, my wife?"

"I sure did," Jack said. "And a fine lady she is, too."

"Ah, shit," said Jane, pulling on Hickok's arm. "Let's quit chewin' our cuds and git somethin' to drink." She pulled him off toward a saloon.

"All right, Calamity, you don't need to jerk my arm loose," he said as he was led away. "Wish I could recollect where I seen that feller, though. It'll come to me."

We had decided to leave town the next day. By the time I had got our gear together and saddled the horses, however, Jack had wandered off somewhere. I started looking for him, getting more nervous by the minute as I walked around Deadwood alone. There had been trouble up in the hills between some miners and the Sioux, and several scalps had been brought in for the bounty being offered. My hair looked enough like Sioux hair to do the job, and I could see folks sizing it up all the time.

I finally found Jack in the last place I would have expected— in Number Ten playing poker with Wild Bill Hickok. The smoked glasses were still hiding his eyes and making it hard for him to see much, but he seemed to be getting used to them. He recognized me and motioned me over to meet the men around the table.

I recognized one of the men and decided to keep an eye on him: Charles Rich was known to have won a few hands with the aid of a six-gun, and I sure didn't want to be standing between him and Hickok in case of a quarrel. In fact, I didn't want to be in the same room with them. I motioned to Jack that we should leave.

"There's no hurry," he said. "Besides, I want you to look at something really curious." He pointed to where Hickok sat, his chair against the wall and facing the door. The only thing I saw was a good-sized pile of money in front of Hickok. I took a closer look. It was the silver bullet with the initials "C.K." carved into it, lying next to a stack of coins.

"I don't know how that could have got here," Jack was saying, "but it used to belong to my father. I remember seeing it when I was a child. I've decided to win it back."

I looked at the small pile of money in front of him. "Look like you lose," I said. "Maybe quittum now?"

"Oh, don't worry," he said. "I had more than this a few minutes ago, and that bullet too. I had planned to quit then, but Mr. Rich suggested that it was impolite to quit when I had won so much of his money, so I stayed. I'll win it again soon."

Hickok stood up. "While you fellas are havin' this nice long chat, I think I'll take myself a pee." He walked toward the back.

The other men stood up and stretched, and some of them decided to fetch glasses of beer back from the bar. There was a general milling about, during which I tried several ways to signal Jack that it was time to leave. He ignored me.

Everyone drifted back except Hickok, who was talking with someone at the bar.

"Let's play cards," Rich said impatiently. "Hey, Bill, you in or not?"

"Deal me in," Hickok said from the bar. "I'll be there in a minute."

Everyone was holding cards when he got there, and he stopped with a puzzled look. "Hey, kid, you're in my chair," he said to Jack.

Jack was peering at his cards and grinning. "We can swap after this hand," he said. He hummed a tune and said, "I believe I'll just bet twenty this time."

Two men threw their cards in instantly. "Bet's to you, Bill," Rich said. "If you're playin' this one."

Hickok was still glaring at Jack as if he might just kick him out of the chair, but he was also fiddling with the cards that had been dealt to the empty place. Idly he picked them up and looked at them. His anger faded, and he sat down. "All right," he said. "I'll play these, but then we'll change places." He tossed his twenty into the pot. Rich followed suit.

Hickok drew a card and Jack stood pat. Rich drew two. He looked at them and tossed his cards in. "One of you might be bluffing," he said. "Not both of you."

Jack was humming and grinning furiously now, and he counted out another twenty from his dwindling pile. "I believe I've got you this time, Bill," he said.

Hickok frowned and stared at his hand, trying to decide. But he never got to, because at that moment a man stepped in from the street, raised a good-sized revolver, and pulled the trigger. There was a sound like a snapping branch and smoke rolled across the table.

So did Wild Bill Hickok, sprawling into the pot with his head a bloody mess.

There was a moment of total silence and then the man ran back out into the street and everyone started rushing around and yelling, pointing this way and that, shouting for someone to do something, and generally creating more noise than a cavalry charge. Chairs were flying over backwards as the men jumped up, and a couple of beer glasses crashed on the floor. Jack sat there, the smoked glasses in his hand, blinking as if he couldn't take in what had happened at all.

I scooped up the pot and the silver bullet, then grabbed Jack's arm and led him quickly out into the street. I hoped we could make it back to the stables and out of town before people started rounding up the witnesses, but the town was in such an uproar I decided it wouldn't look good to ride right out then. So we stayed, sleeping behind the stable among some hay bales and manure piles.

Just before I dropped off to sleep, Jack said, "I think I did have him beat. Doesn't three deuces beat aces and eights?"

They caught the young man who fired the shot and held him all night in the saloon under heavy guard. Next day they held a quick trial, and the man was acquitted. (We heard later that he was re-arrested in another town the following month, while he was bragging about how he'd gunned down Hickok. This time they found him guilty and hung him. Children, it doesn't pay to brag.)

Even in Deadwood that day it seemed that not everyone was happy with the acquittal of the young fellow, whose name turned out to be Jack McCall. In fact, Jane was rampaging up and down the street screaming curses at everyone in sight. "You goddamned yeller-bellied polecats, you cain't let that son of a bitch just walk away free. Somebody put him up to it, and you damn well know it." One man tried to calm her down and nearly got a whiskey bottle alongside his head for his trouble. "Did any one of you ever hear of Bill sittin' in a doorway like that?" No one answered. "Course you didn't. He never would'a sat there if somebody hadn't'a took his chair. You jist find out who done that and you'll know who wanted Bill dead." She tossed the half-filled whiskey bottle into the air and splattered it with a clean shot. Whiskey and glass flew all over the place.

I was standing next to the man who had taken Hickok's chair, and I figured sooner or later somebody would remember that and point Jack out to Jane. It wasn't hard to persuade him the time had come to put Deadwood behind us.

We rode south.

In Fort Laramie the talk was all of Custer's defeat and of the Fifth Cavalry, still in the field and swearing to avenge the massacre. I didn't like the looks I was getting from people around the fort, so I decided we should stay only long enough to get supplies. Indians were not popular these days.

We had filled our saddlebags and were mounted to ride out when Jack decided he wanted a newspaper. He went back into the store and came out a minute later reading one, but just as he was about to get on Whitey, a figure came flying over the hitchrail and knocked him flat on the ground.

"You cain't git away this time, you bastard. And them fancy circus folks ain't around to help you, neither. So git up from there and let's git at it." The man was dancing around and punching his fists at the air, waiting for Jack to get his mask straightened out so he could see.

It was Andrew, the mistreated hired hand from our first cattle drive, the one who had jerked Jack out of the saddle in his final circus performance. And he was as mad as if his misfortune had happened yesterday, instead of nearly ten years ago.

Jack staggered to his feet, still adjusting the mask. Before he could get the eyeholes in the right places, Andrew snatched the mask off Jack's face and ripped it in two. "There," he said, "now you cain't hide behind that danged thing no more." He took a looping swing and caught Jack a good one on the side of his head.

Jack stood there, blinking and rubbing his jaw, and then he saw the pieces of the mask in the dust. His face began to get red. He brought his fists up in the classic fighting stance he'd seen pictures of and said, "Now you've done it."

By now a crowd was beginning to gather, cheering both fighters on. Andrew charged in and knocked Jack down again, and when I started to pull Andrew off somebody yelled, "Let 'em fight, Injun." I looked up just as the man heaved a sack of beans at me from up on a supply wagon. I tried to duck, but fifty pounds of pintos caught my shoulder and knocked me backwards into Whitey. He bit my arm. I forgot about Jack and started for the man in the wagon, but someone stuck a gun in my belly and suggested I just stay put till the fight was over.

Jack got up and took a swing at Andrew, but missed him by quite a bit. Andrew knocked him down again, and Jack nearly rolled under Whitey's hooves. Andrew went after him.

That was his mistake. Whitey was getting pretty annoyed by all the ruckus by now anyway, and when he saw Andrew running toward him he danced sideways and let fly with both hind feet. Andrew sailed halfway across the street and came down hard. He just lay there, moaning and looking like he might not get up for a week or two.

The gun was taken from my belly and somebody said, "Pretty good fight," and everyone began to move away to finish whatever they'd been doing. I picked up the newspaper and stuck it in my saddlebag, then helped Jack up.

"I guess he won't try me again," Jack said as we rode past the prostrate Andrew and headed out of the fort.

The stars were so bright and glittery the sky seemed almost alive. An August breeze carried just a hint of the cold days and nights ahead. But it was all lost on Jack, who stared gloomily into his cup.

"That was my only mask," he said at last. "Just when we're ready to get after Hardin again, that crazy man tears it up."

"You gottum glasses," I reminded him.

"No, they won't do. They were all right in Deadwood, under the circumstances there, but they're just not the same. Besides, I keep falling over things when I wear them."

I knew there was no sense in arguing. I saw he had rolled up in his blanket and was probably already half asleep. His white clothes were hanging on a tree limb near the fire, where he had hung them to dry after scrubbing away at the dirt and dried blood from the fight. Masked or not, he meant to look sharp on his quest.

I sat for a while, looking out across the silent prairie as the fire died down. Then I noticed the newspaper lying by my bedroll and picked it up. I stirred up the fire until there was light enough to read by. The first thing that caught my eye was a big headline:

BUFFALO BILL KILLS FIRST INDIAN FOR CUSTER

I read on into the story, which was all about how the Fifth Cavalry was busy driving the Cheyenne and Sioux northward, away from white settlements. I read about two couriers who were sent ahead with dispatches for Col. Merritt. Then I got to this part:

"Several Indians started out after the couriers hoping to cut them off before they could reach Merritt. All this was observed by the famous Buffalo Bill Cody and his scouts from some hillocks opposite the main body of Indians. Cody and his men rode around behind the approaching Indians and as the scouts topped a small rise Cody fired once and an Indian pony went down. He fired again and the Indian fell dead. In an instant his scalp was hanging from Buffalo Bill's hand.

"The dead Indian proved to be one Yellow Hand, a sub-chief of the Cheyennes. It is said that the scalp, along with Yellow Hand's war bonnet and shield, are to be sent to Mrs. Cody in Rochester, N.Y., for display in the window of a local store. . . ."

I stopped reading and tossed the newspaper into the fire. In times to come I would hear many variations of this story, but the two things I know to be true were told to me by a trooper who was there. Cody did wear a black velvet suit with a red satin sash as the papers reported, and he did send the souvenirs back to Rochester, where Mrs. Cody showed them around at tea parties when they were not laid out in the window of Kerngood's clothing store.

The fire was almost out, so I pulled my blanket around me. I lay there for a long time, though, listening to the night sounds of the prairie. And wondering how the white people would feel if an Indian had set up a store window featuring the buckskins and long yellow hair of the remarkable General Custer.

Chapter

9

*In which we go for a
boat ride and become fugitives
from the Hanging Judge.*

Again we drifted.

We held jobs here and there, and in between we sometimes raced Whitey—when the competition didn't look too good. Whitey hadn't gotten any mellower with the years, but sooner or later he had to lose. Somehow I didn't want to see that happen.

It was during one of these between-job times, somewhere in Kansas, that we met Professor Hansen. It was nearing dark when we spotted his campfire, and we decided to see if whoever it was could spare a cup of coffee. So we rode in, cautiously, and called out a hello. A little man in a big frock coat got up from the cookfire and peered into the darkness.

"Come, gentlemen, welcome to my humble repast," he said. He looked at Jack's newest mask, made from someone's discarded hat, and frowned. "That is, you're welcome if you don't plan to rob me. You won't find very much to rob anyway, I might add, unless you fancy three hundred bottles of Magical Mystery Medicine."

We ate his beans while Jack explained about the mask and his quest. The professor listened, nodding.

"Splendid," he said at last. "What better means of furthering your mission than employment with a peripatetic emporium of pharmacological palliatives?"

"Huh?" Jack said.

"He mean medicine show," I told Jack. "Are you offering us jobs?" I asked the professor.

He was. We accepted. He went off to write us some speeches,

and the next day we followed his wagon into a small town to try out the new act.

We helped the professor set up the display of bottles and string up his big sign, and by the time everything was arranged a good-sized crowd had already collected around the gaudy wagon. People were admiring the big yellow eagle on the side, and some were trying to figure out the wanted poster Jack had stuck on under it. It was that kind of town, off the beaten track far enough so that very few new people came through. A dog fight could collect a crowd in a place like this.

"Ladies and gentlemen," the professor proclaimed to the twenty or so people gawking at the wagon, "we are now open for business. And what is that business, you are asking? It is the healing of hurt, the bestowing of balm, the purgation of pain, and all accomplished through the miracle of modern medical science in this little bottle." He held up a bottle of greenish liquid with a flourish. "It is Professor Hansen's Marvelous Mystery Medicine. What does it do? It heals, my friends, it cures whatever ails you. How does it do that, you are asking? Well, still your questions. How it works is a mystery even to me, its humble creator. Only the Lord above knows its secrets."

More people were coming now, drawn by the surprising lung power of the little professor. Even the saloon was emptying, it looked like.

"And now, dear citizens of . . . uh . . . of this fair town, I shall turn the stage over to my assistant, the Mystery Man of the West, who has a remarkable story to tell you." The professor pointed to Jack, who was taking a last quick look at the speech the professor had written for him. "And while you listen to his story, Chief Crazy Fox of the Algonquin tribe will pass amongst you with the once-in-a-lifetime opportunity to cure all mortal ills for the mere pittance of one dollar."

As I started into the crowd with the tray of bottles, I noticed some men crowded around the sign Professor Hansen had put up. It said, "Guess the identity of the Mystery Man of the West and win a free bottle of my Marvelous Mystery Medicine." In the blank space underneath some names had already been written in.

"The Prince of Wales?" one cowboy read off. "What the crap does that mean? I been through Wales, down in Texas, and they ain't even got a sheriff there."

His friend put his finger under the next name and tried to spell it out. "B-u-f-f-a-l-o. What's that spell, Soapy?"

"Buffalo," the first man said. "I seen it spelt out just like that onct when Bill Cody rode scout for our outfit." He stared at Jack, who was beginning his speech. "But that sure'n hell ain't Cody," he said.

"When I was very young and in frail health," Jack began, "it was predicted that I would never live out my childhood. But thanks to Professor Hansen's medicine, you see before you now a man who has—"

"—held up my stage, you sonofabitch!" the man called Soapy yelled. "You're the bastard that done it, and near scared the pee out of me." He was pushing through the crowd toward the wagon.

Yes, Children, that is who it was—the stage driver from that faraway day in Texas. People seemed to have a long memory where Jack was concerned.

Soapy was yelling and shoving people out of the way, and a couple of men started shoving back, and Jack just stood there holding a bottle of the green stuff and staring at the crowd. I handed the tray of bottles to a farmer and ran around the crowd to the back of the wagon. I jumped in and ran out onto the stage, which was really just the side of the wagon let down on blocks. I pushed Jack off the platform, gave Soapy's face a kick and jumped off after Jack. We both hit the ground running.

"Gettum horses," I yelled at Jack. I turned back to see what Soapy and his friend were doing.

"Notice what quickness, what fleetness of foot," the professor was booming. "And that man was not expected to live, my friends."

Soapy had got free of the crowd and was coming my way. His sidekick was not far behind. I fired a shot into the air.

They stopped and stared at me. "Shit, it's just one crappy Injun," Soapy said. "Let's stomp 'im."

"You stomp 'im," the other man said. "I'd as soon not git my ass shot off by no Injun."

The crowd was moving our way, sensing a better show than the professor's. I hoped Jack got the horses pretty soon, before somebody figured out that there was only one Indian and a hell of a lot of white faces here today.

"I don't believe he'll shoot a white man," Soapy said, starting toward me again. I took a few steps backward and fired another shot into the air. And then I heard the horses behind me and made a run for them.

"Ride-um hard!" I yelled at Jack, who was lagging behind. Then someone fired a shot from the crowd, and Whitey went past as if the finish line and the sugar lumps were just ahead.

It was one of our shorter-lived jobs.

We rode south, without provisions and with very little money. We rode most of the night and camped without a fire. Next morning we cooked up the last of our bacon.

Jack was rubbing at a spot on his sleeve and complaining about how he'd had to leave town before he'd even got his suit washed. Suddenly he stopped and stared out across the prairie. He pointed and said, "What in the world is that?"

I could see something big moving way out across the flat land, and I could see riders around it, but I couldn't tell what it was.

"Must be that Horner* fellow again," Jack said.

We watched as it drew closer. "No lookum like house," I said.

And then I began to see what it was—or what it appeared to be, anyway. It didn't seem possible, though.

In a minute Jack said, "Oh, now I see. It's a steamboat. Of course." He sounded as if steamboats went by on the prairie every day.

We sat and watched the most unlikely thing I'd ever seen out there come closer and closer. It was a big boat, we could see, with a large paddle wheel on the back and a deck that went all around a central cabin. I suppose there were much bigger boats on the Mississippi, but I think it's safe to say this was the biggest one that ever crossed the Kansas plains.

In a while the lead rider saw our camp and gave a wave. He motioned for the drivers of that huge wagon to take a break, then rode around the boat to talk with some of the other men. The oxen pulling the wagon began munching grass while the man rode over our way.

*To encourage settlement, town fathers often offered a choice lot to the builder of the first house in a new town. A.F. Horner won the prize in Brookville, Florence, Newton and Hutchinson by moving his twenty-by-sixty-foot black walnut house from town to town. In the 1870s Mr. Horner and his house must have been a common sight on the Kansas plains.

As he got closer we could see that he was wearing pink pants and high polished boots, with a black velvet jacket and a little round hat. He pulled his horse up close to our cookfire and tipped the hat.

"How lovely to take one's tea in the open air," said Sir George Grant. "It does brace one's appetite."

After the usual explanations about the mask, which Sir George seemed to find reasonable enough, we were invited to go for a boat ride. Since we had no jobs and no prospects, we went with him.

As we rode along in front of the creaking wagon, we learned about Sir George and the boat. It seemed that he had bought a tract of land from the Union Pacific and had platted a township on it, to be named Victoria.

"After our queen, naturally," he explained.

"Naturally," I agreed. I hoped his queen would be proud of the honor.

"And we've dammed up a creek there to form a jolly little lake," he went on. "Which explains the boat, of course."

Of course.

We made the trip to Victoria without much trouble, apart from the slowness of the big wagon and a few broken wheels along the way. When we arrived at the site where the town was planned, Sir George's men pulled the wagon up on a small slope, blocked the wheels, unhitched the oxen, and then let the big rig roll down into his little lake. The steamboat settled in the water majestically to a round of cheers and applause from the crowd of Englishmen on the shore.

"Good show!" shouted Sir George. "And now, gentlemen, let us break out the gin and run up the Union Jack."

"Tell me, Mr. Fox, about your aboriginal beginnings," Harry Winton said a few days later. We were lolling in our deck chairs, sipping glasses of Tom Cat Gin with bitters as the boat chugged up the nine-mile lake for the second time that day.

"Oh I say, old man, that seems a rather impertinent question," Sir George said. "Mr. Fox may not wish to—"

"I don't mind, Sir George," I interrupted. I had learned that one had to interrupt him if one was ever to speak at all. "But first, Harry, I wish you'd answer a question for me."

Harry lifted his glass and said, "Carry on."

I waited while the steward filled our glasses, then said, "Harry, what *are* all you Englishmen doing out here in the middle of Kansas. Isn't it rather far from home?" I was beginning to sound British myself, I noticed.

Harry pondered while two horsemen flew by on the prairie, their pink breeches flashing and the black coats changing to the color of Kansas dust as they rode. "Halloooo," one of them called.

"George, old fellow, why don't you bring some foxes out here?" Harry asked. "Running after those bloody hares is getting damned tiresome." He turned back to me and frowned. "What were we discussing? Oh, yes, why are we out here." He chuckled. "And a very good question that is, I might add."

I waited while he emptied his glass and rang for the steward. "Have you heard the term, 'remittance man'?" he asked.

Jack looked up from cleaning his gun. "You mean like a bill collector?"

Harry laughed. "In a sense you are quite correct," he said. "I collect what is rightfully mine, from a family that would prefer not to have me cluttering up the ancestral halls. So, I journey in distant parts, and the family sends along the jolly old sterling, and we are all happy as the proverbial clam." He took a long pull from his fresh drink. "I may try India next," he went on. "They've things to shoot at out there that're rather easier to hit than your bunnies."

Just then the whistle blasted out an ear-shattering hoot that sent every bird within a mile shooting straight up into the air. Harry clutched at his head and moaned.

"Does the bugger have to do that every time he turns this thing?" he complained.

"Yes," Sir George said. "He says it's in the rule book for river pilots."

The whistle blasted again, and Harry held his ears. "Enough, damn it!' he yelled. "I'm going inside." He got up and weaved toward the mess cabin, yelling for more gin.

"Poor Harry," Sir George said. "He just cannot accept his lot in life. Damned shame. Won't change, y'know. Younger sons will always be younger sons."

"How do you spell 'remittance'?" asked a Texas version of a former remittance man as he opened his notebook.

We had nowhere to go, so we stayed with Sir George for a while. We chugged up and down on the steamboat, drank gin, rode "to the hounds" on the prairie, drank gin, shot at jackrabbits we were all too drunk to hit, and consoled ourselves with more gin. Sometimes we rode to neighboring settlements, where Sir George could buy supplies and Jack could nail up his Hardin posters. But mainly we sat on the deck of the steamboat and drank, while Sir George and his friends reminisced about cricket matches and recalled Lady Alice's unforgettable parties back home.*

As we rode around the prairie I began to realize how much the land had begun to fill up with white faces, not all of them belonging to the Americans so many Indians had reason to hate. There were people from all over the world out here now, and many had brought their strange customs with them. In one settlement we met a group of Mennonites who wore long coats that clinked when they walked and who told us in sign language how much they loved this land of freedom. (The clinking, I learned later, was caused by gold pieces sewn into the linings of their coats.) Another group of people pointed with pride to their new sod synagogue.

But most who came knew nothing of The People or their ways, or how they, too, loved the land. These newcomers had probably never seen a buffalo and never would. The herds that had once sustained whole nations were gone now, never to return. The land was changing.

So I rode with a crowd of Englishmen through this white man's world, hoping I could find some way to make money to send back to mine. But pleasant as the days of hunting or steaming up and down the lake were, there was no money to be earned here, and I was growing restless. So when Jack suggested we resume our quest, I was relieved.

Jack explained to Sir George.

"So, you and your faithful companion must continue the fight for law and order," Sir George said. "Quixotic."

"Too right," said a tipsy Harry. "Let's all drink to that."

We did, but the next morning, with heavy hearts and pounding heads, Jack and I rode south to seek John Wesley Hardin in the Indian Territory.

Children, how can I make you feel that place and time? How can People who sit in houses listening to talking boxes begin to

*Sir George Grant's one important contribution to America was his introduction of Aberdeen Angus cattle to the West.

understand the hellhole the Indian Territory had become? Railroads now crisscrossed The People's land, and wherever the rails went the white people followed. Without permission, wild and dangerous towns had sprung up all along the lines.

Some white men leased land from the tribes, on leases that extended forever—as the Indians learned too late. And when The People were wronged by the white men, the only help was the court at Fort Smith, on the Arkansas River just over the Territory line. But Judge Parker's court had many miles to cover and too few sheriffs to cover it, so little help could be expected from the white man's law.

In fact, the Territory was filling up with outlaws of every kind, mostly because the Indians there hated white law so much they gave shelter to vermin that should have been squashed. The Indians had been given the land because it was thought to be worthless, and the rustlers and whiskey runners and murderers had come because it was thought to be safe from the law. And for the most part it was, because the court at Fort Smith employed only two hundred deputies for the whole Territory.

I had crossed this land many times before, but those had been different times. Now you could feel the danger in the air, like the prickling feeling on your skin before a storm.

We camped one morning in a little wash, and while Jack was trying to get a fire going I heard the creaking of wagon wheels and the murmur of voices. I motioned for Jack to leave the fire unlit and come with me, but when we climbed up out of the wash the grass was too tall to see over.

"Let's get the horses and see who it is," Jack said.

"Maybe better we wait," I said.

"Well, let's at least get the horses," he said. He slid back down into the wash and began to saddle Whitey. I followed him.

When we rode up out of the draw, the first thing I saw was a man who seemed to be skimming magically along on the surface of the sea of bluestem grass, his horse completely hidden. I touched Jack's arm and motioned for him to flatten himself along his horse's neck, as I had done. I had noticed another man's head floating along behind the rider, and I figured we'd be wise to see what was in the wagon before we let ourselves be seen.

Just then the man turned toward us, and the sun glinted off the star on his chest.

"It's a lawman," Jack said. He straightened up and yelled, "Hello the wagon!"

The deputy was young, but he meant to grow older. He had his gun out and leveled at us as we rode up. Jack and I held our hands up in the traditional peace sign, and he relaxed a little. But only a little. He had noticed the mask.

"I'm Mike Rogers," he said as we stopped a few feet away. The gun was still pointed in our direction. "And I'd like to hear some explainin', damn quick."

Jack told his story and showed the Hardin poster. "So you see, I, too, am seeking to bring a criminal to justice," he finished.

The men in the wagon had been listening, and now one of them let out a guffaw and poked the man next to him. "Lord, wouldn't you give a nickel to see ol' Parker's face when he hears *that* one?" he said. "Hey, Mike," he yelled at the deputy. "If you'll swaller that story, I got a good one to try out on you." All six men in the wagon began hooting and jeering, and even the driver joined in. Jack waited till the noise died down. He was used to such reactions by now.

"Perhaps my traveling companion and I could ride along with you for a while," he said when he could be heard. That brought more whooping from the wagon.

"Me and my travelin' companions might object," one of the men called. "Shit, you got us all chained up and we ain't even wearin' masks, much less ridin' with a stinkin' Injun."

Mike Rogers was trying not to laugh himself. "Now I don't know about that," he said.

"Ah, hell, let 'em come along," someone yelled. "Lord knows these trips to Fort Smith ain't too entertainin'."

So the deputy put his gun away and we rode on with the wagonload of chained men on the way to Judge Parker's court.

We traveled with them for a couple of days, sharing their beans and answering the deputy's questions about Hardin and Texas and the affair in Benton's Canyon years ago.

"So you see that I have to bring Hardin to justice," Jack said. "To avenge my family honor."

"Well, maybe," Rogers said. "But to tell you the truth, it sounds like maybe it was Injuns that—"

"No, no," Jack interrupted. "Other people were confused about that too, but it will all be cleared up when I bring Hardin in and get his confession."

One of the chained men made crazy-in-the-head signs, and

another said, "Hell, Mike, I'm gettin' tired of eatin' these damn beans and listenin' to this feller's gas. When are we a-gonna meet your boss and head back into Fort Smith? I can't wait for some of that good jailhouse grub."

"You keep your pants on," Rogers said. "If Chris found those whiskey runners where he thought he would, we oughtta be meetin' him at the Little Creek crossing tomorrow. And he'll have some more company for you."

"Why do you try to bring in so many criminals at one time?" Jack asked.

"Ain't profitable no other way. Mileage fees wouldn't amount to enough on jest one or two men, so we leave Fort Smith with a whole batch of blank warrants and write in the names as we go along."*

"Yeah," said one of the prisoners. "And they'd put a dog's name down if they thought Parker would pay up." Everybody laughed.

We camped that night, with the men chained to the wagon wheels, and the next day about noon we reached the Little Creek crossing. Mike Rogers waved to a tall man standing under a big maple tree, and the man raised a rifle over his head in greeting. Three men were chained around the tree, but he paid no attention to them. He kept his rifle pointed loosely in our direction as we rode up.

"Howdy, Chris," Mike said as he got down from his horse. He pulled the red bandanna from around his neck and dipped it into the creek to wipe his face, then scooped water up in his hand for a drink.

The driver stretched and climbed down stiffly from the wagon seat. He went around to the back and let the tailgate down. The bone-weary prisoners tumbled out and headed for the creek, giving Chris quick nods as they passed. He ignored them but continued to stare at Jack and me.

Jack started to dismount, but I touched his arm and he stopped.

*These marshals are never identified; however, some of the men who rode for Judge Parker's court included Chris Madsen (an eyewitness to Buffalo Bill's killing of Yellow Hand), Heck Thomas, Bill Tilghman, and three of the Dalton brothers. Marshals received no salaries, but they were paid two dollars for each man arrested plus ten cents a mile for transporting and feeding prisoners. They averaged about five hundred dollars a year, not counting money from nongovernmental rewards.

Chris went to his horse and slipped the rifle into the boot, then started rummaging around in his saddlebags. When he turned back he had some papers in his hand, and his eyes were narrowed.

"What's your name, stranger?" he said to Jack.

Jack started to answer but I kicked his foot. Whitey danced away.

Chris waited, clutching those papers that looked suspiciously like warrants.

Mike came up, shaking water from his head. "Boy, does that feel good—" He saw the papers in Chris's hands and the look on his face. "What's the matter?" he asked.

Chris gave him a hard look. "I jest naturally assumed this man wasn't chained in the wagon because you didn't have no warrants," he said. "Elseways why would you, employed to assist me in bringing in criminals, be riding with a feller dressed like that?"

Mike gave a nervous laugh. By now the prisoners were all listening with interest.

"I know it looks sorta funny," Mike began. "He did have a purty good reason, though."

"I'd shore like to hear it," Chris said coldly.

"Well, way he told it he's trackin' down a criminal hisself. Fella from Texas name of Harvey. Or maybe it was Hawkins. Anyways, that's how come the mask." He stopped lamely. "Show him one of your flyers," he said to Jack.

Jack handed a flyer to Mike, who handed it to Chris.

"Hey, Mike, I told you not to swaller that story," one of the prisoners said.

"Hell yes," another one added. "Didn't I tell you I had seed that feller down to Belle Starr's place not more'n a week ago? Prancin' around in his white duds and that blamed mask—hell, ol' Belle thought he were purtier'n a new dress."

Chris glared at them and they got very silent. Then he glared at Mike, and then at Jack. Satisfied that everyone had been sufficiently glared, he started reading Jack's flowery prose beneath the odd-looking drawing of Hardin. He shook his head and glared at Jack some more.

"Of course, my address is no longer correct on these," Jack said. "I'll have to have new ones printed up as soon as—"

"Are you a Texas Ranger?" Chris interrupted.

"Well, not exactly, but—"

"Are you a lawman of any kind?"

"No sir," Jack said, "but—"

"Then where did you get this here flyer?"

"Oh, that's all right," Jack said. "I had them made up myself."

"Oh, you did, huh. Then they ain't the real thing, are they?"

Jack looked thoroughly confused by now.

"All right, this ain't Texas and these ain't legal flyers and you ain't a real lawman, and you're under arrest. Git down off that animal." He drew his gun and came toward Jack.

As he got close, Whitey began to snort nervously, and spittle flew all over Chris's shirt front. The prisoners laughed. Chris glared them silent again, then wiped his star off carefully. Then he punched Whitey in the nose.

Whitey staggered and shook his head.

"Hey, wait a minute," Jack said. "There's no call to—"

He never got to finish, because it seemed that Whitey agreed with him. He snorted and brought up a forehoof that sent Chris sprawling. His gun skittered across the hard earth and came to rest in front of the prisoners. One of them stared at it for several seconds, then grabbed it up.

"I'll be damned," he said. Then he pointed the gun at Chris. "Unless you get these chains off us faster'n a fly can shit, you're a dead man," he told the stunned marshal.

Chris was groggy but not stupid. He knew death when he saw it pointed at him. "Get the key," he told Mike.

Chris, Mike and the driver were chained around the maple tree, stark naked, watching while their clothes, money and horses got ready to ride off in all directions. No one had bothered us, but I had done some quick counting and had come up with nine outlaws and seven horses, not counting ours. I signaled Jack that we should go.

"But we can't ride off and leave those lawmen tied up like that," he said.

"We sendum help. Now we go." I turned my pony and headed out, trying not to attract attention. Whitey fell in behind me.

We almost made it.

"Hey, stranger," someone yelled as we crossed the creek.

"No stoppum," I said to Jack.

"Hey," the man called again. "Listen, I'll be riding on into Missouri. You want me to pass out some of those flyers?"

Jack turned and headed back toward the man who had

called. "That's very kind," he said, holding out a handful of his flyers.

The man reached up and pulled Jack out of the saddle.

I was riding back to help, but I had a feeling it was hopeless. And I was right. We both got stomped pretty thoroughly, and they ended up with two more horses.

They were laughing and tossing handfuls of flyers into the wind as they rode away.

"I still think we should have tried to get the chains off those men," Jack said again as we walked over hot, shale-covered ground.

"No key," I said. "And Chris not look friendly anyway."

"Well, I sure hope someone finds them." He was limping and heaving loud sighs. "This sure is a fine mess you got us into," he said. "My horse is gone, my flyers are gone, and we haven't got anything to eat. And my feet hurt." Another sigh. Then he brightened. "At least they didn't take my mask," he said.

We found a little spring that trickled out from a cleft in some rocks and drank our fill. Then we sat down to rest, and to try to come up with a plan. This was no country to be traveling on foot, without guns or food.

I couldn't come up with any ideas so we just sat there for an hour or so, drinking water and sighing. And then I heard the sound of a galloping horse.

"Somebody come," I told Jack. "Maybe we get help." Or maybe we get killed, I thought to myself. Out here it was about even money.

The hoofbeats got nearer, and in a minute a horse came over a little hill and headed our way.

It was Whitey.

He still had his saddle and gear on, but there was no rider in the saddle. And then, as he got closer, I saw the single boot dangling from the stirrup.

Nobody except Jack rode Whitey for very long.

Chapter 10

*In which we return too
late to Texas, and Jack becomes
a literary legend.*

I considered our situation and found it less than ideal. We had no money, very little food, no jobs, and no inclination to hang around where Judge Parker's deputies could catch us, lest we find ourselves literally hanging around Fort Smith. We didn't even have any flyers to post about Hardin, a loss that hit Jack harder than it did me. We did have one horse and some money I carried hidden in my clothes, and Whitey's saddlebags turned out to have everything except the flyers and Jack's money in them. However, our one attempt to double up on Whitey revealed that his opinion of Indians hadn't changed much over the years. He might have been getting older, but he still had the strength to buck both of us off, and he gave us a very convincing demonstration of that before I could get a leg over his back.

We didn't even know where Dulsie was now, to get the loan of a room and some money. In fact, we didn't even know for sure where we were ourselves, except that we were much too close to Chris and his two friends for comfort. So we started moving south, Jack riding and me walking, without even a tail to hang onto up the slopes. We made very poor time.

In a few days we saw a small cabin with smoke rising from its chimney. We approached it cautiously, aware that people in this country didn't always welcome strangers but too hungry to pass it by. About a hundred yards from the cabin I saw a puff of smoke and Jack's hat went sailing off behind us. I hit the ground, with Jack landing close beside me. About then I heard the crack of the rifle.

We lay there, considering the possibilities. Either the shooter was a very good shot to hit a hat at that distance, or else he had been aiming at Jack and had missed. It was not reassuring either way. But we couldn't lie there all day either, so after a few minutes I stood up, my hands held high over my head. Jack waited a few seconds to see if I would draw fire, then stood up with me. We started walking in, slowly, with Whitey clopping along behind Jack.

"That'll do it, right there," a voice said as we got close to the house. It was a woman.

"We're friends," I said. "We were just hoping for a little grub and maybe a drink of water. We mean no harm."

"Course not," the voice said from a window. "Why in perdition would anyone be suspicious of an Injun and a man wearin' a mask, I wonder."

"Oh, I can explain that," Jack said, lowering his hands and starting forward. The gun banged and a bullet whined past his ear. His hands shot back up and he stood as rigid as a post.

We stood there, considering the possibilities, for quite a while. It began to seem likely that we would all grow old standing there, in fact, if someone didn't do something.

"I'm not wearing a gun," I yelled at her. "My partner isn't either. Can we talk?"

"You ain't wearin' a gun! Why in purgatory not?"

"It's a long story," I yelled. "Can't we talk?"

There was another long silence. Then: "All right, you boys walk over to the porch and set down."

We did.

In a moment a tiny woman came out, lugging a long-barreled rifle that must have been older than she was and nearly as heavy. She sat down in a rocker several feet away with the rifle across her lap and began to talk.

We learned that her husband and his brother had gone after supplies almost a month ago, and they should have been back by now. She was worried about them. She was also worried about us, but as we talked she began to relax a little. Finally she leaned the rifle up against the wall and fussed with her hair. "I must look a sight," she said. "We don't get company much out here, and you fellas didn't give me much of a chance to neaten up." She went prattling on, as if we had dropped in for a neighborly visit. "I reckon I've got to trust somebody," she said, "though to tell you the truth I would have preferred somebody a mite more customary in appearance."

We stayed with the woman, Maude Hunter, for a couple of weeks, helping with her chores and sleeping in the barn. There weren't too many chores, actually, because Indians had run off most of her stock soon after her husband had gone. She had a couple of horses and a milk cow, but she had been afraid to ride out to see how many cattle were left. There weren't many.

We weren't earning any money, but at least we were eating decently. And to be honest, I didn't want to leave until her husband got back anyway. Despite her marksmanship, a woman alone in this country didn't have the best of times.

I knew we would have to leave eventually, but the whole thing was decided for us when a rider came in with news that wasn't altogether surprising, though Maude still took it hard. Her husband and his brother had been ambushed and killed before they had gone twenty miles from home. It had taken all this time before anyone came across the bodies.

After the burying we convinced Maude to go back to St. Louis, where her folks were, and stayed to help her pack up. We offered to buy her unneeded handguns and a riding horse, but she refused the little money we had.

"You warn't the likeliest looking hands I'd ever seen, but I don't know what I'd have done without you," she said. "You take what you need, and my blessings."

We rode with her a few days, till we reached a little town that was on a stage line. We helped her sell her horse and wagon and then left her waiting in the stage office, alone and tiny. She never should have come to the Territory, she or all the other white trespassers. Still, she was a good person, and she had treated us fairly despite her misfortunes. I wished her well.

With the few supplies Maude had given us, we rode out of town. That night we camped near a little stream that looked familiar, and as I sat by the fire with a belly full of beans I realized we were probably pretty close to the cattle trail we had traveled back in '71.

Jack must have been thinking the same thing, because he suddenly turned to me and said, "Crazy Fox, I'm going home."

I couldn't think of any reason why he shouldn't. After all, there was the CK Ranch. There were a lot worse things in the world than owning one of the biggest spreads in the West, even if you didn't have a real gift for running it.

Next morning we headed for Texas.

How many times had I ridden under the big swinging "CK" sign? How many times had I been impressed with the miles of range, the dozens of well-kept buildings, the big house in its park-like setting? Enough times to know that this time it felt different.

As we came up the long road, the fences looked in need of paint. Not falling down or even close to it, but still not as spanking white as Mr. Knight had kept them. And there weren't many hands around as we crossed the little bridge and rode into the barn yards. A few Mexicans watched us ride up, but they didn't have to stop work to do it because none of them seemed to be working.

No one came out of the barn to take the horses, so we hitched them to a fence and started toward the house. I could feel eyes following us from under sombreros, but nobody said a word.

"Good Lord," Jack said. "It's a good thing I came home. It doesn't look like Judge Gannon hired such a good foreman."

The front door opened and shut, and we saw a rounder Elena staring at us. We walked toward her, through dead stubble of grass and weeds where flowers once had bloomed. She watched us silently.

At the steps Jack took off his hat and said, "Hello. I guess you're Elena. I suppose this is a surprise for you."

She stared, her eyes wide.

"Elena, it's me. Jack. Jack Knight."

She sighed. "I know," she said. She turned and went back inside, leaving the door open. We took that as the only invitation we were likely to get, and followed her.

The house was jammed with people. The chairs, the floors, the very air was filled with Mexican faces, and every one of them was staring at us. It looked like a Mexican village had been picked up all at once and squeezed into this house.

Jack stared unbelievingly. He walked past some old women and down the hall to his father's study. When he opened the door I heard guitar music. He closed it and came back, shaking his head in puzzlement. He turned to Elena, who was standing motionless, a small boy clinging to her skirts. The child already had a familiar stockiness about him.

"Who are all these people?" Jack asked Elena.

"Go see Judge Gannon," she said. And that was all she said, despite Jack's questions.

Finally he gave up. "All right, I will go see the judge. And he'd better have a good explanation about his hiring practices, too. I said a foreman, not a whole Mexican town." He started toward the door, then noticed his mother's shawl around the shoulders of an old man snoring on a chair. A good jerk on the end of the shawl sent the old man sprawling on the floor, which woke him up enough to start searching his clothes for a whiskey bottle. When we went out the door he was gurgling from it, still on the floor.

"I just can't believe this," Jack said as we pushed through the crowd on the porch and headed back for our horses. "It looks like Judge Gannon must have misunderstood my instructions."

Cottonwood was still there, a little bigger but not much prettier. Even the new buildings looked old, and the sign over the freight office still serviced the South from one dangling chain. The only sounds came from Sam's saloon.

We climbed the steps to Judge Gannon's office, above the feed store. When we opened the door he was waiting for us. Evidently there was still one horse at the CK that could travel, and one Mexican who could ride.

He stood up behind his desk, all smiles. "Jack, my boy, how good to see you," he said. "You set yourself down in that big chair there and tell me what you've been up to." He gave me a glance but said nothing to me, so I remained standing.

"Look, Judge, there's something going on out at the ranch I'm sure you're not aware of," Jack said. "That woman Elena has moved half of Mexico in there, and they're even wearing my mother's clothes!" He waved the shawl at the judge.

"Now, Jack, don't get all upset," the judge said. He went behind his desk and took a long cigar from a box, then made a big project out of lighting it. Finally he smiled at Jack again. "Now, my boy, tell me what the problem is."

Jack waved away a cloud of smoke from the cigar. "Judge, I just told you, a whole Mexican village is living in my house, and I—"

"In Elena's house, you mean," the judge said quietly.

I felt sick.

"No, I don't think you understood," Jack said. "I wrote you to hire a foreman while I completed some unfinished business. Now, instead of a foreman I find my ranch—"

The judge blew an enormous cloud of smoke at Jack and said, "My boy, it's you that don't understand. I just told you it ain't your ranch, it's Elena's."

Jack looked at him in complete puzzlement, then turned to me as if I could translate.

"Judge Gannon, I believe that Mr. Knight—"

"*You* believe? Who in hell are you anyway?" He knew who I was, and he knew that I knew. But you had to put the Indian in his place.

"My name is Crazy Fox," I said patiently, "and I have reason to believe that Mr. Knight left letters of instruction with you concerning both Jack Knight and myself."

"Oh, you have reason to believe that, do you. I suppose then you can show me some proof?"

"We have letters. Not with us at the moment, but they exist." Somewhere out in the Territory, probably blowing around where some prisoner had thrown them. They'd left Jack's letters in his saddlebag, probably meaning to unwrap the oilcloth package at their leisure, but I had been carrying the letters from Mr. Knight in mine.

"Well, maybe you'd better go get them," the judge said. "'Cause I ain't ever seen any letter of instruction like the ones you mention." He carefully tapped his cigar into a marble ashtray I remembered used to sit on Mr. Knight's desk. "What I *do* have, however, is a will that leaves everything to Elena Knight and her son, Charles Junior." He pulled a document from his desk drawer and tossed it to me. "It's right there, if you can read it."

I read it. He was right. Everything to his beloved wife Elena and his beloved son Charles. There was no mention of Jack at all, much less me.

While I was reading Jack was pacing up and down, staring at the judge and then at me with a look of pained confusion. Finally he said, "I can't stay here and listen to this any more. I'll be across at Sam's if you need me." He stalked out.

I finished and looked up at the smiling judge. "You know this will can be contested," I told him carefully. "I doubt if a Texas court would let a will stand that doesn't even mention the eldest son."

Judge Gannon's eyes narrowed. "Well now, you are an educated Injun, ain't you. All right, you go on and tell me all about what a Texas court will do."

I picked my words carefully, sensing that it was now a lone Indian against a Texas judge. "I'm sure Jack has no wish to cause trouble for Mrs. Knight," I said. "Still, I'm sure he'd have no trouble hiring a lawyer to represent his interests in this matter."

"Is that so?" the judge said, stubbing out his cigar. "Well, now, here's the way I see this matter, Injun. What I see is a loony man who runs around making a damn fool of himself. And this here loony has got himself an Injun friend who puts on airs you wouldn't even take to in a white man. And the two of them is just maybe in trouble in some parts of this here world to boot." He pulled a wanted poster out of a drawer and shoved it across the desk. I read about a white man wearing a mask and an Indian who were wanted for impersonating officers and for a dozen other things, including assault on a U.S. Marshal and aiding prisoners to escape. There were no pictures, but the descriptions couldn't fit too many people.

"So I reckon you can take this matter to court," the judge said. "Course I'm the judge in these parts, and the jury would be bound to have people on it who recall some of Jack Knight's scrapes in years past, so you might find things goin' a mite different than you'd want. In fact, some folks might even think Jack belongs in one of them institutions for fellas that act strange. Or could be the both of you might find yourselves extra-dickted up to Judge Parker's court."

I sat there, listening and thinking frantically of some way we could get around what he was saying. There was just no way I could see to win this pot with Gannon holding all the cards. And for us the stakes were too high. But I tried to keep my face from showing what I felt.

"You may be the judge here, and it may be that some people don't remember Jack in the best light," I said. "But they remember his father, and I doubt that they would let someone get away with a thing like this."

He smiled. "Like what? He left the ranch to his wife and son. What's wrong with that? And he disinherited his crazy son, who he hadn't even seen for years and probably wouldn't have wanted around anyway." He shook his head. "No, I doubt that you've got much of a case, Injun."

We stared at each other for a while, but I couldn't think of an answer. At last he sighed and opened another desk drawer. "I don't want folks to think I ain't got a heart, however," he said, taking out some more papers and a packet of money. "I mean, it's clear you boys will be leavin' town right away, and I wouldn't want you to ride out empty-handed. So if you'll just get these papers signed I'll turn over this thousand dollars Jack's pappy would have wanted him to have, and we'll all be done with this thing."

I read: ". . . undersigned hereby relinquishes all right, title, and any claim whatsoever against Mrs. Charles Knight or any property in her possession . . ."

"Jack will never sign this," I said.

"No, maybe not. But you will. Bein' an Injun, you know when the battle is lost."

He was right. I signed.

"Good," he said. "Now I'll just put this little document away, along with this wanted poster and the will, just in case your friend ever does decide to have his day in court, which I'm hopin' you'll persuade him not to do for his own sake."

He pushed the money across the desk. I picked it up and stared at it, unable to speak because of the stone in my throat.

"Now no need to thank me, Injun," the judge said. "It's the least I could do for my old friend's son. I know he had good reason to think like he did about the boy, but I can tell you it grieved my heart when I read that will for the first time."

Can you scalp a fat Texas judge and make it out of town ahead of the posse? Not likely.

I put the money inside my shirt and left.

Jack was slumped against Sam's bar, ignoring a girl in a red dress who was trying to talk to him. I thought the dress looked familiar, and then I realized it was the same one Dulsie had worn so many years ago. I guess if you didn't fit the dress, you didn't work at Sam's.

"Jack, we need talk," I said.

He didn't turn around.

I shook his shoulder, and he turned slowly to face me. Tears were running down his bare face, and he held up his hand with the torn pieces of the mask in it. He dropped them on the floor and picked up his bottle, weaving away toward a table.

I turned to Sam. "What happened?" I asked him.

"How the hell do I know," he said. He poured a drink from a special bottle for the girl in the red dress, who carried it back to a table where a cowboy was waiting. "All I did was mention about Wes Hardin bein' in jail, and next thing he's carryin' on like a crazy man. Which he probably is."

"Hardin's in jail?" I asked stupidly.

"That's what I said," Sam snapped. "Why, are you a-gonna commence cryin' too?"

I shook my head. Now I understood about the torn mask.

"They caught him back East somewheres,"* Sam was saying.

*John Wesley Hardin was arrested in Pensacola, Florida, in August of 1877. He was sentenced to twenty-five years hard labor in Huntsville Prison.

"They brought him back to Texas for his trial, and Lord knows they had enough crimes for a hundred trials." He looked over at Jack and raised his voice. "'Ceptin' they never did bring out nothin' about no massacre," he added.

The girl was back for another drink, so Sam went to get the special bottle. "I do declare, I think I'm gettin' a mite tipsy," the girl said in a carrying voice. "If I have another drink somebody may have to help me upstairs to my bed." She headed back to her grinning cowboy, glass in hand.

I walked over to Jack's table and sat down. I took a long pull from his bottle, then another one to wash the first one down. The bottle was running low when Jack finally looked up at me.

"What does it mean, Crazy Fox?" he said softly. "I come home to find my father has left everything to that bunch of Mexican cabooses. And now someone else has caught Hardin." He took several gulps from the bottle. "I'll tell you what it means. It means I haven't got a home, and I haven't got a quest, and I haven't got . . . anything." His voice trailed off.

I went to get another bottle. I knew the judge would be watching to see that we left town that day, but he'd just have to wait a while.

Right now it was time to get drunk.

Sometime later that day we were shooting at a row of bottles out in the middle of the street. We had dragged a rickety bench down off Sam's porch to line them up on, but we fell down more than the bottles did.

"Come on, Crazy, if we emptied them we ought to be able to shoot them." Jack lurched and shot. The bullet pinged off a chain, and the South was no longer being served. He fired again and a window flew out of the feed store. "Come on," he said. "I'm doing better than you are."

He started to take aim at the bottles again, but I grabbed his arm. There was a wagon coming up behind them, and I figured the lady driving it might not appreciate bullets flying around her. Jack wasn't likely to actually hit her so long as she was near the bottles, but Judge Gannon might take a dim view of such things anyway.

"S'matter?" Jack said, falling flat on his back.

The wagon was coming nearer, and I tried to focus on the figure driving it, but next thing I knew I was lying next to Jack and staring straight up. The wagon stopped.

"Move your little butts, boys, or I'll put wagon tracks on your chests," Dulsie said.

When I woke up next morning my head was pounding so hard I was afraid to open my eyes. There was a creaking sound, and I tried to remember where I had heard it before. Then I remembered. It sounded just like that windmill, years ago. Slowly I opened my eyes.

It was the windmill. I could see it through the window, creaking and clanking just the way it had back then. I closed my eyes again, trying to figure it out, and then I caught the smell of coffee and bacon. Slowly, holding my head so it wouldn't fall off, I sat up and got out of bed. It had to be the Morgan place, out by Quit Well. Mr. Knight must have had the windmill rebuilt, before he died.

Dulsie was in the kitchen, humming and mixing something in a bowl. When she saw me she poured a cup of coffee and put it down on the table. "Better set down before you fall down," she said.

"How did we get here?" I asked her.

"Sam helped me throw you in the buckboard," she said. "And when I got out here I just opened the tailgate and you rolled right out. Then I dragged and wrestled you into bed." She laughed. "I'm stronger'n I look, as many a drunk cowboy has discovered."

I sipped the scalding coffee, which took my mind off my pounding head for a minute. "Where is Jack?" I asked her.

"In the other bedroom, in Daddy's old bed. He may not wake up for a week or two." She was still humming as she slid the biscuits into the oven. "You did know that Daddy had died last year, didn't you?"

"No. I'm sorry to hear it."

"Yeah, so was I. He never was worth much, but I guess you've only got one father."

"So are you living back here now?" I asked. It didn't seem likely, but here she was cooking just like any farm woman.

"Not hardly," she said. "I'm just here tryin' to straighten out the mess Daddy left."

"Mess?"

"Yeah, a right big one, too. I was plannin' to sell the place cheap to Lonnie Harper, so I signed it over to him last time I was down here. Hell, ol' Lonnie ain't ever had three cents, but they was good to me when my Ma run off."

Something clicked in my aching head. "Were you down here in seventy-six?"

"That's right. I wrote and told Jackie I'd be here."

That burnt letter. The ". . . wood" hadn't been Deadwood, it had been Cottonwood.

"Anyways, Harper had to show the deed in court after I left, and when he did Judge Gannon said it wasn't any good, and that Stumpy hadn't ever registered a deed on this place. So Harper wrote to me, but I was out in Colorado and the letter didn't catch up to me for a spell. But when I did get here I had Judge Gannon show me the records, thinkin' I could square it away by signin' some papers. And it seems that in the meantime somebody else had gone and filed a deed on the place, all legal like." She smacked an egg down on the side of a skillet and it splattered all over the stove. "Whoa, girl," she said, and tried another one. This one plopped nicely into the pan.

"The person who filed the deed. That wouldn't be Judge Gannon himself, would it?" I asked her.

"How'd you know that?" she asked me.

I told her what had happened to us yesterday.

She was quiet for a while, then she began to laugh. "You know, friend, I do believe that old bastard was in our drawers when we wasn't lookin'," she said finally. She noticed that I wasn't joining the laughter. "Oh, come on," she said. "Things could be worse."

"How?"

She giggled. "I knew you'd say that sooner or later."

And despite headaches and misfortunes, I found myself laughing too.

"What's so funny," Jack said from the bedroom door. He looked sleepy and confused—and different, without the mask.

"Oh, nothing," Dulsie said. "Come and have some coffee. Did you sleep well?"

"No, not really. I kept dreaming, all night long. Dulsie was in some of them. And I'm all worn out this morning."

I couldn't resist. "Tellum dream, Jack."

He looked at Dulsie and a red flush spread over his face. "Not now," he said quickly.

Dulsie was grinning like a little girl as she put a plate of bacon and eggs in front of Jack. "Eat up, boys," she said. "That old bastard Gannon gave me till noon to pack up and move out of here, so let's get going."

At the mention of Gannon's name Jack's face got sad. "Did you know that my father left everything to Elena?" he asked Dulsie. "I never knew he felt that way about me. Do you think it was all because of that windmill?" He looked as if he might start crying again.

Dulsie put a hand on his shoulder and stood behind him. "It's all right, Jackie," she said softly. "We'll go up to Dodge together and forget all about Texas."

She glanced at me, and a hard look was in her eyes. "Yeah, to hell with Texas," she said. "But there is one Texas judge who may find it ain't so easy to forget Dulsie Morgan."

I drove Dulsie's wagon, with my horse tied to the tailgate and Jack riding along on Whitey. Dulsie kept babbling on about Dodge and how interesting it was, what with folks like Wyatt Earp and Luke Short and Bat Masterson coming and going all the time. As she talked, I noticed that Jack was falling behind and slowed the wagon so he could catch up.

"He doesn't seem to want to go," Jack said when they'd come up to the wagon. "It's almost like he feels as bad as I do about everything."

We started up again, and in a little while we reached the fork in the road. I turned north, toward Kansas. Whitey tried to go the other way, and Jack had to yank on the reins.

"We might even go on out to Colorado," Dulsie was saying. "Maybe even to California. I hear San Francisco is a mighty nice place. What do you think, Jackie?"

Jack was still having trouble with Whitey and didn't hear her. In fact, Whitey was fighting the reins in a way I'd never seen before. "You dumb sonofabitch," Jack yelled, kicking at the horse's side.

In a second he was sprawled on the ground and Whitey was skittering away, whinnying like a colt.

I stopped the wagon and jumped down to help Jack, who was dusting off his pants and glaring at the horse.

"You come right back here," Jack ordered.

Whitey moved a short way toward him, then backed off, pawing the ground and whinnying. And then he turned and trotted away across the prairie.

I untied my horse and told Dulsie to wait there for us. Mounted double, we followed Whitey. And in a little while, I realized where we were heading. Benton's Canyon.

We came to the place we'd stopped at years ago, and once again we got down and waited. Whitey was there, nibbling grass and drinking from the little stream, but this time he didn't come closer. He watched us, and every now and then he'd move away a few yards and then come back, as if he couldn't decide what to do next.

"I think that horse is doing this on purpose," Jack said angrily. "As if I don't have enough troubles, he's got to start acting up. You come *here!*" he yelled at Whitey.

Whitey snorted but stayed where he was.

"He not come, Jack," I said at last. "Me think he go home."

"Home? You mean Benton's Canyon? Why would he do that, after all these years?"

"Maybe him go home to die."

Jack's eyes got wide. It evidently had never occurred to him that he wouldn't always be riding that big, mean-tempered, silver monster. "I don't *want* him to die, Crazy Fox," he said softly, like a child seeing death for the first time. "He's not old enough to die, anyway." He counted on his fingers. "I've only had him for about ten years."

"Him not colt when you catchum," I said. "Men try to catch Whitey many years before that. Whitey get old. Horse know when time come."

"He *can't* die," Jack said. He put his head in his hands for a long time. Then, finally, he looked up at the horse again. There were tears in his eyes. "He's still got his saddle and bridle on," he said. "We can't let him go like that, or he might get sores or . . ." his voice caught.

He got up and started toward the big horse again, and Whitey started to dance away. But Jack said softly, "It's all right, Whitey. I understand." When he got within a few feet of the horse he stopped and held out his hand. "Come on, old friend."

Whitey came to him and stood quietly while Jack removed the gear. Then he shook himself, nickered softly, and galloped away. Jack turned and started gathering up his saddle and bedroll, ignoring the diminishing hoofbeats.

And then Whitey reached the crest of the hill and reared high, outlined against the blue sky. I looked one last time at the most beautiful horse I've ever seen, and he was gone.

Jack swiped at his eyes. "And now, on top of everything else, I've got to carry this damn saddle," he said.

Traveling with a woman and a white man without a mask was a lot easier than I'd been used to. Towns didn't have to be avoided or approached with caution, no flyers had to be posted, no stories had to be told about old war wounds—in short, we traveled like ordinary people, a couple with an out-of-luck Indian they had befriended or hired. Dulsie did the talking when talk was needed, since Jack refused to speak to anyone at all and people sometimes failed to hear an Indian correctly.

We worried about Jack, who traveled like a man asleep, eating what was put in front of him and washing when Dulsie told him to. Even the white suit grew a deeper gray every day. He had gone into some private world of his own, and from what we could tell it was not a pleasant place to be.

One day, as we were heading up through the Territory, it occurred to me that we were passing within a two or three days' ride of the reservation where my People lived. And I still had that thousand dollars from Judge Gannon, though I had never told Jack about it and wasn't sure how much of it I could rightfully claim as mine. I decided to try to talk to him.

It didn't go too well.

"You mean to say you took that man's money?" he said in outraged disbelief. "You should have thrown it in his face."

"Maybe so. But money good, and that all we get." I held it out to him. "Money yours. Come from your father."

He looked as if he might spit on it. "I wouldn't touch the stuff. Throw it away." And he turned and went back into his dark private world again.

I considered the problem. Obviously I would not throw it away—not with so many people in need of it. And yet I could not give it to my People with Jack in his present state of mind. He wasn't really thinking straight, or even in his customary zig-zags. At last I decided on a compromise: I would take half to my People and keep the rest for Jack, for whenever he came out of his gloom and needed it.

I told Dulsie I would be leaving them for a few days, and arranged to meet them again at a crossing on the Cimarron. I was worried about the two of them in this country alone, but she pointed out that they had Jack's six-gun, a rifle, and a shotgun for company, and she was sure Jackie wouldn't let any harm come to her. Jack grunted.

I rode day and night again, and made the trip in five days. My

People were much as before, though times had not improved their lot and didn't seem likely to. Sharp Nose was older and thinner, but he was pleased to see me, and pleased to get the money. I left with a familiar sadness, which grew worse with each visit.

I arrived at the Cimarron crossing not long after Dulsie and Jack, and was pleased to see they had made it with no bad luck.

"Not a single problem we couldn't handle," Dulsie said. "Some cowboys got a little uppity once, but they left pretty sudden, tryin' to outrun a load of buckshot. Other than that, it was like ridin' to Sunday School, if memory serves."

Jack grunted.

Dodge City was going the way of Abilene. It wasn't even a dozen years old, and already it was quieting down. Boot Hill was gone, the bodies moved to an official cemetery. In fact, most of the hill itself had been moved, to pave a racetrack. What was left now had a school on it.

The piles of buffalo bones were gone, and the stench of decaying carcasses no longer drifted in from the prairie. The town had two pet buffalo wandering around in it, begging scraps from kitchen doors and provoking talk about the good old days. Watching them allow their noses to be petted, I felt sad for the days of the great herds that stretched farther than even an Indian's eye could see.

Even the saloons were feeling the pinch of change. There were more of them than before, but the town council had passed ordinances against music or dancing in them, and some had already closed down. Kansas was supposed to be dry, and there seemed to be temperance preachers on every street corner reminding people about it.

I doubt if Jack noticed whether the town was dry or not. We were staying in a little house Dulsie owned in town, and Jack rarely ever went outside it. Dulsie was living back in her rooms above the Long Branch, to preserve appearances (it must have been Jack's reputation she was concerned about), but she often had dinner with us. Even her presence couldn't lift Jack out of his gloom, though. He ate, slept, and sat around, but you couldn't help feeling that he had stopped living back there in Cottonwood.

I worked around the place as much as I could, though Rita and Pedro—Dulsie's hired couple—really didn't need much help. Still, it passed the time, and kept my mind from tilting over like Jack's.

One morning I was replacing a broken window in the kitchen when I noticed a book lying on the table. It was one of those things called "dime novels," though this one was shabbier-looking than most I'd seen, and even lacked the flashy picture you usually saw on the cover. Even so, the title jumped right out at me in big black letters. *The Taming of the Terrible Black Hills Gang; Or, The Mystery Man of the West Rides Again.** I opened it and read a couple of pages. Then I went to find Rita.

"Where'd you get this thing?" I asked her.

"From Miss Dulsie," she said. "She gave to me many book for to read and improving better the English." She beamed at having put together such a long sentence. "You want book? I have been read, so do not more need."

I borrowed the book and spent the rest of the day reading how the Mystery Man of the West struck terror into the outlaws who had preyed on innocent travelers traversing the Deadwood Trail. I could hardly believe my eyes.

The Mystery Man wore a mask, rode a huge white stallion and traveled with a faithful Indian companion. He was of towering stature (the Mystery Man, that is—the Indian could have been two feet tall for all the reader knew), he had smoldering brown eyes and a granite jaw, he was deadly with his twin six-shooters at distances that would have challenged a buffalo gun, and he was the scourge of all evil-doers in the West. The minute the Black Hills Gang laid eyes on his unmistakable figure they knew the game was up. On page fifty-eight he rounded up seven outlaws and delivered them to the nearest sheriff through a blizzard. On page seventy-four General Custer begged for his help, since "your guns are more deadly than any twenty of ours." The faithful Indian grunted a lot.

When Dulsie came in that evening I showed the book to her. "Have you read this thing?" I asked her.

She glanced at it and said, "Lord no, I don't read that trash. People leave them in the saloon and I bring them home to Rita. Why?"

"Because you're in this one, that's why. And so is Jack." I couldn't bring myself to mention the Indian companion. "Maybe you ought to read it."

She read a couple of pages, then looked at me in confusion. "Who's this Mystery Man? Jackie? You're loco."

*We can find no record on this particular dime novel, a fact that will surprise no one familiar with the proliferation of that genre and its lack of durability.

"Read on."

A few pages later she read aloud: "His first and only love is the fair Dulcinda, a lady some say is of noble birth." She clasped the book to her breast. "Lordy, I love it so far," she said. "Even if my name ain't really Dulcinda." She read on.

"Dulsie, skip on to page twelve and read how this fellow describes the Indian," I said.

She flipped the pages, then read:

"His faithful companion watched as the Mystery Man scouted the dangerous trail ahead. Minutes later he raised his muscular arm and signaled for the Indian to follow.

" 'Me come, keensobbie,' the faithful companion replied.

" 'Less noise, old friend,' the tall man instructed, 'lest the scalping, thieving Sioux hear us.'

" 'Me try, Mystery Man,' the savage apologized."

I took the book from her hand. "Enough, Dulsie, please."

She smiled. "Well, maybe that ain't exactly the way it is with you and Jackie, but it makes good reading."

"Good reading!" I moaned. "Dulsie, the Indian talks like an idiot!"

At dinner that night Dulsie showed the book to Jack.

"See the nice book, Jackie?" he said. "It's all about people you know." She often talked to him the way you speak to a stubborn child.

He picked it up and glanced at it absently. "Who's the author?" he asked. "All it says is 'An Old Cowhand.' "

"Probably somebody who was ashamed to put his name to such stuff," Dulsie said. "Why don't you read it and see for yourself."

He started reading, forming the words with his lips. In a minute he got up and left the table.

A little later Dulsie and I took our coffee out to the porch, and we found Jack there, quietly reading. Dulsie and I talked for a while, and then she said, "Well, Jackie, back to work." She got no answer, so she shrugged and walked down the path.

I watched her turn and walk up the street toward the Long Branch. I thought about the time we had spent in her house and all we owed her, and I knew I'd have to get a job soon. The money from Judge Gannon wouldn't last forever.

It was growing dark, so Jack moved back inside to hold his book under a lamp. I looked at the stars for a while, then decided to go to bed, so I could get up early and begin to look for work.

I was asleep and dreaming of a young maid with shining black hair who stood shyly aside as I entered the wedding wigwam. When I turned to take her by the hand to lead her to the scented buffalo robes, she gave me a punch in the ribs and screamed, "Crazy Fox, wake up! Wake up! We're in a book!"

Chapter
11

In which Jack enters
the corrida, and we join Cody's
Wild West Show.

I did find work, now and then at this and that, and we spent the next few years in Dodge. The jobs were mostly what you'd expect: Occasional odd bits of carpentry, some work at the stables, helping out at spring roundup on some of the nearby ranches—mostly not worth talking about. But I will mention the one job I turned down, because I was never offered the likes of that unique position before or since. It came about when one of the two competing stores in town brought in a big wooden figure of an Indian to stand outside its door. The owner of the store across the street at first tried to buy a bigger statue, but when he saw me walking by he got an even better idea: Would I dress up in buckskins and war bonnet and stand in front of his building? The pay was good, but after brief consideration I turned it down.

Jack helped Dulsie in the saloon from time to time, and he appeared briefly in the Dodge City Cowboy Band. He got the job on the basis of his work with Custer in '74, but after his first performance one man said it was a pity Jack hadn't been along at Little Big Horn. With his playing, the Indians would never have come close enough to do battle.

The dime novel occupied a good bit of Jack's time, and for a while he went around showing it to everyone who would listen. He finally figured out that "An Old Cowhand" had to be one of the reporters he had talked with during the Custer expedition, but he had no idea which one.

"Of course, the book isn't exactly the way I told our adventures to him," Jack said.

"Me hope not," I told him, recalling the feeble-minded Indian companion.

"No, I'm sure I mentioned that my eyes are blue, and he has them as brown here on page nineteen."

He carried the book with him most of the time, even insisting that the girls who worked in the Long Branch read how he had singlehandedly rounded up the Black Hills gang—with some help from his Indian friend, of course.

The redhead read a few pages of the book and then showed it to one of Dodge's assistant marshals who was drinking at the bar. "I dunno," she said. "This feller claims to be this here Mystery Man in the book, but I don't see a whole lot of resemblance. What do you think, Wyatt?"

The marshal read the description of the Mystery Man and then eyed Jack. "Oh, sure," he said. "Course this feller ain't wearin' a mask or a white outfit, and he ain't got a big white stallion, and he don't wear two guns. And he ain't really what you'd call 'towerin' in stature.' And his eyes ain't brown, like on page nineteen here. Otherwise he's the Mystery Man to a tee."

"See," Jack told the redhead. "But don't let the eyes bother you, Miss Kitty. I plan to have that error corrected in future editions."

Others who read the book were even less impressed than the marshal and Miss Kitty. One man laughed out loud. "Hell, you ain't near tall enough nor handsome enough, you ain't wearin' a mask and yore suit is a damn long ways from white. You ain't even mysterious. Fact is, we got a feller right here in town folks call Mysterious Dave Mather, and I think I seen him ride a white horse onct. More'n likely this here's him."

Jack was amazed. "But it *is* me," he said with a hurt look. "You tell him, Dulsie."

Dulsie stopped counting bottles for inventory long enough to turn around. "What? Oh. Sure, Bat, it's him."

The man went away chuckling and shaking his head.

After a few such reactions, Jack stopped showing the book around Dodge. "I think it's the brown eyes that are causing the confusion," he told me. "I wish that author had checked his facts more carefully."

Bit by bit, rip-roaring Dodge City slid into history, helped along by those ordinances and some zealous law enforcement. The town fathers were pleased that cowboys no longer gunned one another down in the middle of Front Street, but they were less pleased at the lack of attention being paid to a tamer, duller Dodge. They decided something was needed to bring attention—and business—to the town again.

What was needed, they decided, was a bullfight, the first one ever held north of the Rio Grande.* The businessmen's association raised the money and made the arrangements for the bulls and the Mexicans to fight them, and for weeks you hardly heard about anything else. There were groups formed to promote the event and other groups formed to protest the cruelty to the bulls, who might actually be hurt before becoming steaks on people's dinner tables. But mostly there was a sense of excitement, in a town that had been running short of that particular commodity. If cowboys couldn't shoot one another, maybe they could at least watch a bunch of Mexicans get gored and trampled by some of the meanest Texas bulls ever assembled at one time.

Naturally, we all planned to go. But on the first day of the fights, Jack was busy writing to the publisher of the dime novel, offering corrections and further true adventures of the Mystery Man of the West. He said he'd catch up with us later, so we left him there and headed for a good spot to watch the parade, which was to start in town and end up at the arena about a half mile out. The Cowboy Band played louder than ever and the local bigwigs walked as tall as they could manage, and the bullfighters themselves looked fine in their bright colored, tight-fitting outfits.

We followed the parade on out to the arena, along with thousands of people who had come in from all over the country to see the show. The grandstand, which was built up in a circle around an open area a hundred feet across, was said to hold four thousand people. The seats were all filled, and some of the girls from the saloons even had to double up by sitting on laps.

The crowd seemed to divide itself naturally, with the cowboys and other excitable types sitting apart from the quieter businessmen and their wives. This division had been helped along by an attempt to separate the women as they came in, so the respectable ladies of the town wouldn't have to watch the squeezing and tickling some of their less constrained sisters were apt to engage in. A deputy sheriff was in charge of this operation, and by the time Dulsie and I got

*This bullfight, held on the Fourth of July, 1884, may well stand as the only one ever to be held on United States soil.

there you couldn't help thinking he'd probably rather be doing almost anything else.

"Now, ma'am, if you'll jist head over thataway . . ." he began.

Dulsie gave him a look that must have fried his bootsoles.

". . . or maybe over thataway, if you d'ruther," he finished, his face bright red.

Dulsie smiled. "Since you give us a choice, we'll set over yonder with the girls," she told him. "These other folks look dry as dust to me."

We sat amongst the cowboys, who were amusing themselves handily while waiting for the "athletic exhibition" (as the newspaper had called it) to begin. In fact, some of them seemed so completely amused that you had to wonder whether they'd have noticed a bull if it sat down next to them.

Jack arrived just before the parade of the bullfighters. He was complaining about the crowds and wondering why we had sat over here, where it was so packed, when he could see some spaces over there next to the mayor's party. But then the march of the toreadors began, with the Cowboy Band whaling away at a piece that might have been Spanish. And Jack stopped complaining. He almost stopped breathing, staring open-mouthed at the costumes on the matadors. "Good Lord, that's beautiful," he said, in the kind of voice a man might use on his wedding night.

I had to admit that the outfits made Jack's formerly white clothes look pretty dull by comparison. Especially the suit of lights on the tall bullfighter called Gallardo, who was scheduled to fight the first bull of the day. His was red and blue and he looked like a prairie sunset. Jack wore the expression of a man who had just seen the Red Sea part.

The first bull was a big, mean-looking rip-snorter, and he spent half an hour chasing the matador around the ring and getting his back stuck full of little darts with colored streamers on them. After a while he was carrying more of those little flags than a Fourth of July parade, but he never seemed to tire of chasing the matador. They finally had to rope him and drag him out of the ring.

The rest of the bulls were less enthusiastic. The second one stood around wishing it was elsewhere while the matador waved his cape, so they finally chased it back into the corral and let out a different one. The third and fourth bulls weren't much livelier, and the fifth one tried to climb the fence to get out. The crowd began jeering and yelling for the first bull to be brought back for the promised "confrontation with Toledo steel."

"We ain't gettin' our money's worth!" yelled a girl who was busily stuffing a cowboy's greenbacks down the front of her dress.

The Cowboy Band ripped into something that sounded sort of Mexican, but the hooting and jeering went on anyway. And then the tall matador walked into the center of the ring, a short sword held high over his head, and the crowd got quiet.

The little corral door opened and the big red bull came charging back out, looking as energetic as ever and even more determined. He ran at the matador and rammed his horns into the cape. Then he whirled around and did it again, and again. He stopped, considering the whole thing, then took another run. This time the matador went flying through the air. The crowd cheered and shouted encouragement to the bull, who responded by going after the matador, head down and snorting all the way.

The matador scrambled behind one of the wooden safety barricades and crouched there while the bull knocked big splinters off it with his horns. The man seemed inclined to stay right there, but the crowd threatened to drag him out and let the bull have a clear shot at him.

At last he came back out, shoulders straight, and faced the bull. As the animal charged the matador raised the sword high, pointed downward. At the last second, just before he would have gotten those horns right in the belly, the steel flashed and the man jumped aside. The bull went down, kicking and snorting, and in a few seconds was still.

The crowd, having at last got its money's worth, went crazy. I figured they'd all turn out for the second day of fighting, and that there would still probably be more of them cheering for the bull than for the matador. But I hoped the bulls showed a little more spunk tomorrow, or some of those cowboys might jump down there and stomp them to death.

Dulsie headed back to the Long Branch to help cope with the crowds, and Jack and I wandered around to the side of the arena where the matadors entered. They were all there, standing around in a group arguing with the Scotsman, Moore, who had brought them there from Mexico. I listened to the staccato Spanish.

"What are they saying?" Jack asked.

"Tall one say he not come tomorrow. Say matadors must parade without him. Him go back to real business tonight." In everyday life Gallardo was a tailor in Chihuahua.

Jack's face lit up. "I will take your place tomorrow," he said to the matador.

Everyone was speechless, including me. Had Jack gone completely crazy?

Mr. Moore recovered first. "You? Have you ever done this kind of thing?"

"No, but what's so difficult about it?" Jack said. "I'm pretty sure the suit will fit me well enough."

Moore squinted at Jack and thought it over, then he must have begun to see the possibilities of salvaging something from Gallardo's quitting. "All right," he told Jack. "But I take no responsibility in this matter."

"Oh, that's all right," Jack said. "I'll see that the suit is returned in good condition."

Moore turned to Gallardo and the rapid Spanish began again. I didn't catch it all, but Gallardo was protesting about lending his suit to a gringo and Moore was insisting that he had paid good money and that the suit was damn well going into that ring tomorrow, with either Gallardo wearing it or the gringo. He could take his pick.

Gallardo stripped. Then, with as much dignity as a man wearing only socks and underpants can muster, he presented the suit to Jack. "Good luck," he said. And then, in Spanish to Moore: "See that it is returned to me with all blood removed and rips mended."

"Jack, me think we need talk," I said as the beaming matadors began to pump his hand and slap his shoulders. But he waved me away and headed back to town, surrounded by his new-found friends.

Gallardo watched him leave. *"Vaya con Dios,"* he said, hitching up his drawers.

I caught up with Jack later that evening, but by then he'd put away enough Tequila to make conversation difficult. He was still with the other matadors when they arrived at the Long Branch, but by then he was wearing the suit of lights and couldn't even sit down without ripping the pants or damaging himself. The whiskey flowed again, as it had all night, and everyone drank to Dodge City's own matador. I joined the toasts, waiting for a chance to talk with Jack.

"Now who says I'm not handsome enough to be in that book," he said to Miss Kitty, holding on to her shoulder to keep from falling.

"Quit hangin' on me, Jack, or my boyfriend'll likely jerk a knot in your tail," she told him, propping him up against the bar. A few minutes later I saw her talking to an unusually tall man, and remembered somebody pointing him out as the fellow trying to get a job as a marshal here.

"Where in the world did Jackie ever get that outfit?" Dulsie asked me above the noise.

I started to tell her, but Jack and the bullfighters were weaving toward the door and I didn't want to lose track of them. "We'll talk later," I told her as I headed after them.

We didn't. I finally picked Jack up off the floor of some saloon and got him home, staggering a good deal myself. I didn't have the strength to get that suit of lights off him, so I left him on the bed sparkling like a pile of diamonds in the moonlight.

I don't remember going to bed, but I must have because I woke up there hours later with a blacksmith working inside my head. I went to find Jack, but he was not in his room. In the kitchen I found a note: *You were sleeping so I went on into town to find my friends. We'll meet at the bull ring. Madadoor.*

I went into the parlor and looked at Dulsie's clock, which was ticking away in the belly of a mostly naked lady. When I got my eyes focused properly I saw it was nearly noon. I got dressed quickly and went out to find Jack.

I tried the Long Branch and most of the other saloons in town, but no one had seen him. By then it was getting close to time for the bullfights to start, so I headed out to the arena. When I got there I saw that someone had added to the sign listing the "World's Bravest Matadors." At the bottom, in prophetic red paint, it said "El Misterio."

I ran to the little room under the grandstand, but when I got there the parade of the toreadors had already begun. While the Cowboy Band blasted away at their notion of Mexican music, the matadors marched slowly around the ring, with Jack bringing up the rear waving his hat and yelling "Olé" at everyone. It was a splendid sight, marred only by the thumping and snorting of the bulls in their pens.

As Jack came back into the little room, the crowd was still yelling, "Yay, El Misterio!" He was beaming.

"Isn't this great?" he yelled above the roar of the crowd. "It's almost better than being the Mystery Man of the West!"

I had a feeling things might take a turn for the worse, and I wanted to warn him. But I never got the chance. As the crowd continued to cheer, Moore rushed over and pushed Jack back through the little door and around the barricade into the ring. "They want you," he said.

Jack marched out into the ring, again waving his hat and yelling "Olé" right and left. The cheering increased until it drowned him out completely, but if I leaned around the barricade I could still see him, marching and waving and *Olé*ing for all he was worth.

He was still at it when the cheering suddenly stopped, and the crowd seemed to hold its breath. A door had opened at one of the little corrals, and out came one of the biggest, meanest, angriest-looking bulls ever raised on the Texas plains. It stopped to look around, pawing the ground and grunting. And then it saw Jack.

And then Jack saw the bull. For a long moment he stood there, his hat raised and his mouth frozen in the shape of a swallowed "Olé." He was still in that pose when the bull charged, its long, curving horns aimed directly at his belly.

Just as the horns were about to nail him to the wall, Jack jumped out of the way.

The crowd roared.

The bull turned, located Jack, snorted some more, and charged again.

Jack yelled something that was drowned out by the crowd and dodged again, but this time he kept on going, and before the bull could get turned around Jack was halfway to the barricade where Moore and I stood.

He went past us at a speed Whitey could have been proud of.

"Where in hell's he goin'?" Moore asked me. "He was doin' just great."

I started to tell him that Jack must have figured the bull was doing even better, but I didn't have a chance. The bull was heading our way at amazing speed, considering his size, and those horns were pointed at a part of me I had meant to keep. I grabbed Moore and pulled him through the door just as the horns ripped through the barricade and sent splinters flying all over the little room inside.

By the time I got back to Dulsie's Jack had packed most of our gear and was writing a note explaining that we had been called out of town on business.

And then El Misterio and I rode out of Dodge City, in the opposite direction from the bullring, where I could still hear cheers and boos rising faintly into the Kansas air. There didn't seem to be any good way to return Gallardo's costume, so we took it along.

After all, you never know when a thing like that might come in handy.

We drifted east, picking up a couple of jobs along the way during the next few months. Then, somewhere in Missouri, we hooked up with another circus, heading south. They took us on as roustabouts, and as we moved down through Arkansas and into Louisiana we fell back into a familiar routine—pull into a town, set up the grandstands, help with the animals, and then pull it all down and load it back onto the train for the next town.

The show was called the Sells Brothers Circus. There were four brothers, all from Ohio, and one of the stars of their show was a little girl who could do things with a gun you could hardly believe while you were watching them happen. She was a sweet little thing, and she would skip into the spotlight in her leather skirt and jacket, smiling like sunshine, and then shoot the leather pants off anyone in the business.

There were no phony tricks in her act, either. Other ladies in the shooting business often had to have help, but not little Annie. (One lady I recall used to swing on a trapeze shooting at a big metal plate each time she swooped by. She was all right at swinging on the trapeze, but she couldn't have shot holes in a bag if she was tied up inside it. So each time she swung by I had to throw a stone at the plate from behind a screen.) Annie's tricks couldn't be faked, like shooting glass balls out of the air where you could see them break as she fired. I once saw her break 4,772 of those balls out of 5,000 tossed up in nine hours, and she was loading her own guns in the bargain. She really was what Sitting Bull used to call her—"Little Miss Sure Shot."

When Jack wasn't working on his Custer memoirs he was after whichever one of the Sells brothers he could find to give us better jobs.

"Surely there is something more appropriate," he told

Ephraim Sells one day in New Orleans. (I think it was Ephraim. I never really did get them straight.) "After all, I've been a trick rider, a Mystery Man, and even a matador."

Sells considered it. "We've got more trick riders than we need now, and we're not short on mystery men neither. What's a matador do?"

"He fights bulls wearing a beautiful costume," Jack said.

"Yeah? How do you get the costume on the bull?"

Jack looked puzzled, then said, "You wait here and I'll show you what I mean."

He was back in a couple of minutes wearing the suit of lights. "See," he said, striking a pose. "Isn't it something?"

Sells walked around Jack scratching his head. Finally he said, "You know, I like it. We can't have a bull rampaging around, of course, but I think the suit would add something." He thought some more. "Tell you what," he said. "Frank Butler is feeling poorly, and Annie could use an assistant tonight. You go talk with her and she'll tell you what to do."

Jack was overjoyed. "You see," he told me. "Didn't I say this outfit would come in handy?"

Annie explained his job, which was fairly simple. All he had to do was stand next to a table, bow to the audience while each part of her act was announced, and then toss the balls into the air or hold out the playing card or whatever she would shoot next.

"You cain't hardly go wrong," she told him, expressing a confidence few people shared.

He did get through the first part of the act all right, except for throwing up a few playing cards when Annie was expecting glass balls. She shot them, too, so the audience thought it was all part of the act. She even shot a neat hole through Jack's only copy of *The Mystery Man of the West, etc.,* when he threw that up by mistake. (He'd brought it along for her to read, I guess, but in later years he treasured that neatly perforated copy, drilled dead center by the famous Annie Oakley.) His costume flashed and sparkled in the spotlights, and I thought once or twice the glitter almost caused her to miss a target. But he did look splendid.

Then came the second half of the act, and the part where Annie had to wait till a glass ball was thrown high into the air, then run about twenty feet across the arena, jump over a small table and grab her gun up from a larger table. All the time her assistant is throwing up more glass balls, as high as he can get them, so that by the time she gets to the gun there are three or four of them either going up or coming down. She whips up the gun and starts shooting, hitting first the lowest falling ball and then the others in rapid fire. It was her finale, and a real show-stopper.

Especially that night. Because when Jack set up the tables he got them mixed up and put the big one where the smaller one ought to be. Annie didn't notice, and by the time she'd started her run it was too late. She made her leap but failed to clear the big table and went sprawling into the sawdust, knocking over the smaller table and sending the gun spinning away. While she was scrambling to get the gun, the glass balls started coming down all around her.

Jack was still flinging them up enthusiastically as Annie stalked out of the arena, dodging falling balls and muttering words I didn't even know she knew. She headed for the ticket wagon, where the Sells brothers had their office. I figured it was lucky for them she hadn't been able to find that gun.

We gathered up our gear and headed across town to where Buffalo Bill's Wild West Show was playing. "This is really more our kind of thing," Jack said as we watched the Deadwood stage come thundering into the arena pursued by around forty Sioux, screaming and waving tomahawks. "They've even got proper jobs for you here."

When the performance was over we went to find Colonel Cody. This turned out to be easier than you might think, since the show had a policy of encouraging the public to wander around the campgrounds and see all the performers in the flesh.

We found Buffalo Bill in his tent, the flaps pulled back so everyone could get a good look at the famous scout of the plains as he sipped from a tall glass. A couple of the girls from the show were there, too, in their leather skirts and fancy boots. They were also sipping from big glasses.

"Just lemonade, boys," Cody assured us as we entered the tent. He patted one of the girls on her backside. "Wouldn't want anyone to think these fine ladies imbibe strong spirits. You boys want an autograph?"

"No sir, Colonel Cody, what we actually want is a job," Jack said.

Cody stared at him, his smile fading. "Oh, a job. Well, now, I'm afraid we're filled up tighter'n a lady's corset right now. What do you do?"

"Oh, I've been a trick rider, I've worked in a shooting act, I've even been a matador. And my friend here is an Indian, so he would fit right into the Deadwood stage part of the show." He saw he wasn't causing Cody to look especially interested, so he added, "And I've ridden with Custer, too."

"You don't say. Not at Little Big Horn, I presume." He poked one of the girls and winked.

"No, but I was with him up in the Black Hills in seventy-four. I've had some scientific experience, you see."

"Lord, who in hell ain't," Cody said, taking a long pull at the lemonade and making a face. "I spent months guiding a professor named Marsh all over the Big Horn Basin looking for old bones. Though Lord only knows what they're good for," he added. He scratched his beard and thought about it a while, then said, "All right, we've lost a couple of Indians lately, so you can take their place. Go tell Johnny you're the two new Sioux."

"But sir, I'm not an Indian," Jack protested.

"Course you ain't. But the make-up kit'll fix that." He spotted a girl trying to throw a rope and said, "Excuse me, now. Say, there, honey, let me show you the proper way to hold that thing."

Jack started to follow but I held him back. "We needum jobs," I reminded him.

He shook his head. "All right, but I can't even imagine what it's like to be an Indian," he said. "I may not give the kind of performance a man could be proud of."

We left with the show a few days later, and just before we moved out of New Orleans we acquired a new star attraction. You guessed it, Children—Annie Oakley had evidently gotten a better offer from Cody, so she had packed up her guns and glass balls and had left a batch of disappointed Sells brothers behind. She and her husband opened with the Wild West Show in Louisville, our next town.

The show was something like a circus, only bigger than most. There were well over two hundred performers and twenty-six white-and-gold railroad cars to carry them, along with the roustabouts, scenery, animals, and portable grandstands. The whole thing was run by a man named Nate Salisbury, who rehearsed performers and roustabouts alike until it all moved like clockwork.

We worked Louisville in the spring, and Jack managed to stay out of Annie Oakley's path the whole time. He spent most of his spare hours trailing after Cody or Salisbury, suggesting ways his talents might be better utilized. Or, when he couldn't find either of them, followed around after Buck Taylor, who roped and rode in the show as the "King of the Cowboys." Buck was a talkative man, and one day he started telling Jack about a writer he had met.

"Fella name of Ingraham," he said. "Says he's gonna write about me in a book of some kind."*

"Really? I'd like to meet him, as a fellow writer," Jack said. "Did I ever mention the book written about my life? Annie Oakley shot a hole through it, but you can still read it pretty well. I'll show it to you after the show."

I wondered about the kind of book Ingraham would write. If Jack had been described as "towering," what sort of word would be needed for the six-foot-five Taylor?

Sometime later Sitting Bull joined the show, though he wasn't required to wave a tomahawk at the Deadwood stage with the rest of the Indians. All he had to do was ride out into the arena, sit there in his brocade waistcoat and bright red neck scarf while the crowd booed, then ride slowly out. Later he'd sell autographed pictures to the crowds, keeping the money from them in addition to his pay.

Sitting Bull wasn't new to this life, I found out later when we played New York City. (I think it was in eighty-five, but anyone whose head is that set on the right place and precise date can look it up.) I went out with him between shows to look for some of his favorite white food, oyster stew, and we passed a place called "Eden Musée." He stopped and said he'd been exhibited there the year before.

"Bad place," he said in Sioux. "Much noise and many white faces all around, so close you could hardly breathe."

I was learning Sioux from Iron Tail, who would later pose for the head on the buffalo nickel. He had asked me to help him put his story into English. I'd learned enough of their language by then so that I could talk with the chief pretty well.

In fact, I had just been helping Iron Tail write about the U.S. Commission that tried to buy the Black Hills from the Sioux. Seven thousand Indians had attended that conference, he said. He also said that Little Big Man had wanted to fight, but that Spotted Tail and Spotted Bear had asked for seventy million dollars, while Red Cloud had asked that The People be guaranteed food for seven gener-

*In actual fact, Colonel Prentiss Ingraham wrote seven dime novels about Taylor, as well as a hundred or more about Buffalo Bill. These popular romances, like those of Ned Buntline, were known for their flowery prose and their total avoidance of fact.

ations. But Crazy Horse had said it best: "One does not sell the earth upon which The People walk," he told them.

Unfortunately, what one does not sell to the white man one eventually loses anyway. Most of the Sioux were now on reservations, or working in Wild West Shows. Or writing books about their experiences. It was one big race to the publishers, Children.

Sitting Bull not only had the crowds to face, he also had Jack following him around nearly every day, pencil and notebook in hand. One day Jack and I spotted him standing with his interpreter, Halsey, watching the riding tricks of a young girl who had recently joined the show. She had just picked a handkerchief off the ground with her teeth without slowing the horse's gallop.

"She's pretty good, isn't she," Jack said to the old chief.

"Stupid thing for a squaw to do," Sitting Bull said in Sioux. "I hope she finds a man to give her babies soon."

"The chief says he admires the young lady's skill very much," Halsey interpreted.

"Me too," Jack said. "And I've been wondering, Mr. Bull, why you give money to the children who flock around you," he rushed on, pencil poised. Halsey interpreted.

"Tell him I'm sick of his stupid questions," Sitting Bull said.

"The chief says the children looked hungry, so he helps them in hopes that they will one day help the children of his people," Halsey interpreted.

Jack was scribbling furiously. "And how does the chief feel about the crowds booing him for his crime against Custer?"

Halsey interpreted, changing "crime" to "heroic action."

"Tell him to go away," Sitting Bull said. "Tell him I write my own story."

Halsey said, "The chief says that Custer was a very brave man who unfortunately—"

I left Jack writing away in his notebook.

The season ended in St. Louis, and when the show went into winter quarters we left to spend the cold months with Dulsie. She had sold her interest in the Long Branch to Miss Kitty and had bought a place in Denver all on her own, with rooms in the back for us. We did odd jobs around the place and sometimes tended bar when the regular man was out.

And that was the pattern we followed for many years afterward, joining the Wild West Show in the spring and leaving it to spend the winter with Dulsie in Denver. We did that until the Wild West shows were mostly gone and Dulsie had moved on from Denver to California. But that was some time later.

Sitting Bull left the show to return to his People, and American Horse came off the reservation to replace him. I was always sorry Sitting Bull didn't return to the show with the trick horse Cody had given him, because a couple of years later he was murdered. I heard about that day from one who was there—how the Sioux were shot down in cold blood while Cody's present pranced and performed his tricks to the tunes of death. The horse was brought back to the show, later, and was quite an attraction.

Cody hired more girl trick riders and called them "cowgirls." He added Custer's massacre to the pageants and let Buck Taylor play the General, which might have been almost more than Jack could bear if Cody had not also relented and allowed him to wear his bullfight outfit and ride with the vaqueros in their roping and riding sequences.

I earned money to send my People by menacing the Deadwood stage, the emigrant train, and the settlers' cabins in various pageants. But my favorite was the miniature Battle of the Little Big Horn. I would almost have done that one free.

The high point of that pageant was when Colonel Cody rode out into the body-strewn tanbark at the end of the battle. He sat tall in his saddle and surveyed the silent scene, his handsome face in anguish. Backstage a slide was put into a light machine and the words TOO LATE flashed on the screen in back of him as the crowd roared. But I didn't care what they thought, and neither did the Sioux. After all, they had done this same show once before, with no rehearsal, and had done it better. That time the bodies didn't get up and walk away when the lights went down.

We played city after city and the crowds loved us. Who needed schools or books when they could see the history of the West in an afternoon, with some of the original cast? The Wyoming mountain backdrop might not be as big as the real thing, but it was big enough to hold your imagination for an hour or two. We played New York, and the boxes were filled with famous people, including Custer's widow. She got away before Jack could catch her, but he did manage to corner Mark Twain and tried to convince him to read a fellow professional's thousand-page manuscript about Custer. Twain declined with profuse regrets that his time didn't permit.

We went to England and performed for Sir George Grant's

queen, then toured Europe and saw lots of things—that big tower that had just been built in Paris, several palaces with real kings living in them, and even a few old friends. That journalist, Stanley, who had been interviewing prairie dogs back in Abilene in sixty-seven, turned up in England with some black people called Zulus. Cody hired them on right away as an added attraction, though no one knew their language. Then one day a big Pawnee made some signs to the Zulu chief and the chief answered in sign language so close to the Indian's they had no trouble understanding each other. This was not so surprising, since sign languages around the world tend to be somewhat alike. I've heard it said that Indian signs are similar to those used by the deaf, and that they were the basis for the army's Signal Corps.

I can't remember all the things we did, and the notebook Jack kept got lost in Chicago. It's too bad, too, because a lot of it was interesting—like the time Black Elk got left behind in Paris and then popped up like a cork when the show passed through there the following year. Jack got his story down but I've forgotten it.

How Jack lost his notebook is a story in itself, though. Because he also lost his job, and very nearly his skin.

Chicago was having the World's Columbian Exposition that year, and Buffalo Bill's Wild West and Congress of Rough Riders of the World set up for business on a lot between 62nd and 63rd streets and waited for the world to put its money down. Which it did.

The box office turned people away on opening day, and never stopped doing it thereafter. The crowds came to see the famous Cody, the Cossacks, the Uhlans, the Arabs and Syrians and what have you. They came to see the Indians get the sass beat out of them (except for that one sequence), and if that wasn't enough, they could go around to the Exposition and watch Little Egypt wiggle her belly on the Midway or ride the turning wheel that held thousands at a time.* They could wander through our campground and have their pictures taken with Annie Oakley or Buffalo Bill or Sitting Bull's horse, or with El Misterio if they happened our way.

Jack had set up a little table with pictures of himself for sale. He had wanted to go back to his Mystery Man outfit and sell copies of that dime novel, but he couldn't get more copies of it to sell. The publisher never answered any of his letters, and finally one of them

*Designed by George Washington Gale Ferris, this monster towered 250 feet above the Midway and carried thirty-six glass-enclosed cars, *each* of which could accommodate sixty passengers.

came back marked "addressee unknown." It was probably just as well, because we didn't get a large share of the crowd, which mostly preferred to hear Cody tell of his exploits and to look at the scalp of Yellow Hand that generally decorated the Colonel's table.

One day a little round woman came puffing up to the table and said, "All right, where is he?"

Jack looked startled but launched gamely into his speech. "There is plenty of time, madam, to buy a pic—"

"I don't want pictures, I want Colonel Cody," the woman said shortly. "Now where is he?"

"I believe he's over at the other side," Jack said, pointing toward the area where Cody and the Butlers had their tents.

"Then why did that cowboy send me over here?" the woman demanded.

"Ma'am, I don't know," Jack said. "But if he isn't at his tent I suppose he must be at the house. Let me escort you." He offered his arm.

At the mention of the house her bulldog face lit up, and she took Jack's arm. "Maybe you can help me after all. You're the first one I've talked to who's even heard of that house." She led him away.

I didn't see him till just before the afternoon performance and when he did appear he was a mess. He had a bruise on his jaw, his hat was crushed, and his shirt was half torn from his body. He gave me a weak smile.

"The strangest thing happened," he told me.

I waited.

"I took her over to the Colonel's tent, but the only people there were a couple of those cowgirls who were drinking his lemonade and having a good time. The lady asked them where the colonel was in a kind of harsh voice, and one of them asked her who wanted to know, and next thing the lady smacked the girl right over the head with her purse." He sighed and fingered a tatter of his shirt.

"What happen then?" I said. It never had been easy to get a complete story out of Jack.

"Well, she insisted I take her to that house. I told her I'd never been there and might get lost if I went too far from the campgrounds, but she wouldn't let up. So I went with her to find the house." He stopped again.

"Jack, tell whole story," I said. We'd never make the performance at this rate.

"Well, when we got there she ran right in yelling that she'd caught somebody this time, but there wasn't anyone there. So she grabbed up a poker and started smashing everything in sight. I tried to stop her." He pulled at a button on the ragged shirt and it dropped off. He watched it roll away and sighed.

"And . . ." I said.

"And that wasn't the worst part," he went on. "The worst part was when the owner came in, and it turned out we had the wrong house."

I had already started packing up our gear when Cody came striding our way. "Hey, you!" he roared at Jack. "Are you the damn fool that took my wife over to that house?"

"Your wife?"* Jack said. "Well, Bill, how was I to know—"

Cody started for Jack, but just then a young fellow came up and stared with wide eyes at the famous scout. "Lord, you're him," the boy said. I saw that he was holding a lariat in his hand with a big loose loop, like some of the rope twirlers do, but he wasn't trying any tricks with it now. He was gaping at Cody.

Bill got a big smile on his face. Out of the corner of his mouth he said, "Don't you boys go taking nothing you didn't come with." Then he put out his hand to the boy and said, "Yes, young man, I'm Buffalo Bill. The very same who rode for the Pony Express and supplied the train crews with buffalo meat and scouted for every general worth mentionin'. If you'll come on over to my tent, I have some autographed pictures available."

"Golly," the boy said. He went back to gaping.

"You do rope tricks, son?" Cody asked him. "Maybe you could show me a couple on the way."

"Golly," the boy said.

Bill was beginning to lose steam a little trying to hold up the conversation, but he didn't let his smile fade. "What's your name, son?" he asked.

"Gol— I mean, Rogers, sir. Will Rogers." He resumed his gaping.

"Well, let's head over thataway," Cody said, steering the boy toward the tent where the pictures were sold.

As they went out of earshot I could hear another "Golly," and I hoped the young fellow learned to talk a little better as he got older. "Golly" will stretch just so far.

---

*During Cody's unsuccessful petition for divorce in 1905 several incidents of this nature were cited. In one case Mrs. Cody destroyed a New York City hotel room when a woman answered the phone in Col. Cody's room—in another hotel.

We gathered up our stuff and went back to Denver to get an early start on our usual winter jobs. It wasn't till we unpacked the little trunk we'd been carrying that we discovered Jack's notebook was missing, along with some earlier notebooks he was using for his Custer memoirs. Luckily the big manuscript itself was all there, so the loss did not set him back unduly.

The following summer we tried a couple of other things, even working in Abilene for a while at a place called Parker Brothers that made horses for carousels. But it just wasn't the same as the Wild West Show, and we got tired of it pretty quickly. So we went back to Denver again, to give Jack a chance to finish up his book and arrange for its publication.

He had taken the big box of manuscript around to several publishing offices in person whenever we were in New York, but he never got past the reception desks with it. He said it was amazing how those editors ever got to read anything, seeing as how they were always either having lunch or "in conference." But he finally decided he'd wait till it was entirely finished before insisting that one of them cut a couple of his lunches short to read it.

He worked on it most of the time during the second winter after we left the show, and then began writing to publishers again. One of them replied that he would be glad to read the material, and Jack was all ready to jump on a train that minute.

"But, Jackie, he just said he'd *read* your stuff, not that he'd publish it," Dulsie argued.

"Yes, but I'm sure when I meet with him face to face he'll—"

"Crazy Fox," she interrupted. "You talk to him. Tell him it's foolish to stake so much on this feller's letter."

"Oh, all right," Jack said. "If you insist I'll send the manuscript first. But he'll undoubtedly want me to come East when he's read it."

When the manuscript came back, Jack went into a depression almost as bad as when he'd lost the ranch and Whitey. He burned the editor's letter, but I remember one part of it: "Your story is amusing in spots, but we didn't feel the humor held up consistently or that the events had enough inherent believability." A few nights later we found him burning the manuscript itself.

"Lordy, Jackie, why'd you do that?" Dulsie said. "I'm gonna hide that picture that French lady Rosie Bonner* made of you before

---

*Rosa Bonheur was a frequent visitor to the show in Paris, and her portrait of Cody is well-known. Unfortunately her portrait of Jack is lost to us.

you burn that too." She tried to put a hand on his shoulder but he shook it off and went to bed.

And he stayed there. Day after day. He would barely eat, and only then when Dulsie practically forced him. He wouldn't talk, and the only times he got up were to go the outhouse or to get a bottle of whiskey from the bar. He was making a sizable dent in Dulsie's stock.

One evening as he staggered back from the bar with a bottle tucked under his arm, Dulsie watched him with a frown. "I declare there must be some way I can get him up again," she said. A little later she disappeared into his room.

Next morning she was whistling around the kitchen, all smiles and energy. And Jack came out of his room a little later on, holding his head but asking for a big stack of flapjacks. He saw me watching him and said, "You know, I had some of those strange dreams again last night. This time I was lying in a field of wild flowers when this princess came up, and she wasn't wearing any—" He remembered Dulsie and stopped. "I've got to stop drinking that stuff," he said.

Dulsie's green eyes were sparkling as she brought a huge stack of pancakes to the table. And then she remembered something and went up front to the bar. She was back in a minute with a newspaper in her hand.

"Somebody left this Texas paper behind last night," she said, handing it to Jack. "I thought you might want it."

He opened it idly and then his eyes began to get wider and wider as he read. I got up and went around the table to look over his shoulder. I almost wished I hadn't. I read:

"Among the leading citizens of Pecos City now in El Paso is John Wesley Hardin, a leading member of the Pecos City bar."

The story went on to describe Hardin's wild background, so there could be no doubt about who the leading citizen was.

I looked at Jack's face and knew the quest was on again.

Chapter
12

In which Jack meets two
old enemies, and some scores
are settled at last.

"But, Jackie, that was so long ago," Dulsie argued. "You can't go traipsin' off to arrest a man who's already spent half his life in prison."

"I can too. In fact, I have to do it, for the honor of the Knight name."

Jack was about to launch into one of his lectures, so I headed him off. "What about Judge Gannon?" I reminded him. "If we go back, he arrest us."

"Oh, I doubt if he'll bother you," Dulsie said. "In fact, he ain't even a judge now, or much of anything else."

"How do you know?" I asked her.

"Because I heard about a little habit he had, a few years back, concerning a couple of young girls in Austin. So I fixed it up with them to put a photographer behind a curtain during their next party, and when the flash powder went off the old codger ran right into the streets in his underwear." She laughed. "Wish I'd been there to see it. Anyway, he sold Daddy's old place to Lonnie Harper for a real good price not long after that, and I believe he moved East somewhere."

"So he's not even in Texas," Jack said. "That settles it. I'll face Hardin at last. How do we get to El Paso from here?"

When Dulsie saw Jack was determined to go, she helped him get his white outfit cleaned up and even made him a mask, after another losing argument. Jack was determined to face Hardin exactly

189

the way he would have twenty years before. After all, he reasoned, it wasn't his fault that the man had been out of his reach all this time. Nothing had changed.

We decided to take a train down to Santa Fe and then buy horses there, so Dulsie took us to the depot the next morning, fussing all the way. "Lord knows I may not even be here myself when you get back. *If* you get back. I've been thinking about San Francisco lately more and more. I may just sell the place here and head west. Buy why am I tellin' *you* all this? You're likely gonna be planted down in Texas with Hardin's bullets in you."

As we got on the train she put a hand on my arm, and I could see she was fighting back tears. "You keep in touch," she said. "And try to keep Jackie in one piece, please?"

Jack smiled tolerantly and climbed aboard, carrying the little bag that contained his mask and gun. (Times were changing, Children, and even Jack could see that you couldn't move around Denver armed and wearing a mask.) I gave her hand a squeeze and promised to keep in touch, then followed him.

The train ride was as interesting as most, and I was glad to get down and stretch my legs in Santa Fe. Jack insisted that we go find a livery stable right away, before we looked for a hotel or food, so I asked directions in the telegraph office.

"There's one right down the street," the operator told me. "Run by a gimpy little feller, but he'll treat you fair's any hereabouts. Tell him Horace sent you."

We found the stable without any trouble, but I never got a chance to mention Horace. Because we had no sooner got through the door than a bent-over little man got up out of his chair and started limping toward Jack, fists poking at the air.

"You sonofabitch, I'll get you this time," Andrew wheezed. "You ain't got no mask to hide behind nor horse to kick me, so get ready to take your medicine." He could hardly keep his balance while he waved his fists, and I could see that he was in no condition to do any fighting.

Jack gave me a questioning look. "Do we know this man from somewhere?" he asked.

Andrew took a swing and fell down. I stooped to help him up, but he would have none of that. "You git the hell away from me," he gasped. "Both of you." He looked ready to cry, then started to crawl toward a far corner of the stable.

When he got there he began to pull himself up on the side of a stall. He finally made it, and then I saw why he had gone all the way over there. He was trying to reach a shotgun that was hanging on the wall, just above his reach.

"Dammit, I told Jimmie not to hang that up there," he mumbled. He tottered over to his chair and started dragging it back toward the shotgun. "Sonofabitch ruins my whole life and then he says he don't even know me." He paused and waved a withered arm at Jack again. "Well you wait till I git that damned gun down from there and I'll show you. Maybe after I've blowed your goddamn head off you'll remember me." He started hobbling toward the gun again, dragging the chair and cursing.

Jack shook his head. "There must be a more polite livery man than this around here," he said.

As we left Andrew was trying to get his foot up on the chair.

We bought horses from a stable across town and decided to buy our supplies and ride out that night, in case Andrew did manage to get the shotgun down off its pegs. We camped a few miles south, on the banks of the Rio Grande, which we'd decided to follow on down to El Paso.

In the morning Jack put on his white clothes and mask again and strapped on his gun. As we moved out the only thing that was missing was the big white horse.

"It feels good to be on the trail again," Jack said. "And this time Hardin won't be able to hide."

We traveled at a leisurely pace, making camp early to give Jack a chance to practice with his gun. He claimed he'd grown rusty, but I couldn't see much difference in his markmanship. Behind his target was still the safest place to stand.

I spent a lot of time trying to figure out how to keep this trip from ending up with Jack either in jail or under a tombstone, but I couldn't come up with a thing. I could have refused to go along, but that wouldn't have stopped him. And somehow, after all these years, I couldn't bear to think of him dying alone. I considered getting us lost, but that would have been hard to do with the river right there to follow. So we traveled on, each day getting a few miles closer to El Paso and that well-known member of the Texas bar, John Wesley Hardin.

It was August when we finally rode into El Paso, and nearly hot enough to melt the bullets in your gun. We stabled the horses and went to find a hotel room, a bath, some food, a drink, and Wes Hardin, in that order.

The saloon we ended up in, several hours later, was called The Acme, and it was a middling place even for West Texas. It was early, and there were only a few people in the place when we took a table, so Jack's mask didn't cause quite the commotion it had been known to in the past. It did bring the bartender over pretty quick, though.

"If you're plannin' to rob this place, I'll tell you right now you're wastin' your time," he said. "We ain't took in enough money yet to pay for your bullets."

"It's all right, we're circus folks," I told him, hoping there was a circus somewhere in the area. He nodded, but didn't look convinced.

"I am seeking the notorious outlaw, John Wesley Hardin," Jack told him in the voice he usually saved for lectures about honor.

"Yeah? Well he ain't here. Leastways not yet. He does come in sometimes, though, to shoot dice and have a few belts. Ol' Wes sure does like his liquor," the bartender said, looking at us expectantly.

We took the hint and bought a bottle, to get the dust of New Mexico out of our mouths. A while later we bought another one for the dust of West Texas, and we were halfway through it when the bartender came over again.

"You said you were looking for Wes Hardin," he said to Jack. "Well, he's here."

"He is? Where?" Jack asked, trying to focus his eyes through the slits of the mask. "I don't see him."

The bar was crowded by now, and I didn't see Hardin at first either. But then I did, sitting near the back end of the bar in a frock coat, playing with a dice cup. He'd aged a lot since Abilene, and looked much older than his forty-two years would account for. Prison will do that, I guess.

Jack was still peering around the room, adjusting the mask to get a better view. "Point him out to me," he told the bartender.

"Right down there at the end of the bar," the man said. "But if you got any trouble in mind, you save it for outside or I'll put a load of buckshot in you."

Jack was staring at Hardin. "No, you're wrong," he said finally. "That isn't Hardin. I ought to know what he looks like, after all those posters I've put up about him." He took another pull from the bottle. "It's no good trying to fool me, you know. I'll know him when I see him."

"Suit yourself," the bartender said. He went back to the bar and said a few words to Hardin. Hardin glanced our way and shrugged. They started rolling the dice, and we went back to our bottle while I tried to think of some way to get Jack out of there before he decided to start questioning more people.

I was still trying when Jack took hold of my arm and pointed toward the door. "That's him," he said.

I looked to where he was pointing and saw a stocky man with a heavy black beard standing just inside the door. He was wearing a hat low over his eyes, and peering intently down the bar. In that light he did look almost as mean as Jack's drawing of Hardin, I thought.

The man began walking toward the back, and that's when I noticed the gun in his hand. Jack had started to get up, but I clamped my hand on his arm and said, "Not now. Wait."

The stocky man walked slowly along the bar, toward where Hardin was shaking the dice cup. Hardin rolled the dice out onto the bar and said, "There, now. You've got four sixes to beat."

Just then the stocky man raised his gun and pulled the trigger. There was a blast and a flash, and when the smoke began to clear I saw Hardin sprawled on the floor.

"My God, he's killed another man!" Jack shouted. He jumped and pointed at the stocky man. "I saw the whole thing!"

"Well who in hell didn't," snapped the bartender. He walked over to the stocky man and held his hand out. "Now there, Mr. Selman, maybe you better give me the gun," he said.

"Mr. Selman?" Jack said. "His name isn't Selman. That's John Wesley Hardin, and I have first claim on him."

"What in hell are you jabberin' about," the bartender said. "That's Hardin, there on the floor, like I told you. Somebody go get Young John, or the sheriff or somebody."

Jack stared at the slight figure sprawled on the floor, his head in a widening pool of blood. "You mean that really was Hardin?" he said at last. Slowly he took off the mask and put it in his pocket, then leaned over the body for a closer look. "He doesn't look a thing like his picture," he said, shaking his head. And then he crumpled slowly to the floor in a dead faint.

I got him back to the hotel and dumped him into bed, then returned to the saloon to hear the story of Mrs. McRose and Young

John Selman and the whole stupid business that had cost Hardin his life and that would probably cost Old John Selman his freedom, at least.* Hardin wasn't much good, I guess, but it seemed like a bad way for any man to die.

Walking back toward the hotel in the sweltering heat of an August night in West Texas, it occurred to me that Jack's quest was really over at last. I wondered where we'd go now.

We went back to Denver, stopping to sell the horses back to the stable in Sante Fe. I figured it might help Jack's mood a little to get a couple of good meals and a few drinks inside him anyway. He was not in the kind of depression he'd fallen into after losing the ranch, but he was still very quiet, as if he was trying to figure things out.

After we sold the horses we got a room for the night in a place near the Governor's Palace, and then we went out into the streets of adobe buildings to visit several of their numerous saloons. I kept a wary eye out for Andrew and his shotgun.

Next day, having demonstrated the beneficial effects of soap, whiskey and a good night's sleep, I was ready to start for Denver. But Jack said he had some errands to attend to, and disappeared for the whole morning. When he came back he was carrying a large box.

"What that?" I asked him.

He grinned. "Never mind. You'll find out when the time comes."

The box went with our gear on the train, and I had completely forgotten it until we were back at Dulsie's and had finished telling her all about El Paso.

"So that's the end of John Wesley Hardin," Dulsie said. "Well. Then I guess that's the end of Jack's quest, too. Maybe you boys had better be thinking of what to do next, huh?"

"That was never in doubt," Jack said, smiling. He got up and went into his room, and when he came out I saw he was carrying that box from Sante Fe. He put it down and took the lid off, then picked up a bundle of white material and handed it to Dulsie.

She smiled. "You got me a present? Aw, Jackie, you didn't have to do that." She stood up and shook out the bundle, and as it unfolded her smile froze. It took me a few seconds longer to realize

*The shooting of Hardin occurred on August 19, 1895. Old John Selman was charged and planned a plea of self-defense, despite having shot Hardin in the back of the head. Selman was killed in a gun duel himself before the case went to trial.

what it was, but by then I was paying more attention to Dulsie. I've never seen that combination of pleasure and pain on any face before or since.

"Jackie," she said. "This is a wedding gown."

"Of course. Don't you like it? It is supposed to be white, isn't it?"

"But I don't understand, honey. What's it *for*?"

Jack looked surprised. "Why, for our wedding, of course. Now that my quest is over, I'm free to marry the lady of my dreams." He thought about that a minute and began to blush. "I mean, the lady to whom my life and my quest have been dedicated."

Dulsie seemed to be about to laugh, cry and curse all at once. She stared at the dress, then at me, and then at Jack's expectant face. And then she sat down, as if someone had let the air out of her.

"If it's not the right size we can have it fixed," Jack said in the silence.

She sighed, and smiled sadly. "I know, Jackie. But it has been a long quest, you know? And while you were roaming around looking, you just sorta lost track of the time, I think." She looked at me as if pleading for help. "Jackie, you've spent your life chasing a dream, but the clock didn't stop ticking. The world kept turning," she whispered, "and we got older." A tear was rolling down her nose, and she wiped it away. "You aren't a young man anymore, neither of you." She sighed. "And let's face it. I'm not a young girl, either, though I'll always love you for seeing me that way."

"I dedicated all my deeds of honor to you," he said, his voice filled with more pain and confusion than I could ever remember. "I mean, you are my lady fair, just like in that book about us." He squared his shoulders and set his jaw. "That's just all there is to it," he told her. "You *have* to marry me."

Dulsie seemed to brace herself. "No I don't," she said, "I don't have to do a single damned thing I don't want to do, now or ever, with you or anybody else." She put the dress back in the box. "Fact is, I'm not even stayin' in Denver. I've hired a manager for this place, and I'm leavin' for San Francisco next week. I was hopin' you boys would come along, but..." Before she could finish, Jack stalked from the room.

I found him sitting on the porch swing.

"By God, we've been spurned," he said finally.

He was determined to leave Dulsie's house that very day, and he refused even to say good-bye to her before we left.

"No, she has betrayed a lifelong trust," he insisted. "And I'll probably never have any occasion to use the wedding dress now. Do you suppose I can sell it?"

We left the dress behind and rode out to find the Wild West, but as we rode I couldn't help thinking about what Dulsie had said. We had remained children, living in a dream world. Was that true?

Yes, I decided, it probably was, for Jack at least. But my life was not that simple. Because I had never shared that dream, nor lived in Jack's make-believe world.

My problem was that I had never found a world to live in at all.

We had a pretty wide choice of shows to work, since by now everyone with a dollar and an idea seemed to be in the Wild West business. And we hadn't been blackballed by Buffalo Bill, it turned out. In fact, most owners were so delighted with the idea of Mrs. Cody smashing up the Colonel's love nest that they offered us jobs even before they'd quit laughing.

We worked in several shows over the next few years, but we avoided some, such as the one put together by Frank James and Cole Younger. It wasn't so much that I didn't trust them, but I figured they'd been away so long they probably didn't know what the public wanted now. And we skipped the one with Calamity Jane in it in case she had any old scores to settle. We were with Texas Jack's show for a while, but left when it went to Europe and Africa. I felt there was at least one Indian who had crossed the big water too many times already. Besides, there was always another show.

We did another exposition along in there somewhere, this time in St. Louis. We were with Pawnee Bill's show then, I think, or maybe the one run by Colonel Mulhall. Anyway, we were there and saw the electric lights, ate ice cream and finally rode that big wheel of Ferris's, which had somehow been moved down from Chicago.

It was just after St. Louis that we hired on at the 101 Ranch in Ponca City, Oklahoma. A man named Miller and his sons ran this outfit from a big white-columned house that reminded me of my uncle's place in the Territory. They wore white suits and called themselves colonels, and they liked to hold open house for the public, to show how Western life was lived. The spread looked almost like a small city by the time the father died, and after that the sons got more and more interested in the theatrical side of the operation.

The roundups they held, which the public came out to watch

from carriages or from long picnic tables set up all over the place, got to be almost like Wild West shows themselves. I can't remember the year the first really big one was held, but I do remember that Geronimo was there and that it was a fine day for a cattle roundup, and for the calf-roping and riding contests that followed it. They even staged an attack on a wagon train by over two hundred Indians, most of them hired on for the occasion. Jack drove one of the wagons without mishap, and once again I got to play the part of an Indian.

Jack had wanted to enter the calf-roping and bulldogging contests, but after he watched the performance of a black fellow named Bill Pickett he changed his mind. This Pickett fellow had figured out a sure-fire way to throw a calf. He'd jump off his horse onto it, get a hold across its neck, and then bite the terrified animal on the nose. It brought them down every time, but it also brought a look of disgust to the faces of many watchers. One old cowboy wrinkled his nose and said, "All in all I think I'd just as soon bite the other end."

Jack looked at the nostrils of the calves in the pen and agreed. "They all look like they've got colds to me," he said.

At the end of the day they held a big buffalo barbecue, though I can't figure where they could have got the buffalo. By then the herds were long gone and the remaining buffalo were so few that they were being counted and cataloged—so many in this zoo, so many on that ranch or in that Wild West show. But wherever they found it, the buffalo count went down by one that day, and the public ate it up.

The public was so enthusiastic about the whole thing, in fact, that the Millers decided to take their show on the road. We did a big exhibition in Jamestown, up in New York State, and by the time we got back to Ponca City, Oklahoma was a state. The Indian Territories were gone.

We'd avoided Denver since Jack's argument with Dulsie, but we went back there with a party of 101 people just before the big war started in Europe. The occasion was a sad one indeed: the auctioning off of Buffalo Bill's Wild West Show to pay off his creditors. Trainloads of animals and equipment were sold that day, including camels, sacred cows, Cody's horse and silver mounted saddle, even the gilded bandwagon. Everything was sold, and nearly every other show owner was on hand to pick up bargains for his own outfit. Prairie schooners went for twenty dollars, I recall.

I had hoped to see Dulsie, even if Jack refused to, but her manager said she seldom visited the Denver place these days. Her business interests in San Francisco were keeping her pretty busy, he said, but when he found out who I was he rummaged around and found a note on that familiar scented paper addressed to me. It said that she hoped Jackie and I would come visit her, and that there would always be rooms for us in her house.

We didn't return with the 101 crowd, but for once it wasn't because of anything Jack had done. The 101 Ranch was planning a trip to Europe and we had decided not to go along, so this seemed like a good time for me to go see my People, and take them the money I'd put aside. Jack stayed behind in Denver, and when I got back there he had hooked on with the Sells-Floto Circus, which had been put together by some people who owned the *Denver Post*. They had bought the Sells name from those four brothers, but Floto was borrowed from the sports editor on the paper because they liked the sound.

I stopped by Dulsie's saloon again, and there was another letter there for me. She said she had decided to sell out her interests in Denver and San Francisco and move down to Los Angeles. So if we were ever out that way . . .

The Sells-Floto Circus was playing in Cheyenne at that time, so I joined it there and found Jack still driving the wagon pursued by the screaming Indians. I fell right into my usual role. And I found that another old trooper was there in his usual role, too. The owners of this show had been partly to blame for Cody's financial troubles, but now he was reduced to working for them as a hired performer. He was an old man now and often too ill (or too drunk) to entertain the customers in his tent. But when show time came he would stagger to his horse, someone would help him mount, and he would ride slowly around the arena. He no longer helped save the stages or arrived TOO LATE at Little Big Horn or gave shooting exhibitions from the backs of galloping horses. He just rode around, accepting the cheers and applause, and then exited to fall off the horse into the waiting arms of his helpers. Mrs. Cody was traveling with him, but he was so sick and she was so preoccupied with him that neither of them remembered people from the past—even house guides in bullfight costumes.

I told Jack about Dulsie's newest move and suggested that we ought to go visit her, but he was adamant. "She never even apologized for the way she treated me," he said. "If you'll remember, I even paid good money for that dress. No sirree, not without some sorries being said."

A little while later Cody tried to buy the 101 Ranch show, but without success. I guess he had figured the price would be low, since a lot of their horses and equipment had been impounded by the British government as a kind of forced contribution to their war effort. Even so, he couldn't raise the price, and instead he took a job with them, again selling his famous name and his feeble presence for a salary. His creditors wanted their money, so a sick old man was in the saddle again.

We returned to the 101 about the same time, and we were all there for the next couple of years, until the only thing that could stop Cody did. In 1917 he died. That must have disappointed those creditors, and it's a wonder they didn't have him stuffed so they could parade him around those arenas forever. In actual fact, his body remained unburied for six months while Denver and Cody, Wyoming, argued about which one would have the valuable honor of his presence. Denver won.

His old friend Johnny Baker put together a new show with new owners, and we went out again the next season as the Ray O. Archer Presents Jess Willard (Himself in the Flesh) and the Buffalo Bill Wild West Show and Circus. Iron Cloud went along to lead the Sioux and Flying Hawk led the Arapahoes, and as usual Jack was driving and I was chasing the wagon.

Jess Willard was from Kansas and was sometimes billed as the Pottowatomie Giant. The reason the public was eager to see him was that he had also been billed as the Great White Hope when he beat Jack Johnson back in 1914 to become the world champion prize-fighter. But however you spelled it, he was no relation of mine and I steered clear of him. Jack thought he was wonderful, and never tired of hearing how he had put that black man in his place.

Neither did the crowds, because his whole act consisted of demonstrating and explaining how he had done that one thing and showing off his big, gaudy championship belt, which had diamonds all over it and Willard's likeness in two places. In between he would sign pictures in his tent for the crowd while Jack stood by gaping in admiration or ran off to fetch the big man a fresh beer. He was six feet, six inches tall and weighed 250 pounds, so he could hold a great deal of beer. A couple of years after he left the show I read that he had got the tar beat out of him by Jack Dempsey. Well, I can tell you that that wasn't the first time it happened to him.

What happened was this: One day while the Pottowatomie Giant was somewhere else Jack was hanging around his tent talking to the crowd that was waiting for the champion. For some reason he decided to show off the fancy championship belt, and when he had dug it out of its special case one of the people asked how it looked on Willard.

"I'll show you," Jack said.

He put it around his waist and hooked the clasp, but when he let go of it the whole thing slid down over his hips and clattered onto the ground. He tripped trying to untangle his feet from the belt, and when he had finally got back up with the belt in his hands he discovered the clasp was broken. He also discovered Jess Willard, who had come up behind the crowd and was staring at him with bulging eyes and a red face.

"By God, Knight, I'll teach you to destroy the belt of the world's champion fighter," he roared, pushing through the crowd and sending bodies flying in all directions. He made a lunge for Jack but tripped over a tent rope and went sprawling in the dust. He sat up looking dazed and gave a thunderous belch.

"I'll have this fixed in just a minute," Jack told him, fiddling nervously with the belt clasp.

Willard gave another roar and tried to leap up, but this time he landed on his hands and knees. He shook his big head like a dog and belched again. I had a feeling he had been indulging in his favorite pastime, and probably had several gallons of beer in him. He glared at Jack.

"If I can just get this piece here back together with this piece here—" Jack held the two pieces together to demonstrate, and a diamond jumped off the buckle and landed on the ground in front of Willard.

It seemed like everyone wanted to return the diamond to Willard at the same time, and in seconds there was a great pile of people cursing and grabbing at the diamond and one another. One of them grabbed at Jack, who dropped the belt and jumped out of the way.

I picked the belt up and tossed it into the pile of Willard's belongings in the corner of the tent, then grabbed Jack and shoved him out of the way. By then Willard was on his feet, cursing and throwing bodies all over the place. He might have cleared the place if one of the men hadn't snatched up a tent stake and whacked him a pretty good one on the side of his head.

A whistle blew and a policeman came running, and within no time Willard was alone on the ground. The policeman jabbed his nightstick into Willard's ribs and demanded to know what the hell all the commotion was about.

I had been edging Jack away from the scene, but he stopped and said, "Wait a minute. I have to return this to Mr. Willard." He held out his palm with the diamond glittering in the middle of it.

I looked at the diamond, then back to where Willard was staggering to his feet. He shook his big head groggily and peered around him with eyes that seemed not to focus.

The policeman looked up at Willard and took a couple of steps backward. "Pardon me, sir," he said. "But can you tell me what started all that ruction, please?"

Willard blinked. "Some sonofabitch named Knight started it," he said. "And when I catch him I'm gonna tear him apart."

"Well, maybe I can mail it to him," Jack said, disappearing around the corner of a tent.

A few minutes later we were standing on a strange street in a strange town, with everything we owned in the world in one little bag apiece.

Jack looked up the street one way, then down it in the other direction. There was very little to see. He sat down on the front step of a building and gave a long, weary sigh.

"You know," he said. "Circus life just isn't as much fun as it used to be."

Chapter

13

In which we travel to California,
and reach the end of the trail.

As I stood there on the empty street, I had to admit he was right. The Wild West shows were dying out now, and the circuses were changing to give more prominence to acrobats and animal acts and the like. For that matter, the whole West had changed. The cattle drives and the cowtowns were long gone, and the land was filled with farms and herds of sheep where the longhorns had once been driven to market.

It came to me then that there really was no place left for two cowboys to ride, no towns I wanted to see or things I wanted to do. One of Henry Ford's Model-T cars came chugging down the quiet street, filling the air with clatter and stink as if to emphasize what I had been thinking: There was a new time coming, and I wasn't at all sure how Jack and I fit into it.

I remembered that Dulsie had written a while back, when we were still at the 101, and had given her Los Angeles address. I reminded Jack, expecting an argument. To my surprise he just gave me a weary look and shrugged.

So we went to the train station and spent most of our remaining money on two tickets to Los Angeles.

In fact, Dulsie was living very well now, in a big house up on a hill near a little town called Hollywood. She had long since put behind her the saloons of Kansas and Colorado and San Francisco. Now she called herself Mrs. Carruthers, though I couldn't recall that there had ever been a Mr. Carruthers. A small sign near the gate said: "Mrs. Carruthers' Home for Young Ladies."

Dulsie was no longer a young girl, but she looked almost as

202

healthy as ever. Her dresses, though still pretty colorful, fitted her better than the ones in the old days. Her hair still had a lot of yellow in it, and her smile was like sunshine.

"You two look like you've been run over by a streetcar," she told us the day we arrived. "You'd better get washed up or my girls will lose all their gentlemen callers." She looked at Jack's frayed and dirty white clothes and sighed. "Looks like we'll have to get you some new things, though. The stuff you got on looks like somebody's been scrubbing out spittoons with it."

One of the girls took us up to the room Dulsie had for us, and offered to stay and help us get to our baths. Jack explained that we'd be undressing, and that she'd better leave before she saw things a young girl shouldn't see. She went out, laughing like he'd made a big joke.

"Dulsie always was a big-hearted woman," Jack said as the girl left. "Look how she has always taken in all these young girls and given them a good, wholesome home. Not many women would have done that."

He was right on that score. She had made a life's work of it, you might say.

"But she still owes me an apology," he added.

We bathed and put on clean clothes, and then we went to have supper with Dulsie in her own private dining room. She smiled when we came in, and then she looked again at Jack, in his thread-bare white clothes and scuffed black boots, and for a minute she got a funny look on her face. I looked at him too, and saw something I had never really noticed before. His hair was now white, almost as gleaming as the clothes he had once worn. It made me think of that big stallion he'd had, years ago.

And then I looked in the mirror behind Dulsie's chair and saw that my hair had also turned white. Strange that I had never really thought about that before.

The table was set with big silver candlesticks and glasses that caught the light and sparkled. The candle flames made Dulsie's green eyes gleam, and for a minute she looked like the girl who'd had the bug down her dress back in Cottonwood, so many years ago. But when she smiled I saw the lines around her eyes.

"Well, don't you two look purty," she said.

Jack pulled out a chair and sat down, and his knees popped like breaking twigs. It suddenly hit me then that he was an old man, or close to it. I began counting back in my mind from the first time

I'd seen him, and was surprised at the figure I got. I had never really thought about how old we were before. We could both have been grandfathers many times, if either of us had had children to give us grandchildren.

"What's for dinner?" Jack asked. "I could eat a buffalo, hoofs and all."

"I think Cora has fixed some beef, but if you'd rather have buffalo hoofs I can probably find some in the house. With all these girls and their friends, we keep most everything you can think of on hand."

Jack ate his dinner as if he hadn't eaten for weeks, and Dulsie watched him chomp and smack with a smile like a mother watching her baby suck milk. When Jack was finished he looked up and discovered we were still there. "You got any ice cream?" he asked.

We stayed on at Dulsie's, and without ever being asked we began to help with the house and grounds. The property was very large ("My girls are sometimes high-spirited, and neighbors might complain," Dulsie had explained), and California was a place where things grew fast and needed tending. Or planting, since Jack never had got weeds and flowers straight. He could undo a month's work in an hour with his sickle.

It was pleasant enough, even though Jack spoke very little to Dulsie, as if still awaiting that apology. I figured he'd have a long wait, but something else had been bothering me for some time. Finally I caught Dulsie out in the yard one day and asked her to sit down on a bench.

"Something's biting you, I can tell," she said. "If any of those girls have been bothering you or Jackie you just tell me and I'll tan their little bottoms for them."

"No, it's not the girls." I tried to think how to put it. "It's living off you like this, I guess. It just doesn't seem right to sleep in a bed and eat food someone else is paying for."

"Why? I don't need your money, Crazy Fox. You must know that by now."

"I know. But it just isn't right for a man to lay around and not earn his keep."

"You're earning it right now," she said, pointing at the hedge shears in my hand. But she must have understood what I meant, because she put a hand on my arm and smiled. "You're a proud bunch, you redskins. Let me see what I can think of. With all the businessmen I get a chance to meet, there should be something I can find."

Just then Jack came walking toward us, grinning and holding up a big white flower. "Isn't this pretty?" he said. "I picked it for you, Dulsie." He tried to attach it to the front of her dress but ended up dropping it. When he tried to pick it up there was a look of pain of his face, and Dulsie put a hand on his arm to stop him.

"It's all right, Jackie," she said. "We can get another one. But thank you anyway." She turned to me and said, "Let me think about what we were discussing a while, okay?"

As they walked away together I knew one thing anyway. Jack had decided to forgive her.

As it turned out, she didn't have to think about it. Because the next day, while we were trimming the front hedges, a big motorcar came screeching around the bend in the road, followed by a police truck with what looked like about thirty men in uniforms hanging off it. Then more cars came, and before long they were all screeching and lurching around as if the drivers were on peyote and the cars had been eating loco weed. They kept heading straight at one another and then swerving off at the last minute. And by now the policemen had either jumped or fallen off their truck and were running all over the place. We dropped our shears and went down to watch.

After a while I noticed one man yelling and waving from across the road. "Hey, you guys, get outta this shot," he roared.

We hadn't heard any shots, so we didn't move.

"What're you, deaf?" he screamed. "Move outta the scene."

Dulsie had heard all the commotion and had come down to see what was happening. The man turned to her and shouted, "Miz Carruthers, can't you get those fellas to move? They're gawking in the scene." He was talking through some kind of horn, pointing toward where the cars and policemen were still racing around in circles.

"Hi, Jerry," Dulsie yelled, and gave a big wave. "Come on, boys," she said to us. "If they have to shoot a scene more than once they get in a snit."

We went back to the porch and sat down, and Dulsie told us about the pictures that moved. She seemed to know all about them and how they were made. "Lordy, you just wouldn't believe it, Jackie. They build whole towns just for one movie. And one of them looks just like Cottonwood, I'll swear. The buildings haven't got any backs to them, but if you just stand out in the street you can almost hear old Sam yelling in his saloon, rest his soul."

"Do they pay people to ride in these moving pictures?" I asked her. It sounded almost like the Wild West shows to me.

"They sure do. They have actors playing the main parts, and they hire lots of other people they call extras to make up crowds in saloons and the like. You know, like if they were doing a story about Abilene, say, and they were filming a big gunfight between Hickok and some cowboy—"

"You mean like Wes Hardin?" Jack interrupted.

"Right," she said. "Then they'd need people to be Hickok and Hardin and lots of others to be the people in town."

Jack hadn't been paying much attention up till then, but I could see he was getting interested. "You say they pay people money to just ride around or stand in the street?"

"Sure, honey, and good money too. If I was a mite younger I'd try it myself." She got a dreamy look on her face. "Might be kind of fun being back in Abilene in those days. Specially if it's only pretend."

We sat sipping drinks Cora brought out while the cars kept racing around and the policemen kept running into each other down in the street. Finally, when I'd begun to wonder how much more punishment they could take, the man with a horn yelled, "That's great, boys. Everybody back to the cars and we'll go do Gloria's railroad scene." In a few seconds they were all gone. The street was dead quiet in the California afternoon, except for the wind rustling the palm trees.

The next day Jack disappeared. No one had seen him leave, and no one knew where to start looking for him. And, since he had not been away from the place on his own, Dulsie was sick with worry. She paced around the big house wringing her hands, and for once she even lost her temper with the girls.

"You girls quit giggling and get some clothes on, in case we get company," she shouted at them. Then she saw me in the doorway and said, "Lordy, Crazy Fox, the police may be bringing what's left of him home any minute and they're running around in their drawers."

We had several cups of coffee and finally lunch, but still there was no sign of Jack. Dulsie went outside and began pacing up and down the walk. "Where could he have gone?" she kept asking. "How would he get there?"

She wondered if she should call the police. "Lord knows they owe me a few favors," she said. "But I don't want Jackie coming home in a paddy wagon." She didn't call them.

And then suddenly he appeared, strolling up the walk as if he had never been anywhere. Dulsie ran to him. "Are you all right, Jackie?" she asked. And then, "Where in blue hell have you been? We've been worried sick."

"Why?" he asked innocently. "I just went down to town to find out where they made those moving pictures." Then he saw me and said, "Hey, Crazy Fox, we're in the movies!"

He was breathing hard and looked tired, but he also looked as happy as a kid with a new pony. Dulsie made him sit down on a bench and yelled at Jeannie to bring out some water. I watched Jeannie running across the lawn, as graceful as a young filly, and wondered if it was true that she could twist herself around things like a pretzel.

"Are you listening?" Jack said. "There's this big place called a studio, and they're making a moving picture about a fellow we knew back at the 101, Tom Mix. I got us both jobs as extras." He gave me a serious look and said, "Of course, I had to agree that you'd play an Indian."

Dulsie insisted on driving us down to the studio for our first day as actors, so we all got into her big blue Pierce-Arrow ("It's the same color as them little Texas flowers," Dulsie had explained) and roared off down a big wide street, with Jack pointing out the trail he had followed the day before. It turned out he didn't remember it too well, so we ended up driving around for a while, with Dulsie showing us the sights.

"That's where I hear tell the first picture was made," she said at one point, waving toward a kind of ordinary looking building. But a little farther on we came to something that wasn't ordinary at all, and she didn't have to point it out. It was a mess of big fat columns with elephants and the like on top of them, and a flight of stairs you could have driven a Texas trail herd up with room to spare. "That's where D.W. made one of his big pictures a while back," she said. "I believe it was called 'Intolerance,' or something like that. I don't guess all this stuff is much use for anything else, but I suppose they hate to tear it down after going to so much trouble to build it."

Finally Jack recognized a street and we drove down it to a big gateway. "This is the studio," Jack said. "I just hope we're not late for work."

Dulsie was reading the big sign over the gate. "You know, I think I own stock in this company. I'll have to get Marvin to check out my portfolio, but I'm pretty sure I do."

A man in uniform came out of a little building and walked slowly toward the car. Dulsie squeezed a big bulb on the door and a cow mooed at the astonished man, who walked faster. When he saw who it was he waved her through the gate, yelling for Dulsie to give Jeannie his love.

We drove down a wide street through crowds of people in all kinds of strange looking clothes. They were all rushing around in every direction, just like at show time in Bill Cody's company. Dulsie swung the big car around a corner into a street called Front Street and stopped right behind a man with one of those speaking horns. She gave a squeeze on the bulb again, and when the cow mooed the man nearly fell down jumping out of the way.

"What the hell do you think—" the man stopped yelling and started laughing. "Dulsie, you do that once more and you're liable to see a grown man wet his pants." He came over and helped her out of the car.

"You boys stay out of trouble now," she said. She walked away with the man toward a building whose sign said "Jail," and they disappeared inside.

So we stood around for a while, which turned out to be good practice for our new jobs as extras. Whether the cameras were running or people were arguing about who was supposed to be doing what, the extras mostly stood around. Sometimes we walked back and forth, but standing was the biggest part of it.

In a while Dulsie came back out of the jail with the man, and I heard him saying, "Dulsie, honey, I don't even know how that fella got in here yesterday, but I never told him we'd hire him. I just said for him to come back tomorrow. God, Dulsie, I thought they'd stop him at the gate."

"Well, they didn't stop us," she said. "And now that they're here, I don't see why you can't use them. I mean, one of them's an honest-to-God Indian, and you ain't got a lot of those around here."

The man looked toward us and shook his head. "Okay," he told her. "But you'll sure owe me one for this."

She laughed and gave him a big kiss, then called over to us to behave and do what the man said. "I'll come and get you this afternoon," she said, and drove off down the street. We could hear that cow mooing all the way to the gate.

So we became actors.

The first thing we learned was that you weren't supposed to get in front of a camera unless told to by your "director." The second was that you had to look where the action was. During the seventh or eighth try at filming a bank robbery, I noticed that one of the girls from the dance-hall scene was having some trouble getting the top of her dress to stay up. She reminded me of Dulsie, a long time ago, and I guess I was staring.

"Hey, you Indian there!" somebody was screaming. "Jesus, Manny, get that guy to quit watching the dame and pay some attention to the goddamn bank robbery, will you?"

In this particular movie I was supposed to be an old Indian, which was fairly easy, and Jack was a storekeeper. After the first day he flatly refused to pretend he was an old man any longer.

"I don't see why I can't be an outlaw," he told me. "They've got a whole bunch of them in this picture, and they even wear masks some of the time."

After a while I could see there was no way to talk him out of it. I went to talk to the director.

"What do you mean, he wants to play an outlaw?" the man said. He was pretty short-tempered most of the time, and I figured he wasn't likely to spend a lot of time discussing the matter. "Hell, he's probably close to sixty."

Not so close, I thought, but I didn't talk about age any further. Instead I pointed out that Jack was tall, that he was wearing his own outfit which was authentic (a word the director liked to use a lot), and that you wouldn't see his face behind the mask anyway. Besides, one of the men playing an outlaw had busted his leg pretending to fall off a horse just a few days before. I figured Jack could do that without breaking anything, with all the practice he had had at it.

"All right, all right," the director said. "I'll try him in Irving's role, but if he fouls up he's out."

I thanked him, and as I left to tell Jack about it I was wondering how he could foul up when about all he had to do was stand around and not say anything.

That afternoon, while they were doing scenes that didn't need extras in them, I walked over to another place where other pictures were being made. This was a story about really mean outlaws who wore black hats and very clean-looking cowboys who wore white hats. The main white hat was a new actor named Buck Jones that everybody said was better than Mix, though I had doubts about what either one of them would be worth on a cattle drive. Still, I stopped to watch while they were doing a part of the story about Jones being chased by some of the outlaws. They kept riding in a big circle around a large rock, and every time the outlaws started catching up someone would jump out and wave at them to ride slower.

On about the fourth time around the rock, one of the outlaws fell off his horse. Something about the way he landed looked very familiar, so I walked over and helped him up. He was a young fellow, and his mask had slipped around till he could hardly see.

"Thank you," he said, fixing the mask. "I think they gave me a bad horse. I'm a good rider, ordinarily."

His voice sounded like an Easterner, but his face kept looking familiar. And it wasn't just the mask, either.

I stayed around till they finished that part of the story, and when the young man went to get coffee I joined him at the lunch wagon. He had taken off the mask.

"You keep reminding me of someone," I told him. "Are you from Texas, maybe?"

"No. I grew up mostly right here in Los Angeles, though I did spend several years in a school back East." He looked at me oddly, probably noticing that I was an Indian. "My mother is a widow, you see, and she felt it would be better for me to attend school back there, since her business interests here keep her so busy."

"I see," I said. "My name's Crazy Fox," I added, prompting him.

"Jack Carruthers." He stuck out his hand. "My mother runs a girls' school here. And she has a lot of other business things, too. I have an apartment not far from the studio."

I sipped the tasteless coffee and watched him. Without the mask I could see that the resemblance was even more pronounced. "Did you say your mother was a widow?" I asked.

"Yes," he said. "We used to live in Colorado, years ago. My father was a famous lawman out there. He wasn't written about as much as Hickok and Earp and some of the others, but my mother says he was braver and tougher than all of them." He had a sort of wistful look on his face.

"That must have been a long while back," I said.

He nodded. "I never knew him. He was killed in a shootout with a gang of outlaws just before I was born. After that my mother moved out here, to get away from his memories." He shook his head, as if to say that women's ways were a mystery. "She said she didn't want me to get shot down the way he did, but I've always felt I could have been just as brave and tough as my father if I'd only had a chance."

I nodded. I had been thinking of how to tell him about his father, and even of how to introduce them, since Jack was working only a short walk from where we stood. But his words stopped me. He had a picture in his mind that no reality could measure up to.

"That's why I'm working here," he was saying. "My mother wants me to go back East again, but I told her I wanted to *act* like my father at least, even if she wouldn't let me *be* like him."

I watched while he got back on his horse, on the third try. *You are more like your father than you know,* I said to myself.

I only saw him once again, and I never discussed him with Dulsie. Or with Jack. I wouldn't have known how to explain the whole thing to Jack anyway. But now I understood why Dulsie had left Denver, and why she called herself Mrs. Carruthers.

Jack's new part called for him to stand around pretty much like before, but now he had a mask on so he was happy. "They've begun to see what I can do if they give me a chance," he told me after a day in which we had all stood around while the director and the main actor argued over which side of the actor's face should be toward the camera.

The next day we were doing a scene in which the outlaws are all standing around outside town, getting ready to rob the bank, when a stranger rides in and tries to join up with them. The stranger was wearing a big white hat, so I figured he'd probably turn out to be one of the lawmen trying to fool the outlaws. I never got to find out, though, because we never finished the scene.

I should have noticed, I guess. Since this scene didn't call for an old Indian I was free to look wherever I pleased. In fact, I should have known something was up the night before, because Jack had been complaining about the mask they had given him to wear and had gone off somewhere to fix it. But I was watching the big stranger in the white hat now and didn't even think about Jack until the director yelled for the cameras to stop. "Get that damn fool out of this scene, Iggy!" he screamed.

I looked to where he was pointing, and sure enough there was Jack, in his white clothes and black boots and a black velvet mask with little sparkly things all over it. It turned out he'd made it out of part of a costume worn by one of the young ladies in Dulsie's house, and he was very proud of it. He tried to explain that to the director, but the man just kept staring at him and shaking his head. Finally he turned to his assistant and said, "I want this idiot off this lot, and I don't give a shit what C.B. says."

I thought that would end our jobs as actors, but Dulsie must have talked to somebody because a few days later we were working again. This time the movie had a famous actor in it, and he played two parts. In real life he was a kind of fussy Mexican fellow who worried a lot about his clothes. But then later he would put on some kind of disguise, someone said, and would ride out to fight outlaws with a kind of long, skinny sword they called a rapier. He was always slashing a big letter "Z" into things with that rapier, which seemed to get everyone else all worked up.*

We had finished shooting the scenes inside the hacienda and had moved out to the lot for some outdoor shots with horses. This was to be the first time the main actor appeared in his disguise, and when he did I nearly fell over in surprise. Because he came riding up on a big white horse, and in addition to a flapping black cape he was now wearing a black mask. I looked around quickly to see how Jack was taking this, but for a minute I couldn't find him in the crowd.

Then I saw him. He had been trying to get on his horse, and now he was standing stiffly beside it and holding his back. He reminded me of the medicine man in our tribe when I was a child. He, too, had stooped with the failing muscles of age.

The main actor had jumped down from his horse and everyone was standing around trying to decide whether he'd done it right or not, or whether they'd have to do it over again the way they usually did. I looked back at Jack, and saw that he had given up

*This description would appear to fit *The Mark of Zorro*, Douglas Fairbanks' famous movie made in 1920.

trying to mount and was just standing there, staring at the masked actor and the big white horse.

And as he stared, an odd thing happened. He stopped rubbing his back and straightened up, pulling his shoulders back and sticking out his thin chest. He seemed puzzled, as if he couldn't remember something. And then, slowly, he pulled the velvet mask out of his pocket and put it on, and started walking toward the horse. He was ramrod straight and there was a bounce in his step I had not seen for many years. He strode quickly across to the white horse as if no one else was there, and when he got to it he gave a little spring and vaulted into the saddle.

"Hey, what the hell's he doing?" the actor with the cape yelled.

Jack seemed not to hear. He was patting the big horse on the neck and saying something I couldn't catch.

"Get the shit off my horse!" the actor screamed.

Jack smiled, and before anyone could move he kicked the horse in the side and said, "Go, Whitey!"

I stood frozen as the silver horse reared and then raced off. It was as if I had seen the many long years fall away, as if the big white stallion of Benton's Canyon had never died and Jack had never grown old.

They were quickly swallowed up in a cloud of dust, but you could hear the thundering hoofbeats of the great horse for a minute or two after they were gone. And then I heard something else, too. It was the insect noise of a camera close to me. I looked around and saw that the cameraman was standing with his mouth hanging open, watching where Jack had gone. The camera was still running.

There was silence as the dust settled on the false-fronted buildings along the street of this fake town, and then I heard the voice of the director.

"Who *was* that masked man?" he asked.

It would be good if I could tell that Jack died well, perhaps in battle against the evil he had pursued so many years. Or even that he had died happy in the arms of his old friend. But truth must be told.

And the truth is that the search party found his body, pinned under the dead horse, at the bottom of a bluff many miles away. It seemed that the runaway horse had kept on running after the trail had stopped at the edge of the cliff. No one could understand why my friend had gotten on that horse at all, but everyone was very sorry for the way he had died.

Later on it was found that the camera that had been left running had caught the few seconds in which Jack had jumped on that horse and ridden off, and the bit of film was used in another picture they made the next year.

I never saw that movie, but I didn't need to. I would see those moments forever, and would always remember the young man who had sprung up on that horse and ridden off from this world. I have often thought that in the final moments of his life, as he soared through the free clear air on Whitey's back, he must have known there would never be a better day to die.

Dulsie paid for a very fancy funeral. She must have had a long talk with the minister, because he had a lot of information about the illustrious Knight family and he made full use of it for about an hour.

I saw the young actor who looked like Jack among the mourners, but Dulsie didn't introduce us and I thought it better not to bring the subject up. After the dirt was shoveled onto the coffin and the preacher had said a few more words, we walked back to the big black automobiles that had brought us to the cemetery. Dulsie walked beside me with her hand on my arm. She looked much older then than she had ever looked before.

"You'll be staying on at my place, won't you?" she said. "You know it's your home as long as you want."

I looked down at her and saw that the green paint around her eyes was smudged. "No," I said. "I thank you, but I think I would rather die among my People."

She nodded and said no more.

I left the next day on the train for Oklahoma. I never saw Dulsie again, though the years have never taken her face from my memory.

I found that there were still those among my People who knew of me, and kin who welcomed me into their homes. And so I would have lived out my days, sitting in the sunshine and remembering as old men do. But then the young girl who is like a grand-daughter went to hear the talking box, and those memories seemed to need telling.

I have told you the way it was, my Children. It may seem a strange life to you, but I hope you will someday understand the importance of a debt, and the need for a man to keep his word.

I will listen no more to the talking box. What it says no longer matters. What was, was, and will always be.